Books by Pauline Hornsby

The Devil's Prophets

This Devil is Crazy

I0607513

This Devil is Crazy

ISBN # 978-1-78686-305-8

©Copyright Pauline Hornsby 2017

Cover Art by Posh Gosh ©Copyright 2017

Interior text design by Claire Siemaszkiewicz

Totally Bound Publishing

The Devil's Prophets

THIS DEVIL IS CRAZY

PAULINE HORNSBY

Chapter One

Jenna

Chrissie placed my résumé on her desk and ran her shrewd eyes across the page. A recent widow, I had to assume that she was as guilty as her late husband.

But if she knew that eighteen years earlier, Hellion, the president of the Devil's Prophets Motorcycle Club, had drugged me, raped me, kidnapped the son I bore him, and arranged my murder, she didn't give it away.

She had brought me to an office that was just a portable building situated at the back of a massive, yet empty, workshop. The room was neat, homey, with worn furniture and photos on the walls.

Glancing up, she licked her cherry-red lips. "Well, you're certainly qualified. Are you sure you know what you're in for?"

"I'd be doing the accounts, booking jobs, that type of thing." I leaned forward and placed my finger on the sheet of paper near my last position. "As you can see, I was responsible for reorganizing a client's entire inventory and upgrading their accounting system. From what I read in your advertisement, you're looking at a complete overhaul."

"Yes, but you've never worked in a garage before." She flipped my application over face down. "There's a lot for you to learn. Costing out jobs, repair quotes, and the like. We do a lot of custom rebuilds here. It can get complicated."

"I'm a fast learner." I smiled back at her, even though she pissed me off.

Two days earlier I'd answered an ad in the *Mt. Xavier Times* for the office assistant vacancy, and if anything, I was overqualified. I was more accustomed to working for large corporations in slick, modern offices and the garage position would hardly be challenging. I'd even gone so far as to downplay my credentials and experience.

I needed this job.

So much so, I hadn't been far off from getting down on my knees and begging her. Hell, I'd work for nothing, if it wouldn't have made her and the rest of the club suspicious.

"I'm not doubting you." She raised her perfectly filled in brows.

It had been a long time since I'd been anywhere near this close to Chrissie. Years, and it shocked me how little she'd aged. She appeared pretty, refined and delicate under her heavy makeup. But then again, most of my observations of Chrissie had been obscured by whatever I'd found to hide behind.

I hated the bitch.

"But you don't see me here?"

She tilted her head, her platinum hair spilling over her shoulder. "Well, in a way, no." Nodding at me, she screwed up her mouth. "I'm not sure you're the right fit."

I glanced down at myself. My neatly ironed pants, my crisp white shirt worn under a pale pink cardigan, hardly the clothing of a club babe. I was her polar-opposite. Chrissie's skintight jeans and revealing top, more the kind of outfit a woman wore around a biker gang. I started to doubt my choices, but this wasn't far from my normal attire.

"But you agree, I can perform the job. The accounts side of things." I met her eyes, my gaze steady, while hers wavered.

"Oh, I don't doubt that. But you have to understand, this isn't a normal workplace. We have different rules here."

"All businesses do," I said.

She sighed. "Let me say this bluntly, Jenna. The boys are going to think you are fair game. We don't want to open ourselves up to a lawsuit because they've said something offensive. They're not going to change their behavior to suit you."

I didn't appreciate the reminder of my biggest fear about the MC. I knew what bikers were like all too well. But that wasn't going to stop me working here. Nothing could. I started to reconsider her reaction to my getting down on my knees, or working for free, when she let out another huff of breath.

"To be honest, you're our best applicant. But you're" — she waved her hand out in front of herself — "well, you look like the before part of a porno. The scene right before the secretary rips off her glasses and shakes out her hair. Only I think you're genuine, that it's not an act."

I sat back, startled, and burst out laughing. I had to admit, the last part came from nerves, but Chrissie joined in with me.

"I can assure you, that's not what I was going for." I swiped my damp palms down the front of my pants, hoping she didn't notice. "I can do this job, I just need a chance."

"I guess there's not a lot on offer in town," she said.

There were a few positions, actually. A couple that paid a lot more than this one. But here, if I could convince Chrissie to take me on, I'd get to see my son. All the risks I took by being around the club would be worth it. The Devil's Prophets had done everything to me that they could, apart from killing me, but it wasn't as if I had much of a life, anyway.

"Not a lot, no," I said.

"There's other things, too." She flipped my résumé back over, giving me some hope. "When shit gets out, not that there's shit. But people just assume, you know? It's citizens we think of first."

I nod. "Of course. I could sign a confidentiality agreement if you'd like."

I smiled at her shocked expression. Assuming I did talk out of school, the club would definitely have a way of

7

dealing with me. I doubted anyone bothered with contracts here. Not unless they were the type that you set upon someone you wanted gone.

"Ah, we don't have to go that far. Jenna, if it were up to me, I'd hire you in a flash. I think we'd get along, and it would be nice to have another woman around here to work with. But…"

"Thank you for your time," I said, rising and putting my hand out. "I won't waste any more of it."

Calling her bluff could have had me dismissed, but I had nothing to lose in risking doing just that. Of course, I would have to find another way into the club. The obvious method needed to accomplish that made my stomach twist.

"Wait," she said, glancing around her office, her hand fluttering about. "I'll give you a two-week trial. Can you start tomorrow?"

I gave her a practiced smile as she shook my hand. "Thank you."

We'd been alone when I'd first arrived, but as we exited the office, that had changed. The heavy thump of tools being used and discarded assaulted my ears. Some kind of air-powered device hissed and whirred, drowning out all the other sounds.

"Noisy, right?" Chrissie said. "Lucky for us, the office is soundproofed."

There had been a window covered with a Venetian blind, but I had to assume double glazing had been responsible for the near silence, and not the flimsy bit of cheap plastic.

"It's fine. I don't distract easily."

"We'll see."

Skirting the wall, we made our way outside. No one bothered us, and I tried to ignore the men who worked on the bikes and occasional car. All of them were bikers as well as mechanics. Every man there a member of the Devil's Prophets. A brief, cold prickle slid up my spine, threatening to snap it in two. I shook it off. I couldn't afford to show fear.

Despite the overcast weather, typical for Mt. Xavier, a town that sheltered behind a massive mountain range, Chrissie slid on a pair of designer sunglasses. She seemed to think I needed escorting to my car. I wished she'd leave me alone, bad enough we'd be working together.

When I spotted my vehicle, I hurried over to the parking lot. I had little doubt that my car had been searched. Not that I had anything incriminating inside it, they were the criminals. Everyone knew that the Devil's Prophets operated outside of the law.

"Thank you for the interview," I said, as we loitered. "I appreciate your time and the opportunity. I guess I'll see you in the morning."

But Chrissie's attention had gone to the double gate that I'd earlier driven through, allowed access only after I'd shown my driver's license to a camera.

She twisted her hands together at her chest. "What the hell?"

Following her direction, I watched as two thunderous motorbikes roared into the compound, coming to a synchronized park fifty or so feet from us.

The engines cut at the same time, both riders removing helmets and the bandannas that covered the lower half of their faces as they dismounted.

"Ali," Chrissie said, a warning tone in her voice as she shot off over to them. "Where is he? He's meant to be with you."

Ali, as she called him, pronouncing the name like the boxer, had to be six and a half feet tall. Built huge with dark hair that fell over his forehead. Even from where I stood he looked good. Young, too, he had to be only in his mid-twenties.

Despite his size, he put up his hands as if deflecting the five-foot-eight Chrissie. "Stop your worrying, Mama Bear, Jack made a new friend."

Oh, my God, he talked of my son. If I read this right, Jack was supposed to be with them.

I hurried over, even though I wanted to leave. Luckily, I pulled up short and tamped down my demand to know why my son wasn't there.

"He did?" Chrissie's mouth twisted. "I'm guessing a female friend."

"Yeah, unless shit changed after I left. He'll be home when he's ready."

The other rider gave a quick nod in Chrissie's direction and rushed off toward the second largest building situated on the opposite side of the compound.

Chrissie let out a sigh. "Great, I'd planned dinner." She whipped a pink, sparkled iPhone from her pocket and started dialing. I guessed I'd been forgotten. As she headed away from us, handset jammed to her ear, she looked back over her shoulder. "Ali, can you see her out?"

The biker pressed his lips together in a firm line, narrowed his eyes and clenched his fist. "Right, sure."

With that, he turned and headed for the gate.

"Nice to meet you, too," I said under my breath.

Not that it should have concerned me, but the rudeness from Chrissie not introducing us, and the look the biker had given me, irritated beyond measure. I was going to be working with a bunch of people who didn't even have common decency. Not that I expected much more from them.

As I pulled open my car door, I became aware of a presence behind me. Ali's body cast a shadow that had me spinning back to him.

"Nice to meet you," he said, his words slow and clear. "Is that better?"

I bit the inside of my cheek. Getting on the wrong side of these people wasn't going to secure my job with them. Better to play nice. I was good at that.

"I'm happy to meet you too, Ali."

"And you are?"

"Oh, sorry, Jenna. Jenna Mitchell." I stuck my hand out. If he recognized my name, he didn't give anything away.

"Chrissie just hired me to work in the office."

He waited a beat before reaching out and capturing my fingers, not overly hard, but firm. His palm was warm, dry and calloused. We shook, and his eyes pinned me in place. When I went to pull back, he held for a second too long before releasing me, still staring.

I broke the eye contact and glanced back at the garage. "I guess I'll see you tomorrow. If you work in there, I mean."

"Sometimes," he said.

That would be right. Likely he spent his days selling drugs and beating people up, his job as a mechanic, just a front. He looked handsome, with his blue eyes and silky dark hair. But I had always been a realist. This was a bad man.

"Okay, see you then." I slid into my seat, but Ali's hands gripped the edge of the door, preventing me from closing it.

When I tugged again, he let me shut myself in. It wasn't until I found myself in the relative safety of my car that I started to breathe normally.

I'd survived.

The interview, anyway.

When Jenna drove away in her little hatchback piece of shit car, my closest brother, Cage, approached me from the side.

"Are you going to hit that?"

"Nah, she's not going to last out tomorrow." Jenna Mitchell may be hot—no doubt there—but she appeared fragile as fuck.

"So, you're not bothering." At that, I saw Cage's interest jack up.

"Maybe," I said.

He snorted. "Crushing on the secretary."

"Careful, fucker. I've had an uneventful few days, could do with pussy or a fight. You're closer, and I don't find you attractive."

"Keep telling yourself that," he said, his top teeth working his lower lip piercings. "So, how was Melbourne?"

"Usual bullshit. How's it been around here?"

"Usual bullshit." Cage looked over toward the clubhouse. "Speaking of which, Wraith wants to see us."

Frowning, I pulled my phone from my cut. Seeing the president hadn't messaged me, I wondered if I'd be able to get out of it.

"Don't even think about it," Cage said. "I told him I'd drag your ass in with me."

"Thanks for that." Seeing I'd been off on a run for the club, I'd hoped I'd be repaid with a moment's peace. Guess that shit wasn't happening for me.

I fell into step with Cage as we crossed the packed dirt of the compound. My thoughts were drifting to Jenna as we lapsed into companionable silence. She had unusual-colored eyes. Not green, not blue, aqua maybe? She wasn't tall, a foot shorter than I. That's normally a turn off, logistics mainly. But she had nice tits under the conservative clothes, and a curvy little body that I'd bet was soft as all hell in all the right places.

She was still on my mind when I took a chair in front of Wraith's desk. Our president seemed to be making us wait. Not his normal style, him not being a total asshole and all, so I assumed something had come up.

"Damn woman." The meeting room door flew open and Wraith stomped in. At just under six foot and built like a bull, he wasn't someone most people messed with. His fiery Italian temper was something he normally kept under wraps. He tended more to the quiet, menacing type of behavior.

Cage crossed his arms over his chest and leaned back, keeping his voice low. "Which one? Wife or girlfriend?"

I chuckled, only to have Wraith glance my way. "Something funny, Ali? Tell you what, seeing you think my problem is a barrel of laughs, you can go and talk to the new secretary in the morning and scope her out."

I sat up straight. "Huh? Are we looking at her being an issue?" I couldn't see how, the little blonde was no cop, and I doubted the Diamonds had planted her in the club.

"Chrissie failed to run hiring her by me," he said, landing heavily in his chair behind his desk. "She forgets her place. If she's not too careful, I'll put her ass on the other side of the gate."

Seeing that Chrissie had only been widowed for a few months, I got that she might not have been firing on all cylinders. Wraith wasn't what anyone would call a soft touch, but this was harsh, even for him.

Cage raised a brow at me before giving Wraith his attention. "We're talking Chrissie, Prez."

"Yeah, I realize that." He shook his head.

"Then ease up," I said.

Wraith's eyes widened and he reached for his laptop, spinning it to us. "What do you see there?"

I leaned forward. "February's books."

"Right," he said. "And what do you see afterward?"

"Ah, nothing." I took my eyes off the screen. "You can't just blame Chrissie. Where's Jarrah on all this? And with Kitty taking off again, shit is bound to be behind." I referred to both our treasurer and the brother who was supposed to be running the garage.

"Don't worry, I'm on their asses, too. Well, Kitty's, if I can reach him. He appears to be off the grid. As soon as I hear back from him, he can come in and sort this mess out. As for Jarrah, he's been working on our other project." Wraith snapped the computer shut. "Thing is, when I asked Chrissie if she's on top of things, she says, yeah, she needed the distraction of work to help her deal. God knows what the fuck she does all day, but the books aren't it."

"Bank balances seem healthy," Cage said. "Not like we're struggling."

"No, we're not. But we're in the midst of a deal concerning the truck company. Having shit fall down like this isn't gonna look good. The bastard of the situation is, Chrissie's hire is necessary. Despite the bullshit application she gave us, she's in. Well, at least until we get things up to speed."

"Bullshit?" I said.

"Yeah, I scanned her background check. She's downplayed shit. She's no bookkeeper, she's an accountant, she even has a master's in fucking marketing. Gotta wonder why she'd want to work here."

I took the sheet of paper that he handed to me. I ran my eyes down the dossier. Single leaped out first. Never married, second. No kids, third. There wasn't a great deal there, education and work history mainly. She was thirty-two, almost thirty-three. I handed it back to Wraith.

"Maybe we shouldn't look a gift horse in the mouth?" I said.

Before Wraith could take the information back, Cage snatched it out of his hand. Quick fucker, he grinned as he read it. "Not bad," he said.

"You" — Wraith pointed a finger at my brother — "keep the fuck away. She's got more to do around here than suck your dick."

"Not my dick you need to worry about," Cage said, cutting a glance to me. "Ali's already called dibs."

"What about creditors?" I asked, ignoring the comment, as did Wraith.

"All paid. We've got a few outstanding accounts, but nothing a few phone calls won't hurry up." At that he smirked. People didn't normally take too long to pay us their debts. But if they hadn't been billed, I guessed it wasn't their fault, but ours.

"Wonder why she never married?" Cage asked, making me wish he'd shut the fuck up talking about Jenna. "Reckon she bats for the other team?"

Wraith shrugged. "Couldn't give a fuck. Either way, Ali, get on her in the morning. Find out why she applied here in the first place. If you don't like what she has to say, toss her ass out. I don't want shit at the moment."

"On it," I said, and Cage snickered. I loved the man, but

there were times when there was nothing more satisfying than smacking him in the mouth. Nothing. "What are you, ten?"

"Sensitive, brother?" Cage said.

"With Hellion up and dying on us," Wraith said, a slight crack of worry entering his voice, "we're in a fucking vulnerable position as it is."

"I get that," I said. "I'm surprised that Geezer and the Diamonds haven't made a move on our territory already."

Seeing as Geezer, the president of the Diamonds, was basically a nut job, surprise didn't even cover what I was thinking.

"Exactly," Wraith said.

Cage cut me a look and I shrugged back at him. I couldn't see Jenna as being a problem. At least I hoped she wasn't.

Chapter Two

Jenna

I'd spent half an hour that morning changing clothes. I never did that, cared about what I wore to work. As long as I looked polished and didn't stand out, I was good to go. Yet, I'd spent valuable time going from business suit, to casual pants and jacket, to jeans. I'd finally settled on black skinnies and mid-heeled ankle boots with a blazer.

Attracting the attention of the club members with my usual office outfit was not an option. But neither did I want to match Chrissie in her stilettos and low-cut top. I figured I'd go somewhere in the middle. Still, I felt very casual for a work day. The real pity being that my mood didn't harmonize with what I wore.

After swiping up my keys from the small dish on the hall stand, I took a final glance in the mirror and left for work.

Ten minutes later, I ducked under the workshop roller door and looked about, assuming I was alone. But my eyes landed on the back of a man over in the corner whose arm jerked up and down as he operated a wrench. It wasn't Ali, the one I'd met the day before. This man, although not small, wasn't as wide.

He stood when I entered, but kept his back to me.

"Morning, princess," he said.

I froze in place, not sure what to reply with. More accustomed to my fellow male workers in suit and tie, not T-shirts with the armholes stretched tightly around huge biceps. As for the tattoos, I wasn't unused to them, but again, if my coworkers had ink, they were covered. The colorful display on the biker's arms drew my eye.

"Hi," I said, and lifted my hand in an unseen wave. I am that lame.

He turned. Not only adorned in artwork, this member had facial piercings. Gun-metal-gray rings through his brow and lip, but his ears were strangely hole-free. He crossed his arms and tilted his head to one side.

"You're early."

"I wasn't sure. Chrissie didn't say, but I figured nine would be a bit late. I looked up the garage hours, it opens at eight, I supposed that meant coming before then." After babbling away, I clammed up.

"It's okay. We're capable of answering phones." He lifted and flexed a hand. "Opposing thumbs and all that."

"When does Chrissie start?"

He stepped forward. "Nine, nine-thirty. Whenever the fuck she wants."

"I'm Jenna, by the way," I said.

"I know. Cage."

Funny name, but seeing he had me feeling trapped, I considered it apt.

"Nice to meet you, Cage. I guess I can just go in and start." I looked over to the portable office way on the other side of the workshop. To get there, I'd have to pass the biker.

He ran his hand over his short, dark hair, shaved almost to the skin at the sides. He had an edgy look. Not classically handsome like the other one I'd met, but more dangerous. He grinned, taking on a feral quality. I could see how some women would find him attractive. Personally, I was almost peeing my pants. I backed up, only to hit a wall.

Not a wall, another biker. Two hands clamped down on my shoulders. I shuddered and tried to move away, but fingers dug in hard.

"Where you going?" the voice sounded young, in that it had a higher pitch than Cage's.

As much as I'd told myself that I had to show no fear here, that doing so would make me vulnerable to a bunch of predators, all my best intentions bled out of me as I stood between the two men. One might have been several feet away, but that made little difference. And the one holding me, well, that embarrassing bladder malfunction threatened to occur any moment. I started to tremble, my body on vibrate.

"Prospect," Cage snapped. "Let her go."

"Aww, Cage, you're no fun."

"I said get your hands off her, or I'll cut the bastards off." Cage moved forward. The fluidity of his walk caught my attention as the prospect dropped his hands. He grumbled something but made it easier for me to get away from him.

Only problem was, I got closer to Cage when I did so.

The pierced, scary biker dug into his pocket and I wrapped my arms around my middle. I'd been a complete idiot, this likely being a set-up. They knew my identity and were about to shoot or stab me. To make it even worse, I'd not yet seen Jack.

A jangling noise sounded and I saw a flash of keys on the end of a chain. Cage sorted through them and, when he found what he was looking for, crossed the floor ahead of me to the office.

"Come on, princess, I don't bite."

I bet he did, and lot of other things, too.

But I followed.

The office was adorned with some new accessories. Animal shapes of all things. A penguin pen holder, a stapler in the form of a ladybug among the menagerie. I stared at it all, shocked. None of it had been there the day before. It seemed that Chrissie had gone shopping.

Cage picked up a pen topped with a rabbit then dropped it back onto the desk. "I think Chrissie is excited for another female around the joint."

Under the bright lights, I could see that he had hazel eyes. They were pretty, with flecks of gold.

He raised a brow and my cheeks heated. Chuckling, Cage nodded to a coffee machine. "Make yourself at home. I'll give your boss a call, hurry her ass up."

With that, he left.

I sat down and opened a new laptop. It needed a password, making it useless to me. When I tried the drawers on the desk, they were locked. I stood and attempted to open the filing cabinets. No luck there, so I set about making coffee. At least it gave me something to do.

The photos on the wall called to me. I'd been avoiding them. But when I started to study the pictures, I saw how many contained Jack. They appeared to have been taken at club functions. A lot featured small children with laughing faces, scattered among the men in their leather. Some from summer featured the bikers with nothing under their vests. Tan muscles and tattoos everywhere. I found one of Ali. He was clean-shaven, his head back and mid laugh. It appeared recent, and I jerked away when I noticed the other two in club outfits he stood with.

Hellion didn't murder my sister by his own hand. Despite my sister Sophie and I looking similar and being close in age, Hellion knew me well enough that I was certain he'd ordered someone else to kill her. Or me as the case had been, Sophie suffering because of mistaken identity. It was logical to me that a member of the club had committed the crime. Quite a few of the members appeared old enough to have been around at the time. I studied the men who stood near Jack's father. One in particular always seemed to be beside him. On closer inspection, I noticed he had *vice president* written on his jacket and that he never smiled. His lack of humor wasn't enough reason, of course, but his closeness and his seniority made me realize that this was likely to be my first suspect.

"Handsome, wasn't he?"

I didn't turn to Chrissie right away. *What to say to that? Yeah, for a rapist, he's easy on the eye?*

"Sorry, I've been here a while." Lost in thought, of course, I hadn't even realized that I stood in front of a portrait of Hellion himself. I turned from it.

"I should be sorry. I didn't give you a time."

I looked over to her. She had dressed similar to the day before. Only her hair was up, and piled in a messy bun. She placed a handbag that cost more than my car on a bench and came up beside me.

"That's my son," she said, pointing at Jack.

I wanted to stab her.

"He's cute," I said.

"He is that." Chrissie smiled. "I guess we should get to work."

It didn't take my new boss long to set things up, and it took an even shorter amount of time for me to figure out that her work ethic was on the low side. Everything was months behind, but nothing that a few days of constant data input wouldn't set right.

I knew Hellion's death excused the accounts being behind, but as much as I'd normally have sympathy for Chrissie's situation, I just couldn't bring myself to feel any. As hard as it was to reconcile the bubbly, friendly woman as someone who'd had a hand in kidnapping and murder, I knew differently.

"What are you looking at?" Chrissie's voice made my skin crawl. For the past few hours, she'd been content on switching between texting on her phone, and surfing through gossip sites on her computer, but now I'd gained her attention. She slid from behind her desk and came to stand behind me. "Oh, Ali. Can't say I blame you, but there are a lot of cum-drunk women in that man's wake. Not a short list, I can tell you."

I had been staring. He'd even looked up a few times and caught me. But mostly I'd been daydreaming, not riveted by my tedious work.

"Oh, whoops, caught me," I said, focusing back on my screen.

"Interested?"

"No, definitely not. I'm not here for that." Even as I said the words, Ali came back into my view. He'd managed to get grease on his cheek, giving him cute, messy look.

"Yeah, sure. I could hook you up, if you like."

I needed to stop this line of conversation. "No."

She chuckled. "Whatever."

"I met a couple of the members this morning when I arrived." My insides kicked as I recalled the fear that they had caused in me.

"I know, Cage mentioned it." Chrissie reached over to her desk and pushed the lid of her laptop closed. "They were only playing. As for Pony, he's just a prospect, but his uncle is a fully patched senior member, so he tends to think he can get away with stuff."

"I'm not trying to make trouble." I didn't like the way her face had become serious. "They caught me off guard."

Chrissie shrugged. "Look, Jenna, they're testing you, and it's to be expected. One piece of advice I can give you is to at least not show them they're getting under your skin."

"I'll take that on board," I said, promising myself that I'd not mention any clashes with the bikers to her again. There was no point of me getting this job only to be fired before Jack even came home.

Chrissie giggled. "You're doing it again."

"I am?" I realized that I was facing the window. I couldn't help it, it was either that or look at Chrissie, and that churned my stomach even more.

But then I had a thought. When Jack returned to the MC, it would be strange if I took much notice of him, he was way too young. Better that I had a decoy, and the good-looking biker was not a bad option. As long as Chrissie got over her matchmaking ideas, I couldn't see the harm.

Chrissie moved from behind me and over to the wall of photos. "I suppose you heard that I lost my old man some time back?" She tapped on a picture with Jack, Ali and Hellion. "That's what I meant before when I said he *was* handsome."

I stared at her for a beat. "Oh, I'm sorry."

"Not even fifty." She slid her finger down the image.

"Heart attack. No warning signs. None that he told me about anyway. He was so fit. But, of course, he was no angel."

No, her late husband had been the devil. And I had willingly entered hell.

Chapter Three

Ali

I let myself into the office the moment Chrissie left to do the banking.

"You settling in?" I said, picking one of the pens out of the stupid penguin holder that Chrissie must have bought.

"I have a lot to do," Jenna said and swallowed. "Can I help you?"

She appeared skittish and I had no plans to alleviate that.

"Maybe." I slid the pen back into the container. "Funny place for someone like you to work. Did you know it was an MC?" I waited for her to say no, to tell me that she had no idea that the garage had a link to an outlaw motorcycle club.

"I worked it out from the address, so yes," she said.

"You've lived here, what, a month?"

"Six weeks. Is there anything else? I'm kind of swamped."

I reached across and closed the laptop, her perfume hitting me sharply. Roses, unusual when most women around the place smelled of spices and sex. I liked it, though, the aroma lighter, more subtle than I was used to.

"Take a break."

Her eyes went to my mouth like she lip-read me.

"I could make coffee," she said, her hands shaking before she closed them into fists.

"So, where's Mr. Mitchell?" I asked, her eyes widening in surprise.

"I thought you checked all that out?" Her mouth lifted at one side.

"We did, just wondering if you have one hidden away somewhere." I leaned closer. "You don't look single."

"I don't? What does single look like?" She appeared interested, her head tilting.

"Not beautiful like you." I cocked my head to the side. "But you don't look very content, so you're either not being fucked properly, or you are on your own."

Her breath hissed in. "I don't appreciate that."

"Being fucked properly?" I didn't back away, leaning down a little more.

"Being spoken to like that. It's disrespectful and unprofessional. I'm here to work, not have you come in here and harass me like this." She rolled her chair back and I held down the chuckle that started making its way up my throat. "I think you should leave."

"Babe, you don't get to tell me shit." I straightened up. Fuck, my dick had been getting hard the entire time I had been talking to her. I had been caught up in the discussion, but still, how the hell had I not noticed? "I'm just making conversation. Besides, it's you that's harassing me."

"What?" Her eyes grew rounder. Had she noticed? I really hoped so. "I've said nothing to you."

"Yeah, but you've been checking me out. I saw you watching me. I'm not an object, you know." I smiled, softening my words. I'd liked her watching me. Of course, she'd checked out my brothers too. We were probably like animals in a zoo to the pretty little citizen.

"You're being ridiculous," she said, her voice wavering. I'd caught her, she couldn't really deny that.

"It's okay. I think I like you harassing me." I scratched my chin. "Yeah, I've changed my mind, you can harass me as much as you want."

"Ali," she said, and the sound of my name on her lips made my fucking balls ache. "All I want to do is my job. Even if the garage wasn't staffed by…"

"Scumbags?" I suggested.

"…bikers, it would be full of men. I'm not stupid or naïve.

24

Any group of men can get out of hand when you're all acting like little boys and trying to impress each other. But seeing I've done nothing to any of you to warrant this kind of…"

"Inquisition?" Again, I obliged her.

"…questioning. Look, I'm new, I understand the curiosity. But I'm an open and very boring book. I live by myself, I go to work and the gym. In my spare time, I read and study." She stood, her hands on the desk supporting her. "I'm really very uninteresting."

I doubted that, she was hotter than hell and the spark that started in her turned me the fuck on. That, and the cleavage she displayed. Even better, I was pretty sure she didn't realize the show she put on.

I smirked when Jenna pulled the edges of her shirt together. Seeing the women around the club showed a hell of a lot more, and quite happily, the brief look I had gotten kicked things up a bit. Easy was…well, easy. This woman wasn't that.

But ripping her shirt open to get a better look wouldn't go down well. I stood. Wraith hadn't been specific about what to find out. My feelings went that Jenna Mitchell was without malice. She couldn't possibly be a threat to the club. As much as I thought there was more to her than she'd let on, I planned to find out the rest in my own time.

"Relax, Jenna." Even to my own ears, my voice sounded strangely soothing.

"That's a bit hard," she said, her eyes flashing fire at me. "If you're all going to have a go at me, I might as well leave now."

"Tell you what," I said, alarm that she might make good on that promise causing me to back up. "I'll guarantee they'll leave you alone."

"How?"

My brows shot up. The woman had to be crazy. None of my brothers were going to argue with me. "I'll ask them nicely," I said.

"Why?"

"Because, seeing your beautiful face every morning might make coming in here more bearable. There's a lot of ugliness, Jenna. Who wouldn't want to look at you instead?"

Where the fuck did that come from? I found myself backing away. It was one thing to show a woman interest, but that had sounded like the weakest thing I'd ever uttered. I needed out, I needed to punch something, no, shoot something — even better — and I needed to do it right-the-fuck-away.

Jenna looked startled again, but the small smile playing on the edges of her mouth made it worth my acting like a pussy. She blushed, two tiny red spots on her cheeks that bloomed to a pale pink. If I'd thought her attractive before, I was a goner with that expression. Who the hell blushed anymore? I didn't miss that there were other ways to cause that coloring and warming to her face. I stared at her speechless, licking my dry lips.

I never could see the point in romantic notions of love. I expected to find a woman I'd make my old lady one day. She'd be beautiful, tough as nails and able to hold her own. Sure, I'd protect her, but she'd have to look after herself too. Kids were a great idea, as well, but not for at least another ten or so years.

This woman wasn't that. She had the looks, but the MC would kill her. No way could Jenna survive the Devil's Prophets. As much as I loved my club, she'd need a certain amount of steel inside to endure the life.

Even with Hellion gone, the place ticked like a time bomb of violence and corruption. If she knew how we made our living, of what went on behind our walls, she'd run. If this woman was as smart as I suspected, she'd put her head down and beat fucking feet out of here.

Jenna wasn't stupid. She'd have a vague idea like anyone else as to what we were about. *But how will she feel if she learns my capabilities? Of what the entire brotherhood can do when pushed?* She'd hate us all, turn her back and think that we were the scumbags we joked we were. Jenna Mitchell probably didn't have a bad bone in her body. I'd seen her bank records. She had five charities she donated to on a regular basis, even with her massive student debt.

But the truth stood in front of me. Beautiful, vulnerable and hopefully less fragile than I suspected. I wanted this woman, on my bike, by my side and in my bed. It would happen, I just needed for her to catch up.

"I'll be watching you," I said, realizing that we'd been standing there not talking for minutes while I mentally rearranged my entire world and changed long-held priorities as fast as deciding what pair of boots to wear that day.

"Okay," she said, catching herself. "How long have you been a member here?"

It might have been a clumsy attempt to turn the questioning around, yet I was grateful for it.

"A decade, give or take."

Her eyes widened. "You would have been a teenager. That's so young."

Jenna didn't need to know the details of my life, I wasn't ready for her to judge me yet, even though that warranted some kind of answer or explanation. The door flinging open saved me from responding.

"God, remind me to get Cage to service that damn car." Chrissie hurried into the office, slamming the door behind herself. "Oh, am I interrupting?"

"No," Jenna said, her words coming out fast. "Ali was just showing me something. How to read the job sheets."

Her lie seemed a little quick and obvious. I had to wonder at it, seeing Chrissie didn't mind any of us coming into the office and just hanging out. She'd put the couch in there when she'd found Jase asleep on the floor once after a big night. Hellion had never liked it, but he hadn't gone into the workshop much in the day, so it hadn't been a real problem.

"Okay, if that's what you kids call it." She grinned and

threw her bag onto her desk. "Guess I should get back into it."

I left the office, weighed down by a sense of calm that I was pretty fucking sure had been caused by a five-foot-five, blonde-haired, aqua-eyed woman with lips made for my dick. Jenna had, in the space of less than twenty-four hours—a quarter of them spent in my presence—gotten under my skin. And I was okay with that. Especially seeing for the first time since my arrival at the club, the urge to rip the flesh from my own bones wasn't with me.

"Brother." Cage's voice filtered to my ears. "You all right there?" He looked concerned. Out of everyone, Cage got me, or near enough.

"Yeah, I'm good." Schooling my expression, I went to get out of his face.

"Uh-huh," Cage said. "You find anything interesting? Princess isn't a plant for the Diamonds, is she?" He laughed at his own dumbass suggestion.

"Nah, nothing important."

Before Cage could ask anything else, I headed back to finish a job I'd started earlier, concentration impossible. All I could think about was Jenna, and more importantly, what I planned to do where the little blonde citizen was concerned.

Chapter Four

Jenna

"None of this makes sense," I said, as Chrissie filed a nail, splaying her fingers to make sure she'd done a perfect job.

"What, Jen?" She turned toward me, eyes wide as if work questions were out of place in the office.

"We seem to be missing parts. According to the inventory, there's supposed to be three one-six-eight-nine-sixes," I said, reading the part number because I had no idea what they actually were. "But there's an order here for three more because two are needed on current jobs. They're not cheap, so I doubt anyone would have just called for more."

Chrissie frowned, rolling her chair over. "You're right. How did I let that get past me?"

"There's a few of these kinds of errors."

"How much money are we talking?" Suddenly she became interested.

"A few grand." I switched windows on the computer. "I'm running a spreadsheet to keep track. But we'll need a physical count for better accuracy."

"Damn," she said, her finger flying to her bottom lip. "Pop out and see the boys, they need to know about this."

"What about Wraith?"

"This is Kitty's baby. Wraith is working on other things. Just go and see Ali, he can get this sorted."

"He's in charge?" I didn't want to go out there and speak to him, still feeling unnerved from our earlier meeting.

"Yeah, and he's good at finding things. Besides, you're probably looking for an excuse to go and talk to him."

"I'm sorry?"

She chuckled, a knowing look in her eyes. "Don't think I haven't noticed you checking him out again."

The heat surged into my cheeks. "I wasn't."

"Yeah, you were. Can't say I blame you. Ali's a honey, I'll grant you that." Chrissie twisted her mouth. "Look, Jen, Wraith called me at home last night. He wasn't too happy about me hiring you without him approving it first."

"Oh, what does that mean?" Worry crept over me. Losing this job because Chrissie had failed to follow the club's protocol wasn't something I'd considered.

"It means that you might need another reason for Wraith to keep you on." She pointed out to the workshop. "That could be your other reason."

Watching Ali was one thing, starting something was quite another. I shot a glance back out of the window. Of all the men for me to have chosen, I'd picked the biggest one out there. But Chrissie had mentioned that Ali had no shortage of women. Maybe if I played things right, nothing would progress further than his teasing earlier.

"I'm not sure about that," I said.

"Go, I'm your boss and that's an order." The last she said with mock-authority.

I dragged myself to my feet. As she said, Chrissie was my boss.

Ali saw me coming and kept his eyes fastened on me as I walked to where he leaned against a bench, taking a break. The man talking to him looked as if he belonged more at a beach than an MC. When I got closer, Ali said something to him and he walked away. I recognized him as the same one who'd ridden in with Ali the day before.

"Problem, Jenna?" He swiped his hand over his hair, getting more grease on his face in the process.

I halted in front of the huge biker. "Chrissie said that I should see you about some missing spare parts." If that didn't sound like an accusation, I'd heard myself incorrectly. I cleared my throat. "She said you were good at finding things."

"They're lost?" He leaned forward, speaking to me as if I were a slow child. "Do you think they're under something? Do you think you want to get under someone and look?" Not a child, not with the seductive quality to his voice. It wrapped around me like a warm rug, but not the kind your grandmother knitted.

I stepped back. It looked as if his earlier questioning hadn't stopped. Problem was that despite him clearly mocking me, I wasn't hating it.

"This is serious. We're talking a lot of money here."

He nodded and moved his hand to his chin. "What is your suggestion?"

"A stock-take."

His expression became pained. "Shit, really?"

"Shit, really."

"Pony, get your ass over here." Ali kept his eyes focused on me even when the younger man sauntered over to us.

"Yeah, Ali."

"You've been signing the deliveries—any chance you have actually been checking them off?"

"Sure, everything."

"Right." Ali nodded at last, letting his eyes drift from mine. "I'm figuring that Jenna here can count. *You*, not so much. She thinks we got missing parts. You wanna fill me in?"

"What does she know?" Pony shot me a look.

By then, Cage had joined the group, the four of us standing in the middle of the room. Pony started tugging at the neck of his T-shirt.

"Pony?" Cage said to him, his tone even more menacing than Ali's.

"I checked off everything, God's honest truth. Do you think I'm that stupid?"

"Yes," Cage and Ali said at the same time.

It was hardly a funny situation and I put my giggle down to my nerves. Ali cut his gaze back to me, a smile pulling at the sides off his mouth, but not quite working.

"Maybe things aren't in the right spots," I said, not sure why I tried to make things easier for a man who only hours earlier had attempted to frighten me. Tried and succeeded.

"I could tidy up spare parts," Pony said, a hopeful look on his face. I noticed him edging farther away from Cage, who tracked him with a narrow-eyed glare that I would not have wanted directed at myself.

"Not happening," Ali said. "We'll get someone else on it. Jack can do it when he gets back."

Pony's eyes were darting around, landing on anything but the two men with us. When they hit me, they were drawn and angry.

I looked away, returning to Ali who met my gaze as if we were the only two people in the world, let alone the room. I stared at him, my thoughts receding in my mind and replaced with something else that was completely foreign to me. I swallowed and my pulse kicked up a few beats. The spell only broke when I heard a small, dark chuckle. Cage's interruption was a good thing. There was no telling where my imagination had been heading.

"I have work to do," I said, spinning on my heel and hightailing it across the concrete.

I'd been stupid, utterly ridiculous. It wasn't as if I'd never been in the presence of an attractive man. Hell, I'd even let my mind wander on a few occasions. But this man was a criminal, part of an organization that had caused me heartache and harm. That he would not have been a member at the time was hardly relevant. He was a Devil's Prophet and I needed to keep away.

* * * *

I made it to Friday intact. Wraith had yet to cross the compound and visit the office. If Chrissie needed to contact the club president, she either phoned, or met with him over at the clubhouse. Even avoiding Ali proved easy, he was away more than he was at work. But he'd returned that morning. Chrissie called me out every time I looked anywhere near the direction of the single window.

Yet, what I worried the most about was Jack's failure to return. Wraith I'd deal with when I had to. As for Ali, I still hoped to keep a distance. Well, at least until I had no other choice.

When it came to the rest of them, the novelty of the new secretary appeared to have worn off. Most of the men took my presence for granted and I'd even managed to join Chrissie with them a few times for breaks. They were a mixed bunch, rough around the edges for sure, but I learned that a lot of them were married with families. Mostly, they were polite to me. Keeping my guard up was still forefront in my mind, but so far, no one had cast any suspicions my way.

"Alone again," Ali said, letting himself into the office. He placed an invoice down on the desk in front of me. Chrissie had left earlier to do the banking with one of the bikers. "This should be right. Jase checked it off earlier."

"We need to be careful with orders. I stuck my head in the spare parts room, it's a mess and we might just be spending money needlessly." I picked up the sheet of paper and scanned the column with the amounts.

"We?"

"Sorry, *you* need to be careful." Placing the bill back down, I glanced up at him. "Anything else?"

"What do you reckon?" He cocked his head to the side. "You avoiding me?"

"No. I just have a lot to do. Besides, you're never here."

"Notice that, did you?" He grinned, standing to his full height with his arms crossed over his chest. "I'm flattered."

"Don't be," I said, pushing my chair back.

He brought his dark brows together, watching me. "Jack's going to do that stock-take we spoke about."

"He's home?"

He shook his head. "Not yet."

"Guess I should get back to it." I made a show of hitting the keypad on the computer.

Ali ignored the hint, planting his hands on the edge of the desk and leaning down close to my face. His breath warm and sweet. Not a smoker. But it was fast being swallowed by the smell of grease and engine oil. Hardly unpleasant, and about as masculine as it came. Something else, too, the outdoors, crisp and cool. Maybe all that bike riding he did clung to him.

"You don't like me, do you?" The words were serious and he held my eyes tight.

"I don't know you."

"What's to know?"

The question came to me as loaded as the sawed-off shotgun I imagined he kept in those big compartments that hung off the bikes. Saddle bags, I recalled. I'd been trying to learn the parts and the names of the accessories that came with, or were added later to, the bikes.

He startled, leaning backward. "What the hell is going on in that head of yours?"

"Pardon?"

"Shit is going on in there." He swirled his finger around in front of my face with his words making it sound like he wanted to know some answers that I refused to provide. Which was pretty much true.

"Well, you know, sometimes these little female brains, they, um, work shit out."

He chuckled. "I know you're smart, babe. Most likely too smart for me. Looks and brains. There's got to be a third trait, though."

I blinked. I'd never been called that before, the term one of endearment. I hated that I was flattered. More likely Ali called all women babe. Probably his go-to word for when he tried to get somewhere with the opposite sex. Trying to get somewhere? Holy shit, he was flirting with me.

I needed to take control of the situation, as socially inept as I felt. I prepared to reel Ali back in. Or at least slow things down. He'd return to being the criminal biker slash decoy, and I'd become part of the office furniture. "You need to go back to work, I'm sure with all that time you take off, you're behind yourself."

Only, I wasn't counting on Ali's lack of filter. "Could be your tits, but they'd be considered part of your looks." He stood, folding his arms across his chest and studying me.

"Oh, we're back to this again," I said, floundering. "Are you trying to shock me? Doesn't it get old?"

He shook his head. "No, not what I'm trying for here."

I refused to fall into the trap of asking what he was trying for. Instead, I rolled my eyes and turned to my computer. As I did, Ali's hand slid down and his fingers wrapped around mine. A small tug and he had me out of my chair. I stumbled and he caught me around the waist.

"What are you doing?" I froze in shock. "Get your hands off me."

He didn't. "I like you watching me."

"I wasn't."

"Yeah, you were. No need for bullshit here, Jenna." He held me in a loose grip and allowed me to retreat. As I did, he reached out and removed my glasses, Chrissie's porno scene springing back to my thoughts. "So why?"

"Sorry?" My mind was going haywire. I hated the effect he had on me. Stepping farther away from him, I collided with the edge of the desk. "You need to leave."

Chrissie invaded my head again. Being with Ali would assure me this job. But having sex on the office desk was going too far. I couldn't do that, but I couldn't be fired without a chance to see Jack. To have my son in my life while I figured out where to go from there.

When he moved closer, I tilted my head up to him. I could do this, I couldn't see a way out. Ali's hands bracketed my face, and a thoughtful look came across him. "Maybe I read you wrong. Are you scared of me?"

"Of course I am, you're the size of a small bloody car."

Averting my face to the side, he grazed his finger under

my chin, turning me back to him so he could lock his eyes on mine.

"Last thing I want to do is scare you. Was kind of hoping that you'd be into this." He released me, stepping away.

I believed him. I didn't know him well enough to realize if he was lying or not, but he seemed sincere. Just kissing him couldn't be so bad. If it went too far, I could make an excuse, or scream, or bite him. I wasn't sure, but something would have come to mind.

Before I could stop myself, I placed my palm flat on his chest. It was all the encouragement he needed. Our height difference didn't stop him. He bent a little as I stood on tiptoe, then we were kissing. Okay, in high school I'd kissed boys. Messy and clumsy times, but, I recalled, thrilling in their own way. But Ali came at things from an entirely different level. His mouth was hot and his taste sweet.

Having no idea what I was doing, I followed his lead. When his tongue swept along my lips, I opened and let him in. Lucky he'd gone back to holding me. My legs felt fluid as I gave over to feelings and sensations that I never knew I had. This was not what I expected. And I was not supposed to enjoy it. But I did—his searching mouth, hands that didn't wander over me, but kept me in a firm grip—I was lost.

"Well, this is new." The voice hit me hard. I knew who it was, simply by instinct, and I broke contact. Turning, I saw them filing into the office, Chrissie, Cage and Jack.

My hand went to swipe over my mouth, but failed because Ali took hold of it. "Thanks for that," he said to them all. "Great timing."

"Hate to interrupt, but we got church." Cage gave me a smirk. "Nice going, princess. I reckoned you were pining for him the last few days."

I shot him daggers, but I didn't care what he thought, only Jack's opinion mattered. But my son grinned, looking gorgeous and dusty with his hair pulled back in a bun and a Devil's Prophets cut on. He was tall, my boy. Six foot and still appearing as if he'd grow some more.

"This is Jenna," Chrissie said, her heels clacking across the floor while she didn't even bother to hide her knowing smirk. "She's the new secretary. Jenna, this is Jack, my son." She beamed with maternal pride that she owned, but didn't deserve.

"Good to meet you, Momma." The maternal moniker, even if it was a generic term, rocked me.

I knew I was blushing up a storm, but I gathered myself, put out my free hand and Jack shook it. The touch, as brief as it was, went some way to making me feel better. Jack didn't seem to have a problem with me kissing Ali. Only I did.

"Well come on then," Cage said, clapping his hands together. "We got church. You can play with her later."

Jack gave me one more smile, before Cage and he turned to leave. Ali gave my fingers a last squeeze and he left with them. From the window, I watched them go. They roughhoused, Ali's shoulder to Cage nearly knocking the other man to the ground. Jack joined in. If it were another setting, it would have been amusing.

"Good for you, Jenna," Chrissie said, drawing me back to her.

I went and slid behind my desk, ignoring her. Jack had returned and I needed to regain the real reason I had come to the club starting right then.

Chapter Five

Ali

Cage was watching me with one side of his mouth turned up. I flipped off the fucker and crashed down in the seat beside him, shutting down my own stupid ass grin.

"Nice moves," he said. "Really liked the hand holding earlier. Gonna have to try that."

"It's called taking it slow. You *should* try it."

"It's called fucking, you should try *that*." He gave me a last cocky grin and turned his attention to Wraith as the president banged down the gavel.

Yeah, I was planning on trying that. My fucking dick was solid and I was in a room full of nineteen other men. That was not quite right.

Shit was only just getting through to me and I was having trouble concentrating on what was being said. My goal was to get back into that office with Jenna. She was not playing easy, but that fucking kiss... Normally, I wasn't much of one to lock lips with a woman. Sure, it was necessary in some situations, but women tended to get the wrong impression if you paid them that kind of attention. With Jenna, I was hoping she was getting the idea and it was fucking right as far as I was concerned.

"So, Ali and Cage can go and have a talk with Salina. You can check in with that shithead Reed while you are there. Rough him up a little and make it clear that he is fired. Or whatever you both see fit at the time."

I shot my gaze to the left. What the fuck? I was going out again? For how fucking long? Right, talk with Salina, and beat the shit out of some hold-out distributer. One day, two at the most. I could do that. Didn't fucking want to, however. But we weren't talking a week here. No need to show how pissed I was.

Cage, the asshole, was smiling at me. "You want I should go alone so you can go back and hold hands with Jenna?"

"Fuck off." I stretched my arms out in front of me, flexing my neck from side to side. Went nowhere close to releasing the tension that had built inside me.

Wraith eyed me curiously, but I knew he wouldn't ask about me and the secretary. At least I thought he wouldn't. Our lives were our own unless they affected the club.

"Anything I should know?"

"Nope," I said, studying the tats on the backs of my hands.

"I have plans for Jenna Mitchell. I don't want you fucking it up."

Well, that was a complete one-eighty. Last the prez said on the matter, he'd planned on Jenna being sacked as soon as she had the books up to speed. I wasn't complaining, though, he'd saved me the trouble of convincing him that it was a good idea to keep her on.

But then another thought hit me and I looked over at him. Wraith might have finished with his latest woman, Bel, a real looker, who should have kept him going another few months at least. He had better not be going for Jenna as a replacement.

"Really, Prez," Cage said, sounding bored. "What for?"

"I've had a change of heart. Apparently, women downplay shit all the time according to Anna," he said, referring to his wife. "Apparently, we're a sexist lot and don't think women are actually capable of doing much more than sucking dick and being secretaries."

"And they're not?" Dusty, one of the old crew, spoke up. "Jesus, I was sure I had that part worked out."

A few of the brothers snickered.

"So, Ali, don't fuck it up." Wraith's tone went back to serious. "With her skills in marketing, she'll be useful with the expansions."

I had to wonder if it was part of the reason he planned to send me out. There was a chance that he was worried I was so inept that I'd screw this up with her. He had a point, but I was determined to do this right. I glanced around the table at my brothers.

"Not planning to. Anyone got issues with that?"

Jack gave me a curious look. "Shit, I've only been gone a few days longer than you. You found an old lady in that time?"

"Potentially," I said. I wasn't speaking to him. He was just a kid, no chance he'd be chasing that particular piece of tail. But as for the others, I needed to lock this down. Wasn't claiming her — no one would take that seriously, not yet — but I needed my brothers to know she was hands off.

Most of the assembled men shrugged. Those who didn't knew perfectly well they'd meet my fists if they tried anything, and a wave of relief crashed over me.

"You need to get going," Wraith said, standing, ending the meeting. "Reed is out a couple of grand. He'll book it soon and I don't want any of the others thinking they can do the same."

When the meeting adjourned and we'd fished our phones from the box we kept them in, Jack grinned down at his own. "So happens Ma's taking Jenna with her to lunch. What do you say, Ali, got time to eat before you go?"

Well, why the fuck not? I wasn't planning on anything — that could wait until I got back from the run. And when I did, Jenna Mitchell was not going to know what the fuck hit her.

* * * *

My mind was filled with thoughts of Jack being home. But Ali kept filtering his way in too, pissing me off. Mine and Jack's meeting had been too brief, but I planned on making an effort to spend as much time as I could around him. Of course, I'd have to be careful not to make it obvious.

"Do you wanna go for lunch, Jen?" Chrissie pulled on her jacket, hoisting her bag over her shoulder. "I meant in town, just get out for a while?"

I didn't want to leave. I had no idea how long the meeting up at the clubhouse was going to be, but I wanted to be there when Jack got out.

"I think I'll keep working," I said. "I'm on a roll."

Chrissie jangled a set of keys in her hand. "Don't be such a stick in the mud. Jack said he'd meet me there later, but I don't want to sit by myself."

Jack was going? Well, that changed things up. "I am kind of hungry."

"You know," Chrissie said, as we drove to town in her sporty white Lexus, "you don't have to be embarrassed over what happened earlier. That office has seen more action than some bedrooms."

Great. I reminded myself to clean later, not to mention disinfect. "It was just a kiss."

"Sure it was, honey." She flipped down the visor and checked her makeup before applying gloss and touching up her mascara. Clearly my life wasn't as important as how Chrissie looked. That wasn't quite how I imagined myself dying at the hands of the club.

Discussing Ali with Chrissie just wasn't going to happen. I reached across and turned the volume up on the stereo. Bon Jovi filled the car and I stopped myself from rolling my eyes. Who would have guessed? She started tapping her fingers on the steering wheel.

"Ooh, I love this." She increased the level further.

I wasn't a hater, yet to me it was just noise to drown out my company. But seeing it served a purpose, I softened a little to the eighties-style rock.

We pulled up near a coffee shop and Chrissie gave herself one last check before disembarking the car. Despite the chill in the air, she nabbed an outside table.

"The coffee here is good," she said.

Making conversation with Chrissie outside the office proved difficult, but I was saved when a waitress approached and stopped, pen poised over her pad.

"You go first, Jen." Chrissie lit a cigarette.

"Latte please, turkey focaccia, and if you have those chocolate muffins, one of those, too."

"We certainly do." The waitress grinned at me before turning to Chrissie. "And for you?"

"A black coffee and salad." A roar of pipes rumbled close by. "You might want to stick around. We've got company."

The server, who was perhaps twenty and very attractive, sent her gaze in the direction of the bikes. I did too, and watched as both Jack and Ali dismounted.

Jack and Ali pulled out chairs, and because I had sat down opposite to Chrissie and Jack, which left Ali to side beside me. "We've just ordered," I said.

"Yeah, what did you get?" Ali placed the menu that he'd been handed down on the table and I rattled off my order to him. "Sounds good."

"You drink lattes?" I tried to avoid staring at Jack and coming off as a creeper. It was my son I wanted to talk to, but for now, I'd have to concentrate on Ali.

"What's not to like? It's coffee and milk."

I noticed the waitress had flipped a page on her pad. She tore it off and placed it in front of Ali. Chrissie leaned down and read it.

"Oh, honey, he's not on the menu."

The girl blushed. Ali seemed oblivious as she all but ran off.

I frowned — there had been no need to humiliate the girl.

Ali gave me a steady gaze. "Problem, Jenna?"

"Just thinking of the work I have piled up."

Chrissie snorted. "Work? That's doubtful."

"You coming to my eighteenth, Jenna?" Jack picked up his water glass and took a sip.

I knew there was a party planned. Chrissie had been talking about it off and on for the past few days. But, no,

I hadn't been asked, and even though it was for Jack, attending an event at the clubhouse wasn't on my agenda. His actual birthday was the Monday before the party and I planned to bake a cake and celebrate it with him at the garage. I didn't think that would come across as too weird.

"You have to come," Chrissie said.

"She does." Jack pointed with his chin at Ali. "And you can go with him. You'll look after our Jenna here, won't you, brother?"

Ali didn't so much as flinch, but he had to be thinking of all the fun he'd miss out on if he had to babysit me. Kiss aside, the man was definitely about to say no.

"That's fine," I said. "I'd love to go to your party, Jack. But, Ali, you're off the hook."

"Shot down," Ali said. He looked disappointed.

I wasn't sure what to think.

Chapter Six

Ali

Jenna had spaced out for most of lunch and I had the distinct feeling she'd been deep in thought as much as disinterested in Chrissie rambling on. She'd made the right noises, though, nodding and agreeing every now and then.

"I do that," I said, as Chrissie headed off to her car, stranding Jenna in town because she'd decided to go shopping. Jack was already on his bike, ready to go back to the clubhouse.

"Do what?" Jenna said. She was frowning over at Jack, not seeming too fazed by Chrissie's desertion.

"Pretend to listen when I'm not interested." Before she could protest, I added, "But she's right, J's is the best place in town for waxing."

While Jack took off, she turned herself to me. "Really? Is that where you go?"

"Nah, but I've seen the work."

"Oh, classy. I guess I need to get a taxi." She pulled out her phone, but I reached across and took it from her. "Hey."

"I'll give you a ride back."

She glanced over at my bike, shaking her head.

"Don't be a chicken," I said.

"I'm not."

"I think you are. I think you're worried about being so close to me. I'd assumed we were past that." Two small spots formed on her cheeks, blooming to a blush that on Jenna looked incredibly hot. "I like that, too."

Her hand went to her face. "It's called a conscience."

"I think it's recall. Look, babe, I've got to head out again, and I need to get back to the clubhouse first. I don't really have time to fuck around here." Taking her hand, I led her over toward the bike.

She stopped halfway. I followed her line of sight and saw two helmets hanging off the handlebars. Courtesy of Jack, I guessed, because I never carried a spare.

"About Jack's party," I said. "You are with me."

"That's not necessary." She continued to stare at my bike.

"Yeah, it is. Otherwise you're going to be fending off drunk, horny bikers all night."

"Instead of just one. Guess those are better odds."

"You won't be fighting me off." I crossed the distance between us and my bike, plucking the smaller of the helmets and holding it out to her. "Come on, it'll be fun."

"I think you and I have different ideas of the term." She crossed her arms over her chest. "Just give me my phone back and I'll get a ride of my own."

My message alert sounded. There wasn't any need for me to check it, I knew it was Cage wanting me to hurry the fuck up. I shook the helmet at her. "Just get on, babe. Like I said, I don't have all day, and you're the one that reckons you've got a shit load of work back at the office."

She sighed. "Just don't kill me, okay?"

"I think I can manage that." Taking off my cut, even though it would swamp her, I handed it over. She wasn't wearing a heavy enough jacket. Even on a ten-minute ride, she'd freeze her ass off.

Tentatively, she slid her arms into it. It was my turn to stare. The worn leather, the patches, it all contrasted with the innocent woman wearing it.

"Now you'll get cold," she said, but she had taken the helmet from me and was putting it on.

"Don't think that's going to be a problem somehow."

Jenna clung tight. I had expected that, her arms around my waist, her fingers linked over my stomach. I was aware of every part of the contact, not the least her body pressed tight behind mine.

I took corners purposely tight just so she upped her grip on me. At one stage when she adjusted herself, her fingers grazed the front of my jeans. Not low enough, but there was some promise there. She was a natural passenger, leaning with me, even if she was probably terrified. She needed to get over that, but seeing it was her first time, I wasn't too worried.

The ride ended too fast and it felt like mere seconds had passed when we pulled in through the gate. I was tempted to bypass the club, just keep going, especially when her hands ended up flattened against me.

As soon as I stopped the bike, she was up and off, crossing the compound away from me.

"What the fuck?" I took off after her, her fingers fumbling with the strap on her helmet. "Jesus, Jenna, wait."

"I've got to go back to work." She slid my cut from her body, handing it out to me with the head gear. "Thanks for the ride."

"You liked it, didn't you?" I grinned low and easy at her. "Own it."

"It wasn't as scary as I thought it would be," she admitted, her words careful. "But it's not my thing."

"Liar." I slid my cut back on. "Aren't you going to say goodbye?"

Jenna was walking backward as I homed in on her. "Goodbye."

"Not what I meant." I caught her in my arms, planning on leaving her with a lasting impression, when something stopped me. Jenna's eyes widened, but there was a feeling in my gut that she was bracing herself for what was coming. So, instead of attacking her mouth like I wanted, I bent and rested my lips against hers. The softest fucking kiss that I'd ever planted.

I let her go and she stumbled back, righting herself. "Um, ride safe, okay?"

Not like I didn't have a reason to return now.

Not what I expected. The small contact had my lips tingling. Ali had kissed me so sweetly and I half-hated him for that. Shaking myself off, I spied Jack entering the workshop.

"Hey," I said, jogging to catch up with him. "I heard you scored the job of counting spare parts."

The stock-take hadn't come up at lunch—mostly talk had been about his eighteenth, and Chrissie going on about where the best hairdressers, manicurists and spas were in town.

"Lucky me," he said, stopping and leaning against the roller door. "But it's cool, I've had a week off."

"I could help, I'm free in the morning and it'll give me a chance to learn more about the parts. I'm having trouble fielding some of the calls that come in. I don't want the mechanics to get sick of me passing the phone to them all the time."

"It's our job, so no one is going to care. Do you really want to help?" He tilted his head, skepticism written on his face. "Citizens aren't expected to come in over the weekend."

"I don't mind, really."

"I think Ali chose well. That would be great. Say, ten?" He had a beautiful smile. It lit up his face, making him seem young, which of course he was.

"Sounds good." He'd walked in on our kiss earlier and my face heated at the memory. "About what happened in the office…"

"Yeah, you and Ali. Lucky we didn't come later." He chuckled scratching his chin. "You know, technically I'm a minor. I shouldn't have to witness that shit."

"I'm so sorry. It was very unprofessional of me." My face heated, which only seemed to make Jack laugh more. "I'm so embarrassed."

"Don't be. I'm happy for my brother. 'Bout time he got a decent woman. He's had enough club groupies."

I wasn't sure what to say to that.

Thankfully, Jack filled in the silence. "Only problem for

you hooking up with Ali is that you've got to put up with the rest of us. We come as a package deal. Cage, too, and sometimes Jase, but we're usually together." He stopped a beat. "I don't mean you'd have to—"

I put my hand up, cutting him off. "I know that." I didn't want to hear him say what I thought he was going to say.

But apart from Jack and I having a second awkward moment, he was giving me something to think about. Being with Ali not only secured my place in the club, but it meant that I'd have a natural reason to socialize with them, too. Seeing that included Jack, I knew I was running out of reasons to slow thing down. However, that didn't make my plans for using Ali as a decoy any easier.

My problem. Ali might have kissed me soft and sweet before he'd left, but I wasn't a fool. He was going to expect a hell of a lot more from me.

Jack stood straighter, giving me another stunning smile. "Guess I'll get back to work. I'll see you around."

I could do this. There was no other choice.

Chapter Seven

Ali

"Go on, you know you want to say something." I looked over at a silent Cage who sat behind the wheel of the car we were using for surveillance. We'd taken possession of it earlier that day from a friend of the club.

"Nah, I got nothing." He shrugged, worrying the two rings he had through the bottom of his lip. "Okay, why her?"

It was my turn to do the old shoulder lift and drop. "No idea, she just is."

"You're fucking serious. This is not simply a fuck to you."

"Easy pussy is only that, easy. So, no, guess she's not."

"Huh," he said.

"Is that all you've got?" I gave him a cautious glance. Cage was normally a lot more quick-witted, usually with some fucked-up opinion on any subject. My being serious about one woman should have had him coming out with line after deviant line. I wasn't sure if the silence was worse.

"What more do you want? She's gorgeous, not like no one noticed that part. But you spent most of the week ignoring her."

Yeah, like I'd admit even to my best friend that I had no idea what angle to take on my approach. The possibility of scaring her off worried the shit out of me. But in the end, I'd been unable to hold back from making a move. Wasn't going to work if Jenna didn't get the real me. Luckily, she seemed to like me, even if she hadn't admitted her feelings to herself.

Cage put his hands on the steering wheel. Running them over the cracked vinyl, he continued to bite at his lip rings. "It's a good thing. Choosing a woman that half your brothers haven't had their dicks in."

I snorted. "Yeah, it is." Not one of my brothers had, or would, get their dicks anywhere near Jenna. That remained a fact. But her being new to the MC wasn't even a fraction of the reason I wanted her.

"Of course, you're not there right now." Cage smirked over to me.

"You really think any of them would be game?"

He laughed out loud. "No, brother, I do not. Fuck, there he is."

I looked in the same direction. Sure enough, Reed — the man we were hunting — exited a club two buildings up from us. We could have gone inside and hauled him out, but that meant witnesses. So, we'd been sitting out here doing fuck all for the past couple of hours. Time to change that up.

I reached down and hit the built-in compartment, pulling out my Glock, and climbing from the car. Cage started the engine and followed as I walked the short distance between me and our mark.

"You going somewhere?" I watched as fear replaced the doleful look on the skinny prick's face. A chinless, pin-eyed little man. Fuck, we could have sent Jenna in to take care of this piece of shit.

"I can explain," Reed said, putting his hands up in front of himself.

"Bit late for that." I reached out and took hold of his upper arm. His entire body vibrated and his heart was likely bursting near out of his chest. I had a vision of a cartoon I'd watched as a kid where the characters' hearts did that and chuckled to myself.

"Look, just give me a few days." Reed's eyes went left then right, not landing on my face straight away. When they finally did, he made a real big mistake. "Tell you what. I gotta sister."

Cage leaned over the passenger side. "Just get in the fuckin' car. We don't have all night."

I shoved Reed. He stumbled, steadying himself on the side of the vehicle.

"Listen to me," he said. "You can have her, you and your mate here. She's fifteen, real sweet."

"Just get in the car, you piece of shit." I pushed him into the back seat and climbed in.

"Hey, Sunshine," Cage said as both the mark and I slid across the filthy interior.

I doubted he'd forgotten his name. With Cage, they were always 'Sunshine,' and that tag never boded well for them.

Sunshine's next problem would be the chosen location. If Cage drove to a park that we both knew was at the end of the street, he would receive a beat-down that could end with him spending a few days in a local hospital. But if he took him back to the house where we got the car, then Sunshine's ending would be a fuck lot more permanent. After the comment about the underage sister, it was anyone's guess what my brother would do. He was no angel, but most men with an ounce of morality would have been pissed off about being offered a little girl. I know I was.

Personally, I hoped for the park. Not that I gave a shit about what happened to the little fucker, and it wasn't like he didn't deserve it, but I didn't want to go back to the house. The owner, an old club associate, had a daughter in her twenties. She was a nice enough chick, pretty, fairly intelligent. But after I'd bent her over the family kitchen table a few months back, she seemed to think she had some entitlement. She'd greeted me hours earlier with a squeeze to my cock. Interestingly, this time when she'd touched me, the thing hadn't even so much as twitched.

Which was funny, when I thought about it. Because every time I played back Jenna's hands brushing along the edges of my jeans, sprawling over my stomach, her tits against my back, the damn thing started to try to punch its way free. Jenna hadn't even so much as tapped my happy place and she was causing all kinds of trouble.

Even as Cage pulled up at the curb near the park, memories of those tiny hands with their short fingernails started to jack me up.

"Right, out you get, Sunshine." Cage had gone all business.

Reed looked over to me like he wanted my help. *Fat chance.* I ignored him and climbed out of the opposite door, adrenaline that had nothing to do with Sunshine surging through my body. He pissed me off. It had taken too long to find his sorry ass, and I could have been home locking things down with a certain woman.

Cage raised a single brow at me. Translation— *You want this?*

I shook my head. Translation— *No, brother, I might get carried the fuck away.*

He lifted one shoulder at me as he got behind Sunshine, guiding him to a secluded area. Translation— *No problem, I got this.*

This had never happened before. Normally, I was looking to take the edge off with a good beat-down. Jenna was distracting me from my club duties. No big deal. At least I told myself that.

With nothing better to do, I followed them. It was cold as fuck out, not likely that anyone would venture as deep into the area as we were, so a look out was unnecessary.

When my brother pulled up short, he turned to our company. "You don't so happen to have a few grand stuffed in your pockets, do you?"

The man's eyes widened. "Nah, but I can get it for you. No problem, just give me a couple of days." He was sweating, fucking rivers going down over his pasty skin. An acrid smell filled the air as he pissed his pants. At least that hadn't happened in the car.

Cage stared at him with disgust. "Really?"

Shoving my hands into my jacket pockets, I started kicking at the grass. I needed this to be over with, we still had Salina's to visit.

The grunts that followed had possums and other assorted wildlife skittering up the trees that filled the parklands. The sounds of Cage's fists smacking against Sunshine's skin were only a few decibels lower than a resounding crack that had a bunch of birds rising and squawking as they sailed into the starless dark sky.

The shitty light didn't hide the fact that Cage had busted Sunshine's jaw with the final punch. It looked like someone was going to be drinking store brand soup for the next six or so weeks.

My brother sauntered over to me, throwing a careless arm around my shoulders, and we left the park. "*Now* to get laid."

"We're gathering intel," I said, reminding him of why we were heading over to the brothel.

"*And* getting laid." He looked over his shoulder, back at where Sunshine still lay on the ground. "Yeah, and you're fired."

* * * *

Salina's was a popular whorehouse only a few minutes' walk from the main business center of the city. It was tucked behind an iron fence that shielded pink rose bushes. The plants were all cut back for the cold, but I knew their scent. Nice, though not as good as Jenna's.

The madam herself greeted us. Tall, willowy, with a prominent Adam's apple that bobbed behind her jewel-encrusted choker. A couple of decades ago, Salina had sported a full set of cock and balls.

"Boys," she said, putting her arms around me and kissing my cheek. "It's been too long."

True, we hadn't had cause to be in her establishment for many months. Her greeting was about as genuine as it got from our sources.

For Cage, she delivered a full-on lip lock. I'd often

wondered about that. Maybe it was an idea to ask him if he'd ever been up close and personal with her post-op pussy on occasion. But then again, there were some things concerning my brother that I was afraid to ask.

She led us away from the main area with its women in lingerie, business types, bucks' parties and assorted other losers, to a room she referred to as her parlor. It was full of the kind of furniture a man my size was wary of sitting on. As usual, I chose the sturdiest thing in the room—a short blue couch with too many lacy cushions on it.

As much as the room gave off a visit with an elderly spinster aunt vibe, the porn that played on a huge screen across from me cut that idea to pieces. Cage remained standing. It appeared as though questioning Salina came down to me. Fair enough, he'd done the last job.

On cue, two women appeared. Both working girls, both looked like they'd make just as much coin modeling as renting out their pussies. Not that they weren't throwing a freebie our way—or Cage's way, to be more specific. I had not the slightest interest in Salina's girls.

They knew their business, sidling up on either side of my brother, who didn't seem surprised that I kept myself planted on the couch.

"Ali found himself a woman," he said, grinning over at Salina. "His dick has a sold sign on it."

I stifled my laugh as Salina gave me a smile that seemed both indulgent and calculating.

As soon as the three of them cleared the room, the madam poured us out two glasses of bourbon and sat down on a fragile-looking chair, crossing her legs, the hem of her dress rising a good few inches.

"So, what is she like, this lady of yours?"

I shrugged. "Perfect."

"You meet her at your club?" She took a sip from the cut-crystal glass.

"She's working at the garage, helping Chrissie."

"A citizen. How lovely." Her face fell. "How is Chrissie?"

"You know, coping."

She smiled. "Poor thing, losing Hellion like that. Terribly sad. And Jack?"

"Same."

She nodded. "Speaking of a different kind of Jack, I had some Diamond Jacks here a while back. I didn't know you kids were playing nice."

"Meaning?"

"They were here all of ten minutes and your boy Kitty showed up. I didn't think it was anything shady. They danced around wary for a while, but they were deep in conversation pretty soon after."

Salina wasn't a girl who caused us, or anyone else, trouble. With my club, she liked to assume that any help or information she gave us was done in the name of friendship. But Kitty's meeting with the Diamonds should have been reported. Wraith would have given her the heads up if we were using her brothel as a meeting ground.

"Anything else?"

"Three nights ago, two other Diamonds arrived, which was interesting."

"Yeah. Why so?" This had me sitting up.

"They asked about the others, if they'd been here. You'd reckon being from the same club that they wouldn't have to come and see me about it, wouldn't you?"

Very much so, but seeing Kitty's visit was a surprise to me, I didn't say anything on the subject.

"Yeah, you would," I said. "Who was asking?"

"The VP, Chops. Had his sweet little nephew with him. Now that boy, he revs the girls up as much as Cage does. They were practically arguing over who was taking him up the staircase." She smiled over her glass. "Not that he went."

"Chops and the nephew didn't stay?"

"No, here for all of five minutes."

"Who's the nephew?" As I asked the question I mulled over what she had said. The Diamonds who had come originally had probably dropped by for purely recreational purposes. It gave me the impression that they weren't supposed to be in the area, that the VP didn't know for sure where they were.

Dissension in the Diamond Jacks' ranks could mean good news for us. Guess that was going to mean some more digging. This of course meant that I'd have to stay longer in the city. Maybe the rest of the weekend. Cage was unlikely to complain, but I was starting to become very pissed off. My only real hope was that Wraith would want us back to discuss the situation with Kitty.

"His name is Tyler," she said.

Never heard of him. "You know him well?"

"Well enough."

Funny, she'd failed to mention this particular biker to me. I didn't show that she'd pissed me off, however. We all referred to Salina's place as Switzerland and it had become a home to a hell of a lot of rival club and gang meetings. We all needed this venue and no one caused trouble within its walls.

Added to that, there was not a single camera or listening device. The law was paid well to keep their noses out, making the meetings as discreet as those things could be. The difference for the Devil's Prophets was that Salina gave us the occasional piece of information.

She did this for personal reasons, even six-foot madams ran into trouble on occasion. Hers had come in the form of a live-in boyfriend who got handy with his fists whenever he needed to get his point across. Like a lot of women, she had tried to keep it a secret, but when one beating had landed her in hospital, Cage and I had taken it upon ourselves to relocate her boyfriend. He currently resided in bush land, buried deep, and not in any state to lay a finger on her again.

"This Tyler, he's loyal to his uncle?" That stood to reason. As much as club took priority, bikers were only human. Blood was blood.

"Very. Chops raised him. He comes across as a sweet boy,

but there's something dangerous inside of him. Wouldn't turn my back if I were you. Geezer would be smart to keep an eye on them both. That's my thoughts."

"What's his actual role in his club?"

"Officially, he's just a member like any other boy."

"Unofficially?"

"He's you—a smaller version, but he's enforcer."

I frowned. My position was not something that normally got spoken out loud. I wore no patch saying what I was. Salina's mentioning it was out of line, despite my knowing that she'd never breathe a word to anyone. Or at least I hoped that was the case.

"Smaller?" I said, cocking my brows.

"Compared to you," she laughed. "He's a big boy where it counts, so I heard. But darling…" She waved her hand at me.

"We might need a meeting set up in the future with Chops and Tyler. You can arrange that?"

She nodded, her lips pursed. "Of course, darling. Now tell me more about this citizen who has captured your heart."

That wasn't happening. I glanced over at the porno, pretending to pay attention to the two women strapping electrodes to a dude chained down on the bed. I winced.

Salina laughed again, patted my leg and left me to wait it out for Cage. That bastard had better not take all night.

I settled back, staring at the wall to the side of the screen and contemplated this latest shit with the Diamonds and what it could mean for us. Dixie would never work close with Geezer and his mad ways, neither would he be happy if we simply walked. But Chops was a whole other issue.

Shit just might work out if we kept our ears to the ground.

Chapter Eight

Jenna

Jack wasn't there when I was let into the compound the following morning. I'd arrived early and headed over to the workshop. The roller door was partially up, so I ducked under it, finding the place lit up bright.

"Anyone here?" I called out, not wanting to be surprised by one of the mechanics putting in overtime.

The office door was open and a man appeared in the frame. A long black beard streaked through with gray hung down to his mid chest. He wore his hair, also showing signs of age, tied back tightly, small wisps framing his forehead. Clearly a member, his cut was adorned with multiple patches.

"Well, look at this." He smiled and lumbered down the steps. "You'd be the new secretary. I'd be your boss, Kitty."

He had a faint English accent and a gravelly voice to go with it.

"I'm Jenna." I kept a wary distance. "I'm supposed to meet Jack. We're doing a stock-take in spare parts."

"Good of you to come in on the weekend. Seeing you likely didn't know I'd be back, I'm guessing that wasn't to impress me." He closed the distance between us, my heart thudding hard in my chest. Kitty appeared friendly, but he was also of the generation that would make him one of Hellion's men. I liked Wraith for what happened, but that didn't mean I was ruling out anyone else.

"It benefits me, too," I said, standing my ground because there was no point trying to outrun him. I'd never make it off the compound, let alone escape the garage. "I haven't done this type of work before. It helps with the learning curve."

"Smart girl," he said and stopped walking. "Well, come over here and let me get a look at you. I can already see why Ali's a little taken."

Word sure traveled fast around here.

"Oh, Ali and I aren't anything," I said, wondering if that was a mistake.

"Not what I heard. But as long as it doesn't interfere with your job, I'm happy about it." His hands went to his waist.

"Kitty!" Behind me, my son sounded delighted. "When did you get back?" His boots thudded on the concrete as he ran over to us.

I was startled when they shared a warm embrace, Kitty stepping back and inspecting him with an obvious fondness. It was almost a paternal gesture. But his face clouded. "Jack, this young lady is here to help you, and you're late."

"No, he's not, I'm early," I said. "Bad habit, I'm afraid."

"I doubt you have anything bad about you." Kitty smiled, revealing a gold tooth. "Well, I'll leave you two to it. Put the reports on the desk when you're done. I'll look them over, see what that stupid nephew of mine has been up to."

This man is Pony's uncle?

With a nod to me, he exited the workshop, leaving me in one piece, still breathing and alone with my son. My fear dissipated only to be replaced by a nervousness that I hadn't seen coming.

"Let's get to it," Jack said. "Sooner we finish, the sooner we can get out of here."

He led the way to the spare parts room and we entered, both of us giving doubtful looks to the boxes on the shelves.

"I think this is going to take a while," I said, not minding one bit.

Jack picked up a laptop off the bench, flipping the lid. "You're not wrong."

He'd worn normal clothes. Baggy jeans and a hoodie with

a skull cap pulled tight over his head. Pretending he was just a typical teenager was easy with him dressed that way. When he yawned, he didn't bother to cover his mouth.

"How do you want to do this?" I said. "We can work together, or both take sections?"

"How about you enter the numbers and I count?" He handed me the computer. "Or we ditch this shit and go grab coffee."

"Coffee sounds good, but I think we might get started first."

He groaned, but walked to one of the shelves. "What did you think of Kitty?"

"Terrifying." The word just came out.

Jack chuckled. "He's a teddy bear."

"So, he's back for good?" I wasn't sure of Kitty's story, or his reason for being absent. I was even less convinced that Jack would fill me in.

"I don't know. He's basically nomad. Comes and goes." He was scribbling on a pad as he talked. "He's strange sometimes, but it's fair enough."

"Oh?" I came closer and started typing in the information from his notes.

"Yeah, lost his entire family. It was years ago, before I was born. Their house burned down."

"Oh, my God. That's so sad. He had kids?"

"Yeah. Three and an old lady."

Pity filled me. That poor man. I ruled him out as Hellion's henchman. It didn't reason with me that someone who suffered that kind of loss would so blatantly murder a teenage girl.

"So what's your story, Jenna?"

"There is none really." I put my head down and concentrated on my task. "I'm really getting to know Chrissie."

"Ah, she loves you." He snorted. "She doesn't like office work so much, but she gets bored at home. She's not really my ma, you know?"

No one had mentioned that to me, but seeing as I did know, I had to feign my surprise. "She's not?"

"Nah, some junkie whore had me."

"You don't know your birth mother?"

"All I know is her name was Sophie, that she gave me up to my old man not long after I was born. Chrissie raised me."

"I'm sorry, Jack." And I really was.

"She's special," Jack said, my heart breaking a little more. "She had the proof that her old man cheated and she never made me feel bad for it. It was years before I worked out that that was how it all went down. You'd never know with Chrissie, though."

There it was again, Jack's habit of calling her Chrissie. I can't say I didn't find it easier. But his hating me, or who he thought was his actual mother, was like being physically hit. I was wrong, the worst thing that could happen to me wasn't being killed by the club, it was Jack rejecting me.

"It was good of her," I said.

"Are you okay?" He stopped working, pulled over a stool and sat on it.

"I'm fine, just great." I put the laptop aside. "You know, maybe if I helped with the counting, this might go faster."

* * * *

"Okay, break time. You're some kind of workaholic." Jack lifted a box out of my arms and set it aside on the bench.

"I'll make coffee then." I went off to do that, Jack on my heels, following me to the office. We'd been hard at it for four hours and were making some progress. I'd been relieved that there wasn't as much out of place as there could have been. It wasn't all that bad, just a few wrongly shelved items and some missing parts.

While I pulled out a chair, Jack settled on the couch against the wall, his long legs sprawled out in front of him. "Are you going to tell me your story now?"

"Nothing real interesting, I can tell you that much."
I crossed my legs and when I noticed my foot tapping, I
stilled it.

"What are you doing in the sticks?"

"I got tired of the city. I grew up in the country, not far
from here. I went to Mt. Xavier Secondary, actually. Well, a
couple of years, anyway."

"And now you're here."

"Now I'm here." Although I wasn't sure he was going to
like that fact when I had the chance to tell him who I was.

I'd been thinking on it since he'd told me he hated me.
Seeing I'd come this far, I had to keep going. If Jack had an
opinion on me, and there was no one around to dispute it,
then I'd have to let him get to know me for me. That was no
guarantee, but I was out of options.

"I'm meeting a girlfriend for drinks tomorrow night,"
I said, referring to an out-of-the-blue invitation from the
woman in my Pilates classes. "Any suggestions? Casey's
new in town, too."

"Jimbo's," Jack said. "You can't miss it, it's that big joint
on Forest and Main."

"Okay, we'll try that."

Jack just grinned, yet all I could think about was how
much my son hated me.

Chapter Nine

Jenna

I arrived for my drinks date with Casey with a heavy heart. But when I saw her coming toward me, I plastered a smile on my face. She'd walked as well. Dressed similar to me in skinny jeans and ballet flats, she waved when she saw me and hurried over.

"I haven't been here before," she said. "What's it like?"

"No idea, one of the guys from my work recommended it. Looks okay, though." I glanced up at the old-fashioned façade, the striped awnings over windows that held boxes of flowers.

"Oh, well, as long as they serve alcohol, I'm in." She started tugging off her scarf as we headed for the door. "Don't know about you, but I could do with a drink, or five."

I laughed, even though it was the last thing I felt like doing as I followed her through the entrance. Inside, the interior had been restored to original. Dark wood paneling, red patterned carpet and lots of lead light features. Booths with dark green upholstery lined a far wall, but we headed for the long, curved timber bar.

The nods to modern times were a loud sound system pumping out rap and a few big screens playing a football game.

After hanging our jackets and bags on the back of the stools, we settled ourselves in. A man in his sixties with a neatly trimmed gray beard and a black shirt with the name *Jimbo* embroidered over the left pocket approached us. The other servers were female and all wore tight black T-shirts with *Jimbo's Pub* screen-printed in white over a picture of a full beer mug, so I assumed he owned the place.

"Evening, ladies," he said. "What can I get you?"

A triple something of take-the-pain-away is what I need. But seeing no such drink existed, I ordered Sav Blanc, as did Casey.

"Nice place," she said to him as he poured our wines.

"Thank you." He waved his hand when we both went for our purses. "First is on the house, you both make my bar look good." He winked, but it seemed more a fatherly than a sleazy gesture.

After we thanked him and he left to serve other patrons, Casey turned to me. "He's either sweet, or an ax murderer."

"I'm thinking sweet," I said.

"Well, he didn't try and look at our boobs, so you're probably right." She glanced around the crowded room. "I'm thinking this is the place to be on Sunday nights."

She was right. The crowd varied, young and old, all looking as if they were sending off the weekend in their happy place.

"Here's to our first date," I said, lifting my glass.

She clinked her drink against mine. "So tell me about you."

"Not much to tell. I work in the office at a garage." I shrugged. "Nothing as exciting as a hospital."

Casey worked as a nurse, I'd found out that information from our few text messages.

"Believe me, the ER here is not that hectic. Which garage?" She leaned an elbow on the bar and took a sip from her glass, her expression interested.

"The one just out of town."

"The biker garage? The Devil's Prophets garage?"

"That's the one. I only recently started there."

"Wow, you are a dark horse." She shook her head. "Now, that's an exciting job, or at least an interesting place to work. What are they like?"

I wasn't surprised she knew about the MC, it would be hard not to notice a group of men who wore leather and rode huge, loud bikes, but her lack of judgment and simple curiosity had me more relaxed.

"Mechanics, I guess. I don't have a lot to do with them." *Except for one who kissed me and one who spent the preceding morning breaking my heart.*

"Some of the girls at work have been out to parties there, pretty wild from what I hear." She leaned down. "Have you partied out there?"

"No, but I'm invited to one next week. An eighteenth. I've been assured there will be families invited, too." I frowned. I hoped she didn't have the wrong impression of me. Now that I'd jumped in and actually gone out for drinks with her, I found I liked Casey.

"Sounds about right. I think the real stuff happens pretty late. You'll just have to Cinderella yourself out of there." She grinned, finishing her drink.

"I plan to, no point turning into a pumpkin. Still, it would have been rude to say no. Jack's a nice kid. He's, um, he's my boss' son." I took another mouthful from my glass as this time one of the female bar staff arrived and produced fresh drinks for us.

"Any of them cute? They come in for blood drive, but I don't handle any of that, so I've never been up close." She paid for the round. "The girls at work reckon there are a few hot guys out there."

"A couple, I suppose." It would have been weird if I said no. Chances were that most people would assume they were all beer gutted, filthy with long flowing beards. I'd seen a few of those types around the garage and compound, but they contrasted with the gym-enthusiast younger members.

"Anyone of them in particular catch your eye?"

I dropped my head. Sure, but that was going to be nipped in the bud as soon as I had the chance. Ali—hardly the man for me—no way.

I'd been thinking on the subject, telling myself that I'd

only gotten carried away because I'd been so happy to have met Jack properly. It was understandable that I'd go with that enthusiasm and give off signals to Ali that I hadn't meant. But with distance, I realized my mistake. Ali was a persistent man, but I could be stubborn, too.

Strangely, she didn't push for another answer as two men came up on either side of us.

They wore polo shirts with the Mt. Xavier Golf Club emblem on the pockets. "What are you ladies drinking?" the one beside me said.

I put him at late twenties, early thirties. He looked nice, neat hair weighed down with a lot of product and a faint pink to his skin.

He was the opposite of Ali who I doubted owned product. The biker had more of a shower and shake, messy short thing going on. I had the feeling it would be soft too, silky if you ran your fingers through it. I pushed the thought away as Casey rolled her eyes at me.

"Moët," she said.

It didn't scare off the intruders. "I'm Gary," the man said, putting out his hand. "I work over at Barnes and Collins."

I had no idea where or what that was. "Okay," I said.

Casey just laughed.

"I doubt they have champagne here," the other man said. He had blond hair, and he, too, owned shares in L'Oreal for Men.

"Yes, we do." Our server was back, winking at me as she produced a bottle of champagne and an ice bucket from beneath the bar.

It proved expensive and I frowned as she pulled the cork, though the men didn't seem too worried as our wine was poured into flutes.

"You have to give us your names, now," Gary said. "He's Brett."

"Casey." My new friend pointed to me. "That's Jenna."

"Pretty names, pretty girls," Gary said, nodding. "Been on the course all day, got a hole in one." He leered when he spoke, leaning closer to me.

"That's nice," I said, 'what the helling' it and picking up my drink. Who didn't like the French stuff?

Casey made short work of her own wine and placed the glass down steadily. That made three drinks each in half an hour. I may have been at a low point, but I knew that I needed to pace myself better. It didn't stop Gary from pouring us more.

"So, what are you girls doing out?"

"Um, having a drink," Casey said, meeting my eye. Brett had draped his arm over the back of her chair.

"Funny," Brett said. "I like this one."

He seemed awkward, unsure of himself, despite his words. His demeanor completely different to the way Ali behaved around me. The biker knew exactly what he wanted and went for it. I smiled to myself, but lost it when Gary followed Brett's lead and encircled his arm around my chair. It wasn't intimidating—neither of these men was threatening—but I was annoyed.

They started to talk about their work. It turned out they were both in insurance, had gone to school together, they even shared a house. They high-fived over our heads and were happy to speak about their lives and offer an occasional question as to ours. Mostly the answers to those went uncommented on.

Casey looked as bored as me, her eyes darting about as if for escape. "We were thinking of leaving," she said. "Maybe catch some dinner."

"Good idea." Gary took a swig of beer. "Here, or you wanna go someplace else?"

"Just us girls, I'm afraid," Casey said. "It was nice to meet you."

As I went to rise, a hand slid over my thigh. "Not so fast, we're only starting to get to know each other."

The arm around the back of my chair clamped tighter. *Okay, this I don't like.*

* * * *

"Are you going over there?" Jase watched the scene over at the bar along with the rest of us. "Jack's telling me that Jenna had planned on going out with her girlfriend looked more like the double date kind of set-up to me."

"Free country," I said, playing with my empty shot glass. Right, like I wasn't going to be going over and smacking heads in the next two seconds.

"Your girl doesn't look too happy." Cage bumped his shoulder against mine. "I might come with you."

"I think I got this." Relief washed over me as I took in the foursome at the bar. Jenna inched away from the asshat that had just put his fucking hand on her. Her friend was doing the same. Time to end that particular situation.

When I got up and started to push my way through the crowd, Cage shadowed me. Like Salina's, Jimbo's wasn't somewhere we started trouble. Different reasons — this was local and went against the low profile we took, and Jimbo being an actual friend without strings to the club. As sergeant-at-arms, despite his love of a good fight, Cage would make sure this didn't get out of hand. Or he could try, either or.

They didn't see me coming. I approached at an angle, but I was hard to miss. Jenna's girl finally looked up and spotted me. She didn't seem happy, probably thought it was all going to go from bad to worse. *Possible.*

We wore our cuts, so if she knew where Jenna worked, and she was local, then she'd have known who we were.

She tapped Jenna's arm, getting her attention, but I was there behind my woman before Jenna had a chance to turn around. I removed the asshat's arm from her with a hard jerk. Real lucky for him, he took the one off her leg on his own undertaking.

"What's this?" I said. "You cheating on me already?"

Her eyes narrowed. She was a little drunk. Not smart, her making herself vulnerable to jokers like the one currently staring at me wide-eyed. Him, I'd deal with later.

"Ali?" She tried to pull herself together. *Cute.*

I got in her face. "Well?"

"Just having a drink with my friend." Her words trailed off as her friend continued her glaring at me. *Also cute, and very fucking pointless.*

"Casey," the brunette said.

"I'm sorry," Jenna said to her. "This is Ali and that's Cage. I work with them."

I'd been reduced to one of her workmates. Well, that wasn't happening. I removed her jacket from where it hung on the back of her stool and held it out to her.

"Maybe it's time to go home." I shook it for emphasis, that rose scent flying in my face. Hard to be mad at someone who smelled so good.

"Yeah," Casey said. "Like that's your decision. We can handle this. You and your buddy here can go back to your little biker friends over in the corner."

"It's fine," Jenna said. "Maybe we should leave."

"Right," Casey said, getting to her feet and wavering slightly. "Let's go someplace else."

Ah, hell no. Jenna was going home and even though I knew I acted like an overbearing asshole, I stood my ground.

"I'll get you a cab." No way was she getting on my bike, not like she was. She'd damn well fall off.

"Look," Casey said, "we're grown women, we don't need—"

"You do not tell me what to do." Jenna's words were steel as she stared me down. "I'm not sure why you think you can, but you do not. You understand that, Ali? Kissing me doesn't give you any damn rights."

Cage's eyes rolled to the ceiling and he muttered, "I'm liking her more and more."

I just blinked a few times at the tiger before me. *Fuck.* I started to get hard, for what it was worth.

She snatched the jacket from my hands and started pulling it on. She had a couple of stabs at the final sleeve, but flinched away when I tried to help. But before she could wrap the scarf wound about her neck, I stepped closer and put my arms around her, lifting her off her feet.

Only two kisses might not buy me any rights—time to find out what a third one got me.

Casey moved in then, ready to rescue her friend from the fucking asshole who held her. I went back a few steps as Cage got in front of her. I'm not sure what he said, but she gave us a curious look and ceased her advance.

Then I kissed my girl. She might have been lit, but she had no problems giving back what I gave her. One hand tangled up in my hair, tugging it. The other she placed around my neck. There were a few cheers in the background as I cupped her ass and her legs came around my waist.

I had no problems with the public display, but Jenna pulled her head back, either to get air, or to return to her senses. I grinned at her.

"Well?"

"You still don't get to tell me what to do." She wasn't smiling, there was some kind of war going on behind her eyes. Eyes that had pupils too wide for her half-drunk state.

"We'll make a deal. There's one place where I call the shots, and we ain't been there yet, so I don't want to hear you argue." I nuzzled her neck. "Not happening tonight, as much as I want it. You're going home, babe. We'll pick this up tomorrow."

When I put my head back up, she looked surprised. She wasn't the only one. But I had no intention of taking her to my bed, or getting in hers, seeing it was closer, without her being one hundred percent certain as to what she was doing.

I slid her down my body and set her on her feet. "You too, lightweight," I said to Casey who was still at the bar with Cage.

She glanced at Cage, shrugged, and wandered over to us. "Me too, what?"

"You're going home, unless you wanna stay and play

with my little biker buddy over there. But I'll warn you, his games might be a little more than you're used to."

Cage watched us with a blank face. If he was disappointed that I'd taken his toy from him, he wasn't letting on.

As soon as we hit the pavement, a cab eased up alongside and a couple of women tumbled out. As much as I wouldn't have minded pulling Jenna into me again, I knew that the temptation to start something when she wasn't operating on a full eight cylinders would rear up.

I put them both into the car, before going around to pay and instruct the driver.

We had time, Jenna and me.

Chapter Ten

Jenna

The aspirin fizzing in the glass of water sounded way too loud. This was my second dose and I hoped it did the trick.

Chrissie eyed me with amusement. "Fun night?"

"Drinks with a girlfriend." Casey had texted me earlier that morning, saying she'd had a great time and we needed to do it again. That bucked me up a little. I'd been worried that after our date had been crashed by the Devil's Prophets, she'd have run a mile.

I was pretty sure that when Cage came into the office before Chrissie could answer, he banged the door on purpose.

"Morning, princess," he said. I was wrong, the aspirin hadn't been that loud, but Cage was.

"Hey," I said, downing the disgusting painkiller.

"Did she tell you she was out drinking and picking up men last night?" His grin was killer as he turned to Chrissie. "Ali was very unimpressed."

Chrissie snorted a laugh. "Jenna! Good for you."

"I'm paying for it now, and I wasn't out picking up men. They simply happened along." I got up and found myself another bottle of water, my third for the morning.

"Whatever," Cage said. "Results were the same."

"He didn't do anything, did he? To Gary and Brett?"

"Why do you care?" Cage folded his arms across his chest. "You said they just turned up."

"That doesn't mean I want them hurt."

He sucked in his bottom lip. "I'll let him tell you. Come

on, Chrissie, move your ass, I got a lot on today."

He slapped her backside as she walked past him, putting on her sunglasses. She giggled and they left me, only to be replaced by Ali.

He landed on the edge of my desk with a heavy thud and a scowl on his face. I was taken aback. He'd kissed me last night, seemed happy with the act, and now he'd done a complete turnaround.

"Do you know who you were talking to last night?" His eyes fired beneath his brows as he leaned down to me. "Do you?"

"No, but I assume you're going to tell me." I wrestled the urge to sit back in my chair, keeping my back rigid.

"Do you know why Bel is here?"

"I assumed because she is Wraith's girlfriend." I wondered what his wife, old lady, or whatever he had back at his home thought of that. Chrissie had mentioned her name was Anna and that was all I knew of her.

"She came here the night of Hellion's wake, someone brought her here, one of the girls. Her boyfriend had beaten her up."

"Oh." I shivered a little, wondering which one of them had done that.

"Yeah, he'd been doing it for a while. Lost his shit in public and when…it doesn't matter who, saw, she brought Bel here for protection."

"Right," I said, dragging the word out. "This is really a women's shelter, how stupid of me not to notice that."

"I wouldn't go that far." Ali's face relaxed a little. "There's always a trade-off."

For me, too? "And your point?"

"Last night you were talking to Gary Hemlock, her ex."

Do I have a sign on me or something? Abusive men apply within. I eyed Ali. He was big, intimidating, with more than an air of violence, but I never once felt it directed at me. Then again, that might have been wishful thinking.

"Jenna? You got anything to say about that?" He sat back

a bit, no longer in my face.

"I was having a drink with Casey, they came up and started talking to us. That's all that happened. When you barged over we were leaving." Or trying to.

"I already figured that out. Babe, I'm not angry at you. I just didn't like you talking to that piece of shit." He tilted his head to the side. "Now, I have to hammer him again. Not that that is a problem, the prick deserves it."

"Wait? You beat him up over Bel?" I frowned.

"Sure. He wanted to hit someone smaller, it was only right that someone bigger laid into him." He appeared totally confused that I was questioning what he'd done.

But I could see the sense, not that I agreed with violence. Hitting a man who hit women had some logic. I just couldn't see a member of a biker club thinking that way. Their own treatment of women was hardly gentlemanly.

"Wait," I said, trying to get a handle on things. "You don't believe in hitting women?"

"Is that what you think of me?" He shut down any expression on his face.

"Ali, I hardly know you, I haven't made any assumptions." Yes, I had, but my preconceptions weren't without warrant.

"But you wanna get to know me, right?" He was still staring at me.

"I guess."

"You guess."

"I mean…" *Shit.* I had nothing.

"Keep going."

"At some stage last night" — *maybe the third drink* — "I'd decided that you and I were not going to date."

"Good, because I don't date. Anything else? By the way, you kissed me back." His face morphed into a smartass grin. "Don't you dare deny that. You might have been drunk as fuck, but you were well aware of what you were doing."

"You think you have me all figured out, don't you?" I shook my head. "I didn't come here to bag a member of the MC, if that's what you think."

"Actually, I've barely worked you out." He looked at me thoughtfully. "One minute you're a timid little kitten and the next, bam, out come the claws. Gotta say, I like it, though."

Timid? Quiet mostly, but seeing I'd left home just before my fifteenth birthday, I'd hardly have survived if I was a coward. Ali could never even guess that I'd walked into this compound aware that I might never leave. My body could end up buried somewhere out in the mountains and I'd never be missed by a single soul.

"You like me telling you off?" That made no sense. Ali was more the kind of man who liked to be in charge. He'd said so himself, at least in one area if I recalled. The thought of the exact location sent heat surging through my body.

"If you didn't, it would mean you didn't care."

"How the hell did you come to that conclusion?" I had to laugh. Ali seemed intent on his opinion as to my reasons.

"Oh, you care, but you don't want to admit it."

He was as sure of himself as I was unsure about myself. One of the hundreds of reasons why this was not going to work out with us. I stopped my thoughts from derailing. *Physical*, I reminded myself, *this is just physical, a means to an end.*

"What are you thinking?"

God, the constant way he watches me. "Nothing. You don't date."

"Don't see the point."

"You never go to the movies with a woman? Out to dinner? Nothing?" That made no sense to me. People dated, everyone except Ali and I that was. "What do you do? Walk up to a random woman and ask to kiss her or sleep with her?"

He scratched his chin. "Half the time, or more, they ask me."

"God, you are so arrogant."

"Why? I'm only telling you like it is. But to clarify it, I never considered actually dating. Until you of course."

Yeah, sure. I'm so special. "Uh-huh," I said. "What am I, the first woman you kissed?"

More chin scratching and an uncomfortable shift on the desk top. "No, but the first where that's all that happened and I'm still trying with you."

"But we'll never go on a date." Then a light bulb moment came upon me. "Hah! Jack's party. You even said it, I'm with you, we're going together. That's a date."

"Sure, if you want it to be." He grinned.

"Wait, I told you I already decided we weren't going to be dating."

Ali rolled his eyes. "Babe, you are so fucking deluded."

"No, I'm not, I get a say in this." I sat back, folded my arms and lifted my chin to him. "Don't push me."

"Get here."

My eyes widened. "If you think I jump just because you tell me to, then you have another thing coming."

"Get. Over. Here."

"No."

"You have two choices. You get that sweet fucking ass of yours on my lap, or I'll bend you over it and spank it raw." His mouth kicked up to one side. "Kind of hoping that you take the latter."

I had no idea why the words he was saying to me had my insides in an uproar, and not in a bad way. It was my turn to move in my seat, my thighs pressing together. Real great time for my libido to come out of hibernation. Right when there was six-and-a-half feet of rough and sexy mere inches from me. Then again, that was most likely the reason.

I knew he was strong—even with all the wine, I'd been aware of how easily he'd picked me up the night before. But when Ali reached over with both arms, plucked me from my chair and dropped me into his lap, I was gobsmacked. At least I was sitting, not bent over him, which was something.

"Are you planning on kissing me again?" I hoped he was, having the choice taken was much easier.

But he shook his head, his mouth a straight line. "Nope."

"Then what?" The spanking, I wasn't too sure about that.

"Work it out."

I frowned, trying hard to think while sitting on hard, muscled thighs, with enormous arms wrapped around me. That wasn't even mentioning the way he smelled, like the outdoors mixed with the garage, a beautiful combination. Something else too, but I had little understanding of that.

"I'm guessing you're not a cuddler." I pushed down the nervous laughter bubbling in my throat.

"Not usually, no."

"Oh."

"Took you long enough."

He wanted me to kiss him. If I did, then I didn't get just to be pulled along like driftwood in Ali's ferocious current.

He dropped his arms, resting his hands on the desk palms down behind him as he waited with patience.

I wriggled a little higher on him. *Is that? Yes, it is.* Christ, I was so in over my head that drowning was not only an option, but a temptation. I gasped before I could stop myself.

He chuckled. "What did you expect?"

I was not going to discuss his hard-on with him. Wrapping my arms around his neck, I kissed him and I damn well meant it.

He brought his arms around me again, opened his warm mouth against mine and slid his tongue inside, between my teeth. It was heaven and it was hell. Exhilarating and terrifying. *Being kissed is one thing, but instigating it? Well, it's amazing.* I was making a promise with that kiss, I was telling him that I wanted him.

I slid my hand down his shoulder, exploring his biceps, moving to his chest, finding his pecs as hard as the concrete floor in the workshop. Ali's hands were in my hair, down my back, sliding under my backside and lifting me so that I was now straddling him. That was a little much and I scooted back. He growled and pulled me forward, grinding me against the front of his pants.

We're almost in a public place, I chanted to myself. This is safe. Over and over the words repeated inside my head until I believed them. His phone rang and he ignored it as he took over the kiss.

I lost myself in him, this beautiful, infuriating man who I had no business associating with, let alone doing what I was doing. I was making out with him. The thought thrilled me to my toes.

The shrill sound of Ali's phone ringing had me pulling back. I didn't want a repeat of what happened last time when Jack had caught us.

"You should get that," I said.

I saw the screen read two missed calls as Ali punched in the lock code and read the message. Averting my gaze, I slid off him.

"I got church," he said.

I told myself the shivery feeling I had was relief—relief that he was leaving again because that seemed to be the constant result of those mysterious meetings.

"I guess you gotta go."

His fingers swiped down my face. "I think I need a minute."

That made two of us.

Chapter Eleven

Ali

"We got a lot to get through." Wraith banged his gavel on the table as I slid into my seat. "For starters, as of this morning, Kitty's returned to the city."

"He speak to you?" I asked.

"Yeah, he's trying to start a dialog with Geezer. He ran into them at Salina's and saw the opportunity. I don't give it much hope. As far as I'm concerned, we're never going to deal with the prick. But knowing his movements won't hurt."

There were murmurs of agreement around the room.

Opposite me, Cage smirked. "I think Ali has some news," he said, his expression something I wanted to smack off his face.

"Yeah, Ali, you wanna clear that up for us?" Wraith turned his focus on me. "Just get on with it. We don't want to be here all day and we have more important business to discuss."

"I'm claiming Jenna," I said, meeting each of their eyes in turn. "Anyone got issues with that?"

I didn't expect any objections and clearly, neither did Wraith. "Right, next point of business is some shit brewing with the Diamonds. It might impact on our plans, so we need to get that sorted."

"I have a problem." Pony had joined our other prospect, Spice, leaning back against the wall. His gaze went to his boots as soon as the words were out.

"You do?" Wraith's eyes widened.

"That shit that went on last night at Jimbo's. I think it needs to be discussed."

Pony wasn't one for highlighting himself. He kept his mouth shut tight in church. I was curious as to his point and so it seemed was every other brother in the room. All eyes were on the dopey prospect.

"You were out watching the bikes," I said. "You didn't see a damn thing."

"I heard, though. Jenna Mitchell was talking to Gary Hemlock. He's an enemy of the club. What if they hadn't just accidentally met?"

"You have a problem with my woman?"

"No," he mumbled, still finding his boots real interesting. "I was just saying, is all. I'm just looking out for the club."

Cage's breath whistled out through his teeth. "Pony, you might want to stick your head back up your ass."

Pony put his face up and blinked. "Sorry."

"Sorry, what?" Cage said, rolling his eyes at me.

"Sorry, sir."

"Right, next order, not that Pony shooting his mouth off was anything worth hearing." Wraith gave me a warning look. I relaxed back in my chair. Pony would keep. "Ali and Cage have some interesting news on the Diamond Jacks. Ali?"

"From what I've gathered," I said, "it's starting to appear as if Geezer is losing his hold on his club, so Kitty's talking with him or his men, more useless than what Wraith first thought. There's obviously some division among the Diamonds, and I get the feeling that Chops is going to make a play for leadership. He's got a nephew onside, that according to my intel looks like he's up for the job of assisting that."

"Which means," Cage said, "they might be in the right place to take over our business with Dixie. An easy way to shake him loose."

For years, we were the hired muscle for Dixie, a medium-sized drug distributer. But twelve months ago, Hellion had pushed us farther into the kingpin's sights. Upping our dealings to interstate distribution. High returns, but high risk to go along with it.

The stupid part of it all was that our legal work was outdoing our shady dealings at least twofold. Wraith's idea to go legit and to buy a trucking company seemed a smarter option. Of course, you don't just get to walk away from that shit. Leaving Dixie shorthanded was going to have consequences — bad ones.

"You learn this all from the trannie?" Trigger asked, his face wrinkling. At thirty, he'd been around a while, transferring a few years back from an interstate chapter. "Dunno if his word is worth shit."

"*Her,*" Cage said, "word is worth more than most. But we talked to a few other blokes. Some of Dixie's crew were flapping their jaws. Starting to sound like Dixie would be keen to give the Diamonds a bigger cut if he didn't have to work with Geezer."

This had everyone's attention. "But nothing real concrete," Wraith said.

"Nah. We'll keep digging." I leaned back in my chair, wondering where that was going to lead.

"You do that," Wraith said. "We already got one brother in the clink, don't need any more of us going down that road."

This comment was met with silence from the assembled brothers. Tucker was twenty-one-years old and newly patched. We weren't expecting to see him in the clubhouse before his twenty-fourth birthday.

When church ended, I was intent on only one direction. I didn't get far.

"Ali, wait up." Wraith's hand came down on my shoulder. "Got a job for you."

Fuck, seriously?

Chapter Twelve

Jenna

Ali's leaving again had been as predictable as the rain that was going to come down any moment. The dark gray clouds floated ominously across the sky as I watched Chrissie climb into her car and drive off to town. Smiling to myself, I headed for my own vehicle and the cooler I'd packed in there before coming to work.

The men had returned from their meeting and back to the workshop. After Ali gave me another of his stupid maddening kisses goodbye, he'd ridden out on his bike. Now was my opportunity.

Hoisting my Sunday morning creation, I shut the trunk one-handed, turning to find Jase watching me. He was one of the quieter members, with his sun-bleached blond waves and his wire-rimmed glasses. I put none of them down as actually harmless, but he came close.

"You want a hand there?" he said, jogging over. "Please tell me that contains beer."

"No, something better. But I think I got this."

He took the container from me, anyway. "So what is it?"

"You'll find out."

"It's a bomb, right? You're actually a terrorist."

"It's cake if you must know. It's Jack's birthday today."

"Starting a tradition. You're really fitting in around here."

He followed me up the steps to the office and deposited the cake onto the desk. I lifted the lid to see that my creation had survived its journey well.

"Shit," he said. "Not bad."

"Made it myself," I said, letting a little pride in at my work. Lifting the cake out, I placed it onto the bench. "I brought candles."

Jase snorted. "Ah, they're not going to sing happy freaking birthday, princess, but the thought's there."

Under the bright office lighting the Harley-Davidson logo had a gloss to it that pleased me. "For chocolate mud cake and two flavor ganache, they'd better." But I didn't hold out much hope.

I pulled out paper plates, napkins and plastic forks.

"You got liquor in it?"

"What do you think the second flavor is?" I laughed, feeling lighter than I had in days. "Well, let's find the birthday boy." I paused on my way to the door. "Ah, should we call Wraith?"

So far, I'd yet to be in close proximity with the president. I hoped that meant my position was so low that he hadn't bothered with me. I wasn't under the illusion I was safe, that he wasn't going to work out who I was, but it wasn't looking like today.

"Nah, he's out for the afternoon, meeting with the lawyers. I'll have his piece." Jase got ahead of me, standing in the doorway and whistling with his fingers in his mouth. "Yo, assholes. The princess has made cake."

The next twenty minutes were a blur, mostly because a grateful Jack had given me a one-armed hug and a kiss to my cheek. I'd beamed and I knew it. But seeing the men were intent on eating, no one seemed to take any notice. They managed to polish off the cake in record time. All of them headed out and only Jack remained.

"I'm sorry Chrissie's not back," I said.

"She doesn't do cake." Jack loitered in the doorway. "I appreciated that, I don't think I've ever had homemade birthday cake. If I knew it was that good, I'd have been asking for it."

"It's no big deal," I said, my heart swelling. I wasn't so stupid as to think this would win Jack over, but he did seem grateful. Small steps, and I'd take a million if I had to.

"I'm glad Ali picked you," he said, sincerity in his words. "He needs someone like you. Someone stable, who gives shit."

Yeah, well, that was another thing.

* * * *

The workshop had shut down over an hour earlier, but I was determined to finish the pile of invoices I'd started. When I finally put down the last one, I closed the filing cabinet with a satisfying *thunk*.

After a quick tidy of my desk, I headed out. The lights were still on, making it easy for me to navigate my way through the various repair jobs that lay under tarps across the concrete floor. I'd assumed no one else was there until a figure moved at my left.

Startled, I increased my pace toward the side doorway.

"What's the hurry?" Pony stepped toward me, his normally placid face screwed up tight. He was no Ali, but he wasn't a small man either. He squared his shoulders and cocked his head to one side.

"I'm just heading home." I didn't stop, continuing my way toward escape. "I'll see you tomorrow, Pony."

"If you reckon," he said, getting closer to me. "You think you're pretty smart, don't you?"

He stopped in front of me, hands resting on his hips. The man didn't like me and I had the feeling it was more than my discovering his lax work ethic concerning the spare parts. Every time I met his gaze, he appeared to be studying me. Seeing most of the other members now seemed unfazed by my presence, his attitude stood out.

"In what way?" I said.

"Hooking up with Ali, getting your ass in here. Lot of bitches have tried and failed. Still, I'm pretty sure he'll get bored eventually."

"You might be right, but it's hardly your business." This

idiot was ruining my happiness over doing something for Jack. "Now, if you'll excuse me, I'm leaving."

I went to move, but he blocked me. Before I could offer up a protest, the side door swung open and Cage entered. He was dressed in gym gear, but looked fresh.

"Left my iPod," he said, sauntering over to us. "You're working late, princess."

"I had some things to do," I said. "I'm finished now."

"She's dedicated," Pony said, a smile plastered on his face. "She was a good find, don't you reckon, Cage?"

Cage slid his gaze to Pony. "She has your number, that's for sure."

"Yeah, great pick-up with my mistakes. At least nearly everything was there." He grinned widely.

Cage continued to watch him as he retrieved his iPod from where he'd left it, and slowly unwound the earbuds cord.

"You want me to walk you out, princess?" He gave me a sideways glance and I realized he read the tension in my body.

Making trouble by complaining about Pony could lead to the club thinking I wasn't cut out for the job after all, so I forced a smile and made myself seem more relaxed. Pony was most likely too stupid to make much trouble for me. So, he hated me. I couldn't expect to get along with everyone in the MC.

"Thanks, it's pretty dark out." Stupid thing to say with the parking area being lit up with floodlights and the path to it was only a short walk.

But it seemed to satisfy Cage who started for the door, only to stop halfway. "Come on then, let's get you safe and home."

I followed him outside, without a backward glance or goodbye for the prospect. "Actually, I'm off to Pilates, meeting a friend."

"You know that's not real exercise?" he said. "If you want, you can use our place."

I'd never seen the club gym, but imagined it to be dark, full of abused equipment, not to mention scary bikers, and couldn't think of a worse place to work out.

"I'm fine, thanks."

"What was going on in there?" He stopped at my car, folding his arms across his chest, his feet shoulder-width apart.

"Nothing, he surprised me, that's all. I thought I was alone."

"You're never alone here." He pointed two fingers toward his eyes.

I laughed. Cage made the move comical, his mouth twisting to a smirk.

"I should go," I said, opening my door. I never bothered to lock my car when I parked at the MC. "I don't want to be late."

"That gym that only lets chicks in?"

I nodded. "That's the one. Well, see you tomorrow."

"Yeah," he said. "Tomorrow."

Cage seemed less scary to me now, and of course, he was way too young to have any involvement in what happened to Sophie and Jack. But he was definitely strange. I pulled away from the lot, determined to put Pony out of my thoughts.

* * * *

Casey released the tie she had been using to hold up her hair and shook out her long, dark brown tresses. "God, that's better than sweating it out."

I grinned. Cage had been wrong, though, the Pilates class had been a great workout. My body certainly felt it after being treated like a pretzel for the past hour.

"You want to grab coffee over the weekend?" I pulled my own hair free, doubting I looked as good as she did when I raked my fingers through it.

"I think you'll be busy." She smiled. "But when you're

free next, sure, that would be great."

"Oh, I think I'll find some time. I offered to help out but Chrissie said she had it all covered. So I got Saturday free until the party." I pulled my keys from my bag.

"I'll come around while you yell at your closet that you have nothing to wear. How does that sound?"

"Like a chick thing." Cage stepped out of the dark. He still wore his gym gear, but this time he'd clearly been out running. His biceps were defined, and along with his face, had quite the sweat going on. I noticed Casey surreptitiously checking him out.

"God, you scared me," I said, my hand going to my chest. "Did you run in from the MC?"

He shrugged. "I took the long way."

"Are you going to run back there?" Casey pulled her eyes off his chest.

"Nah, I have a place in town. I don't live at the clubhouse."

"Oh," I said. "So why are you running this way?"

Instead of a denial, he said, "Making sure you get home."

"Ali put you up to this?" I wasn't sure whether to be flattered by his admission, or feel stalked.

"No, Pony did." He grinned at that piece of bullshit. "Looking after our brother's interests, it's what we do."

"God, and I thought that two brothers and an over-protective father was bad." Casey gave me a sly look. "I'll see you Saturday morning, Mitchell." She leaned over and kissed my cheek.

"Okay." I gave her a quick hug.

"You should come out to the clubhouse," Cage said to her. He didn't bother hiding the fact that he ran his eyes up and down her body. She wore leggings and a fitted top, so he got an eyeful that he seemed to like.

"Night shift for the next couple of weeks," she said. I knew that wasn't quite true, but didn't comment.

"Suit yourself." Cage turned to me. "Well, come on then, home time for you."

After Casey left, Cage got in my car with me uninvited.

"Is this your way of asking for a ride home?" I started the engine. "Well, where do you live?"

"I'll run from your place," he said, glancing around the interior. "This is a mess."

It wasn't that bad. A takeaway coffee container I hadn't thrown out, a few bills on the front seat that he'd had to move, some shoes and a makeup bag. Apart from that, my car was clean. "Sorry, Mum."

He grunted, picked up my iPod and started scrolling through it. If he tried looking for pop songs and girlie ballads, he'd be out of luck.

He whistled through his teeth as we turned the corner. "Not bad, princess. Not what I expected. I might have to start taking you to do the banking instead of Chrissie."

I frowned—he'd made that sound dirty. But I had the feeling that with Cage, he didn't mean anything by it. Still, I planned to download some tunes that might wipe the smug look off his face.

"This is me," I said, pulling into my drive as if he didn't already know where I lived. "You can go now."

He placed my player back on my console and shook his head. "You know I'm going to check your place out first."

I didn't bother to argue. I couldn't see the point.

He inspected my rooms, all of them, then he switched on my back light. He wasn't being curious, he was being security conscious. They were a paranoid bunch.

"Satisfied?" I asked.

Cage ignored me, reached down and scooped my cat from off the floor. The chocolate-brown Burmese purred in his arms. Eventually he remembered my presence. "I think so. Guess I'll see you tomorrow. I'll let myself out."

After he left, I locked my door behind him. Cage might not unnerve me anymore, but now that I found myself alone, I couldn't say the same for Pony. I might have made a mistake not mentioning to Ali's friend about my concern there. Again, I shook off my worry. The prospect didn't like me because I'd found him out. He was just a stupid, immature man who had been bested by a female. I couldn't let that keep bothering me.

Not the easiest thing to do.

Chapter Thirteen

Ali

When Cage entered the gym, I slumped back onto the weight bench and rubbed the sweat out of my eyes using the heels of my hands.

"What the hell are you doing here?" Cage bounded over to me, swept my legs to the side and landed on the bench.

"She's not home." Did he really think I'd be working out down here and not visiting her at her place if she were?

"Least you checked." He tossed me a towel. "Guess you'll have to wait until tonight. It's a fucking madhouse. It might pay us to keep out of the way of the old ladies. Next thing you know, they'll have us icing a fucking cake or some shit."

"It's Jack. They'll go all out."

"Speaking of cakes, did you hear Jenna baked him one." He started laughing. "She's going well, your girl. You talk to her at all this week?"

No, I hadn't. We didn't make a habit of checking in with anyone but club when we were out. It was safer that way, for both us, and those left behind. Still, I'd been gone days and Jenna might have been pissed off about it. I'd just have to deal with it when I had the chance.

"Good for the kid," I said. "Is Kitty back?"

"Nah, and get this, Jenna thinks he's a sweet old man. Her words."

"At least she's fitting in." I toweled off the back of my neck, rubbing hard to ease some of the tension I carried there.

"Whatever."

I knew Cage well enough to know that something else was on his mind. "Spit it out, brother."

"I heard from a couple of the girls that Leanne was planning on showing up tonight." He gave me a grin. "That could get awkward."

"Don't know how," I said. "She was never my old lady, just a woman I fucked a couple of times and lived to regret it. She's got no claim. Last I looked, she was on the back of Dodge's bike." I referred to a brother from a different chapter who had been over paying his respects after Hellion had died. That he'd relieved me of the clingy bitch had been something of a lucky break. Leanne was just a typical groupie. She didn't care which biker she ended up with. As long as he wore a patch, she was happy. Unlike Jenna, who I had the feeling was interested, despite my MC status. That appealed in ways I'd never even considered before.

"You gotta ask yourself why she's back, though. Heard she was asking about you."

"Did you, now?" To be honest, I had trouble even picturing what the woman looked like. It had been that insignificant. It wasn't like I'd led her to believe that she meant anything. Not like spending two consecutive nights together — only because I'd passed out drunk the second time — meant a fucking relationship.

I decided not to worry about it. "Ah, well, she can ask away."

"I reckon you could do with a run. You could use the cardio." Cage seemed keen to get off the subject of club politics and talk of women.

I glared at him. "Meaning?"

"Meaning, wouldn't hurt for you to get rid of some of that pent-up energy. She's little, you don't want to kill her." He laughed and attempted to avoid my arm as I lashed out at him. Nothing serious, just didn't like him talking of Jenna like that. Still, he had a point.

"Why not?"

"I'll go easy on you," Cage said, smirking at me. "Hope princess doesn't expect the same from you."

The next time, he didn't avoid me fast enough.

* * * *

Casey ripped off the tags to the lingerie I'd just purchased during our impromptu shopping trip. I gave her a barely disguised dirty look as I caught the pieces of lace and silk she tossed at me.

"There's nothing wrong with my underwear," I said, holding up the tiny, sexy, bits of nothing. I had to admit they were not only something I'd never worn before, but they were beautiful.

"I'm not saying there is." She grinned at me and attacked another set with her hands and teeth. "It's nice to have some new things, that's all."

"Uh-huh, whatever you say." Apparently, my wardrobe measured up. There were several articles of clothing deemed suitable for the party at the MC. But one look through my bras and underwear had Casey dragging me out of my house and into a shop in the town center.

"He's not going to see any of this, anyway." I captured a pair of black French-cut panties and matching bra as they sailed through the air in my bedroom. "This is not necessary."

"That's denial talking right there," she said, pointing her finger school-teacher style in my direction. "You forget, I saw the way he kissed you. There might have been four of you at the time, but I got the gist."

"It was just a kiss." I hadn't mentioned to her what had happened on Monday with Ali and me before he'd left, yet again, on club business.

"Keep telling yourself that. What top did we decide on, the red or the cream one?" She pulled both hangers in front of her. "Jenna? You need to stop spacing out here, which one?"

"I'm being an idiot, aren't I? Christ, Casey, I can't go to this thing. I'm not going, that's it." I sat on the bed and tossed the underwear to the side.

"Number one, you're not an idiot, you like this guy. And two, if you want to stay home we can order in pizza and watch a movie. It's your choice, no one is putting a gun to your head." She lowered beside me and patted my knee.

"I'm too old for this." I flopped against the mattress. "You know, he's younger than me."

"Really?" She landed beside me. "That's your excuse?"

"As reasons go, I don't think it's a bad one."

"You look good together, I don't think he's all that worried about the age difference." She propped herself on her elbow and looked down at me. "And that boy doesn't appear to have mummy issues, so you need to get your head out of your ass about all that."

She slapped my arm playfully.

"You think?" I said, laughing at her.

"Yes, I do. Now go and put on your big girl pants—your new, sexy, big girl pants—and check yourself out in the mirror. Then come back in here and deny to me that that man is not going to go crazy at the sight of you in them." She smirked. "Or out of them."

Casey had to be assuming that I had a lot more experience with men, that my nerves were down to the fact that Ali was a biker. It made sense, so I went off and tried on some of my new things. It didn't help.

The black I found too sexy, the white too sweet and almost bridal, but the neon pink—Casey's choice—way too wild. I stomped back into my bedroom wearing my robe.

Cotton it was then. I pulled out a cute striped matching set and glowered over to Casey.

"Oh, no, you don't," she said. "I'm not saying that they're terrible, but they do not scream 'take me now', either."

"Not sure if that's the message I want to send." I gave her a nervous laugh.

Casey and I had spent the day together. I'd learned all

about her family, her three siblings, her detective father and her job. She'd asked me questions and I'd dodged answering them. Casey had let me off. She knew that I'd gone to school here, and that I didn't talk to my family, but that was about it. I hadn't mentioned any previous relationships, but she had to be assuming that there had been at least one or two.

"You like him?" she said.

"I think so."

"You want to be his old lady?" When I raised my brows, she shrugged. "That's what they're called."

"I know that. I'm not sure about the whole old lady thing. I'm thinking that Ali isn't the kind to settle down." I took a deep breath. "I'm not into casual sex." Or any sex really.

"Then don't have sex. Put the sweet and boring undies on, and go have fun. Get more of those hot kisses, and hit the road at midnight. Simple." She ran her hands over my coverlet. "Or go and screw a biker, and tick that off your bucket list."

She made it sound all so easy. *Screw a biker, yeah, right.* My face must have shown everything I felt.

"Now what?" she asked, a grimace on her mouth.

"What kind of pizza?"

"I like any. Just no anchovies."

A glass of wine and one pizza ordered and on its way later, Casey sat on the floor in my living room going through my DVDs when my phone pinged a message.

I didn't get many of those that weren't something from a phone company or work-related. I had a short contact list. So sparse that I would have been embarrassed for anyone to see it.

I grabbed the handset and picked it up.

Is our date still on? Swung by to check, you weren't home.

Of course Ali had my number, I should have known. But seeing I'd taken his from the contact sheet at the office, I wasn't annoyed.

"Is that him?" she said, not looking up.

"He wants to know if we're still on for later. He came around here earlier, must have been when we were out shopping." I frowned at the screen. "What should I say?"

"Whatever you want to. We can still eat pizza, it's early." She finally looked up. "Jenna?"

Trying on the lingerie that actually was beautiful, the disappointment that had been creeping over me that I wasn't going to be seeing Ali later swirled through me.

I held my phone with both hands and tapped out a message.

I guess I'll see you around nine.

I flashed it toward Casey who grinned with approval as I hit send. "I knew you'd bend. Part of my evil plan." Right at that moment, she did look like the devil.

An hour later I put the finishing touches on my hair while Casey sat cross-legged on my bed, eying my footwear.

"I love those boots."

They were suede ankle booties with a wedge heel. A favorite pair that I'd barely worn. I'd teamed them with skinny jeans that had designer tears and a tight cream cashmere top. Over that I layered a caramel-colored cropped leather jacket that I'd bought on sale once and hadn't even taken the tag off. Underneath I had on the white lace, which on second try didn't seem quite so bridal.

It was my fourth outfit change and I still wasn't sure.

"The other women will have stripper heels. Are you sure I shouldn't pick something else?" I pulled out my lip gloss and swiped it over my mouth. I wore full makeup. It gave me some confidence but also had me feeling like a fraud.

"Don't you dare. You look like Jenna, only sexier. It's perfect."

Oh, God, I need more wine.

Chapter Fourteen

Jenna

The cool blonde with her slim hip cocked against the staircase was definitely Anna, Wraith's wife. Chrissie had pointed out her picture on the office wall the day before. She seemed to think that it was important that I knew who the president's wife was.

I glanced around the foyer of the huge building. I knew that in its original life, the clubhouse had been a spa resort. It still resembled a Mexican villa on the outside, but inside, the walls were painted a dark gray, there was motorbike memorabilia scattered about, seating and huge sweeping staircase in the center.

I went back to paying attention to Anna as I stood in the entrance way. Surrounded by women and a few young children. It became clear that Anna ruled the room.

They sat on couches in the foyer that were pushed into a grouping with chairs added for extra seating. Most of them held glasses of wine or bottles of beer. Anna, of course, had wine. I doubted she drank from anything but a glass.

I also knew, without a doubt, that the woman didn't own sweatpants. She wore a soft cream jacket with leather pants that looked pricey and heels that were likely designer. Her jewelry looked discreet, but expensive.

To my left, one of the bar doors swung open and the music and laughter spilled out as a brunette in a tight boob tube and the shortest skirt I'd ever seen tumbled drunkenly into the foyer. She pulled herself together the moment Anna fastened her eyes on her.

A few of the women on the sofas teetered as the girl stuck to the wall and made her way to a door, clearly the bathroom.

"Fucking whores," one of the women muttered then spotted me. "Oh, you're Jenna. You can come over here."

I had been standing there for all of thirty seconds. They knew I'd arrived, but this was the first sign of acknowledgment. My choices appeared to be either the group of women or the bar, where I could hear thumping music and even noisier voices. I chose the quieter option and walked over.

I'm no fashionista, but I was glad that I had spent some time choosing my outfit and doing my hair and makeup.

It didn't take a fashion expert to be able to tell the difference between the girls who hung at the club and the old ladies and girlfriends. The two different types of dress styles gave away who was who.

"You look gorgeous," a woman said, validating my choice. "I can see why you've made an impression on our Ali. I'm Marie, by the way, Mick's old lady."

Anna gave her a withering look to which Marie barely flinched. She was an attractive woman with long dead-straight black hair and a baby bump. She had been the one to invite me over. I put Anna's annoyance with her down to some kind of hierarchy.

"Do you know anyone here?" Marie said.

"Only Chrissie," I said.

"Oh, she's in there." Marie pointed to the bar and then proceeded to rattle off the names of the other women, starting with Anna, of course.

They were all friendly — even Anna managed a smile and sent a blonde teenager off to get me a drink.

As the younger girl disappeared into the noisy bar, another woman exited. She wore a bandage dress and the uniform stripper heels. I didn't get much of a look at her as she ignored our group and headed for the ladies' room.

"What the hell is she doing here?" A woman with graying

blonde hair followed her with her eyes. "Don't tell me Chrissie invited her."

"You know that type," Marie said, a downcast turn of mouth. "They sniff these things out. Probably back to get her hooks into you-know-who."

Marie's words met with either scathing comments or howls of disbelieving laughter.

"Who is it?" I asked. In a way I didn't really care, but I was getting pointed looks and had a strange feeling I was supposed to show some reaction.

"Oh, that's only someone who wouldn't mind being where you are now. Don't worry about her," Anna said, waving her hand elegantly, the sounds of her bracelets jangling. "She's nothing but a whore."

Right, someone who knew Ali, and very well going by the way the entire group of women studied me. I shrugged and didn't bother to comment. That she'd come from the bar where Ali was likely stationed wasn't something I needed to be thinking about.

Someone placed a toddler on my lap without asking, as if they were gifting me, and I leaned backward. I didn't hold babies, and had managed to avoid it for a long while now. She smelled beautiful and looked gorgeous with her pink cheeks and wet lips. A physical pain shot into my chest as her soft body formed against mine.

"She doesn't want to get spit up on her," Anna said, moving forward and going to pick up the little girl from my lap.

She halted before straightening up, her eyes going over my head. "Hey, sweetheart," she said.

I assumed it was Wraith behind me. But a different, albeit familiar, voice replied instead. "What's up, Anna?"

"Nothing too exciting, Cage, just us girls. You know how it is." She bent down again and this time extracted the child from me. "I don't think Jenna's too fond of children."

He snorted. "Of course she isn't. Jenna's more interested in the process of making them." Suddenly he put his hands under my arms and hauled me over the back of the couch so that I stood behind it. "Come on, princess, he knows you're here. You're making my brother feel unwanted."

The other women laughed and Cage led me off to a chorus of goodbyes.

"That was rude," I said, after we slipped behind the doors.

"You really want to stay out with them?" Cage smirked and shook his head. "Didn't think so."

But we didn't get far. Jack turned as we entered, his arms opening up. "You came." He looked a little drunk, but that was okay, it was his birthday.

He gave me a quick hug, but Chrissie pulled me back. I had no idea where she appeared from as she proceeded to wrap her arms around me as if we were lifelong friends. I resented her at the moment, as if I didn't already.

Cage rolled his eyes and smacked my backside when she released me, sending me off in another direction. The place was wall-to-wall bodies. I should have been used to the bikers by then, but in this setting, with them so close, I found myself all but clinging to Cage's side. The room was full of muscle, beards, long hair and hungry gazes.

Someone jostled me closer to Cage, his arm going over my shoulders as he looked down, a frown on his face. "You all right, princess?"

I was anything but in a room full of dangerous men. The one who met my eyes with a steady gaze might have been the most dangerous of all.

It took all my willpower not to bolt from the bar stool I'd planted myself on and barrel across the room to punch the asshole who had knocked into Jenna. Didn't matter a damn that it was an unavoidable accident, given the crowd. I wanted to pound that dumb fucker to pulp.

My boy Cage had her, though, and guided her over to me. Saved me wrecking up my knuckles. Not the impression I wanted to make on the angel coming at me.

Fuck, she looks good. Her hair hung down, moving as she

came closer, looking petrified. She must have thought she'd walked into hell with leather and booze instead of flames and pitchforks.

A pause in the music allowed the scream of a woman to ring out through the room. Not an unhappy one, as one of the brothers motorboated her naked tits. *Jenna wasn't looking that way, thank fuck.* But she'd flinched at the noise. Cage leaned down and whispered something to her as she continued to lock her eyes on mine.

Whatever he had said seemed to reassure her. But I wasn't thinking of that other chick as the entire room melted away. Even Cage, who started to piss me off with his arm around her, despite that being kind of necessary to get her over to me, was no longer there.

Fuck this. I stood and shouldered my way over. "I got this, brother."

Cage smirked. "Took your fucking time."

He was right about that, but I'd wanted to watch her for a while. There was a mighty good chance the girl could bolt, and real soon. I needed to get my eyeful of her before she did.

He dropped his arm from her as I reached out and grabbed her hand, pulling her closer to me. I wanted to get the fuck out of there, get her somewhere alone, but knew that was a bad idea, so I took her back to the bar with me instead.

I reclaimed the stool and spread my thighs, getting her in between them and turning her into me. "Hey," I said, forking my fingers through the side of her hair and resting my thumb against her cheek. She seemed tense as fuck, her body all stiff and uncomfortable, but she wasn't looking to pull away.

"Hey," she shouted back, because if anything, it was getting even noisier in the room.

"The women captured her," Cage said, his forearms hitting the bar on my other side. "You can thank me later."

I grunted and went back to paying attention to Jenna. She started to loosen up, but I signaled behind the bar. If there was any other time a drink could help a situation, I didn't know of it.

"Mags, get my girl here a drink, hon." Mags had been around the club forever. She'd started as a sweetbutt and never did rise from there. But she ran the place, worked out in the kitchen and got a wage now.

"Sure." She raised her brows at Jenna. "What do you want, gorgeous?"

Yeah, my woman is gorgeous. I dropped a kiss on her temple. Jenna leaned in, her head going to my chest in an adorably shy way. She turned in Mags' direction.

"Vodka soda please, Mags," she said. "I'm Jenna." She put out her hand and with a surprised expression, Mags accepted the handshake.

The old girl gave me a look that showed how impressed she'd become with Jenna. I winked back at her.

"Coming right up," she said, hurrying away to fetch the drink.

I kept rubbing my thumb against Jenna's soft-as-silk skin and inhaled. As per usual she smelled like nothing but clean and roses.

Leaning back to Cage, I said, "What did you say to her before?" Jenna seemed unsure of my brother, and for him to settle her down like that rattled me.

He shrugged and jutted his chin to where motorboat girl had moved on to another dude who was getting up and close with her implants.

"I got places to be." He pushed off from the bar after giving me that bullshit and smirked.

Before I got a chance to ask again, Jenna tugged on my cut. "He told me you wouldn't do that to me, not in public, anyway."

I threw back my head and laughed. *Christ, that fucker.* "I didn't think you saw."

"Oh, I saw." She pulled back a little from me and took a mouthful from the drink that Mags had delivered.

"Careful, I'm pretty sure that'll be a double."

"It is," she said, and gave me a crooked smile.

Someone stumbled near us and I put up my hand, stopping the man before he fell into us. Normally, I loved these nights, and I shouldn't have cared about what she thought of it, but damn if I didn't. Frowning, I slid my hand back farther into her hair. I had to stop acting like a pussy, this was ridiculous. She was here, she didn't look to be leaving, and it was time to lock this shit down.

I tugged her head back and crushed my mouth against hers. Jenna startled some, but began to kiss me back, her mouth working with mine. I bit her bottom lip, soft at first, but harder as she licked her tongue against me. *Fuck, that was hot.* I tilted my head to the side, pushing farther in. Jenna kissed like she was Marco fucking Polo, exploring the hell out of me.

Imagining what she was going to do with that mouth on my dick had me getting even harder than the initial sight of her had started moments earlier. I moved her body closer with my free hand on the small of her back to let her know what was going on there. She didn't touch me like I wanted though. Just like when we were in the office and she'd ground against me, clearly liking it—hands under my shirt, but below the waist, well, Jenna hadn't been there yet.

Sliding my palms down to cup her ass, I kissed the hell out of her, but still her hands were only on my chest. I liked it, but there were other places. Finally she wound her limbs around my neck, but going way too high in my opinion.

I pulled one of my own hands to the edge of her jeans. Jenna had felt me up on my bike, hands over my abs, the edges of my pants, but since then, nada.

As my fingers searched along the edge of her waistband, a hard sting to the back of my head made my eyes fly open and I was looking at a pissed off Mags.

"What the fuck?" I said, pulling away from Jenna and rubbing the back of my skull.

"Show a bit of respect." Mags gave Jenna an indulgent grin.

Jenna's chest vibrated against me as she giggled.

"Look, seeing I've seen you blow a fucking line of—"

My next assault came from Jenna, her tiny hand forming a fist and delivering a pretty decent pound against me.

"Ali!"

"Sorry, Mags," I mumbled, feeling a-fucking-shamed by that comment. That was low and I knew it. But the woman had fucking startled me.

"You will be," Mags said and went off to serve someone at the far end.

"You wanna get out of here?" I said.

"Now?" Jenna's eyes widened.

"Maybe later." This was not working, something was off. I picked up my beer and took a pull, trying to figure shit out.

I had her here, she'd been kissing me back, fuck if I knew.

"Is anything up?" *Apart from my cock that is.*

"No, I'm all good." Jenna took another sip from her drink.

But if she turned to the left, she'd see a brother nailing a chick up against a wall and a stripper with a huge dildo in her grip, handing over a thumb drive with her music on it to Pony. Normally, I'd be pretty happy right about now, but I was fucking miserable. Well, not quite, I did have Jenna. Time to save this shit.

"Babe, if you wanna watch the show, we can do that. Or you and I can cut out?"

She glanced around, her eyes a little hooded. "To where? Your room?" She looked like the idea landed somewhere between being naked in a desert or a snowstorm.

Yeah, that was the plan. "I dunno, anywhere you want."

"Outside. I could do with some air."

Outside could work. I stood and found her hand. "Let's go."

But the rear exit was wall-to-wall brothers, and women all over them, so I headed us in the direction of the side entrance, landing near the staircase. The old ladies and girlfriends had congregated over to the other side, but the foyer had filled up and we were out of their view.

If I thought she looked good in the dimly lit bar, but out in the bright light she looked awesome. Her lips were swollen from the kissing, her cheeks flushed from what had to be the same reason and her hair tousled from my hands.

Fuck it. I bent slightly and put my hands on the backs of her thighs, tossing her up and over my shoulder. Not sure who I'd been for the last few minutes, but I hated that idiot. Jenna's fists beat against my ass. Like that wasn't turning me on even further.

I pivoted and took to the stairs.

"Ali, put me down."

I spanked her ass, a hell of a lot harder than the tap Cage had given her, and kept moving. I didn't stop until I got just outside my door. Then pulling the chain that held the key in my pocket, I unlocked it and went inside, using my foot to shut us in.

Only then did I let her down.

She breathed hard. "You are insane."

"Nope, sanest thing I've done this evening," I said.

"I'm leaving." She went to push past me, but I stopped her with my hands on her shoulders. "Let me the fuck go."

She was angry now, her eyes flaring widely at me.

"This is what I got, Jenna," I said as my breath increased. "I'm gonna kiss you now. If you wanna walk out of here afterward, that's fine. I'll escort you to your car so you can get out all safe and sound. Otherwise, you're staying in here. It's all up to you now. I'm done playing."

"What, you think you've got some—"

This time, I really fucking kissed the woman. I put every frustrated thought I'd been having for the past couple of weeks out there for her to see. A huge risk, but that skittish act she put on did my head in. I wanted her, had all kinds of feelings for her that I knew were something special, or at least getting that way, but I was done if she kept playing her game.

This time Jenna's hand was on my ass and her other tore

into the skin on my back, having slid up my shirt. I'd never been so fucking relieved in my life.

But I broke the kiss. "Well?"

Chapter Fifteen

Ali

Jenna didn't answer me, not with words, anyway. But her look was enough. I kissed her again and backed us up to the bed, lowering her, putting one hand out so that I didn't completely crush her, despite wanting to. In all practicality, that wasn't going to work.

Shoving her shirt up, I realized the error of not removing Jenna's jacket first, but it didn't matter. I had her bra exposed and one shove upward and yeah, there it was. Her warm skin under my fingers, thumb and forefinger on a nipple. She gasped against my mouth.

Our legs were tangled. I rolled us so she ended up on top, placing my hands to her sides as I lifted her up farther, finding a nipple. I sucked it inside and flicked my tongue against the tight bud. Well, technically it counted as kissing.

Jenna straddled my stomach and I was torn between pulling her down on my dick or keeping her in my mouth. *Fuck, how to make that choice?* But she made it for me, sitting back and staring down at me, tugging her bra and shirt back into place.

"Didn't work, huh?" I said.

She shrugged out of her jacket and tossed it on the floor.

I pointed at her shirt and half spun my finger. "Come on, off with that."

She gave me a look and fucking bit down on her bottom lip as she pulled off her top. I reached out and unbuttoned her jeans.

"Babe, a bit hard to get them off with you sitting on me

like that."

She frowned and rose, taking her leg off me. I gripped her waist and pulled her down beside me as she kicked off her boots. *Fucking awesome.* I took over getting her pants off. Still fully clothed myself, I really needed to check her out first. Couldn't wait.

"The lights." Jenna looked at the single lamp beside the bed, the only one on in the room.

"Babe, that's as dark as it gets."

"No," she said. "Turn them on. All of them."

No complaints from me. I bounded off the mattress, turning on the other lamp and the overhead.

When I shucked off my shirt, Jenna stared at me and paused in wiggling out of her jeans. Appreciative stare, good. Her stopping her undressing, bad. Very bad. Still, I was getting off on her checking me out.

"Don't stop," I said, undoing my belt and toeing off boots and socks at the same time, very economical of me.

"You have many tattoos." She became stock still.

"*Mmhmm.*" I snapped open my pants.

"Oh, no underwear." She averted her gaze before I got a chance to really show her that, but at least she went back to undressing.

I circled around behind her. Strange that she needed all the lights on but stopped looking at me the minute I became completely naked. Sensing her need for privacy, I climbed on the bed behind her and helped her out, sliding her bra off her shoulders and down her arms. I needed another look at those tits, but that was coming. Rushing things wasn't what I needed to do here.

She slid the white satin and lace number off completely and I glanced over her shoulder. Her underwear matched but she drew up her knees, still wearing them.

I began to rub her shoulders, leaning down and kissing one, happy and content to take this slower now that it finally looked like it was happening. But the taste of her skin got me further riled up and I nipped at her while my cock brushed her back.

Still, for me this was taking things the slow pace and I licked softly up her neck. She liked that, leaning back against me. Her earlobe was next, I bit it gently.

Then I pulled her back against me into my lap, wrapping my arms around her. She shivered slightly. Cold? I could warm her up, all she had to do was spin around on me. I loosened my hold, so she could, but she failed to move.

What the fuck is happening?

"Babe?"

When she didn't respond I moved, getting in front of her. Those big blue-green eyes were wide and focused on mine as I slowly tipped her back, climbing over her and leaning down to kiss her again. I kept my body hovering above her, wanting to be sinking down, and, well, sinking in.

She blinked when I lifted my head up. "Sorry."

"Don't be sorry," I whispered against her mouth, dipping back down again. "I'm not."

No, not apologetic in the slightest, just very fucking worried. Which when married up with my incredibly horny state was like putting an ice cube on a roaring fire. It hissed some, but basically was overwhelmed.

The kissing loosened her up again. But there could be no getting around this, my girl was scared and I couldn't for the life of me work out why. Sure, I'd fireman-hold brought her up here, but seriously, I wasn't keeping her in my room against her will. She'd undressed, for Christ's sake, of her own violation. She'd insisted on lighting up the room like an operating room. I couldn't get a handle on what was happening.

But I was a persistent bastard, especially when I wanted something, and I wanted Jenna.

I shifted off her, stretching out along her side, my kisses a lot slower than what I wanted them to be. But Jenna liked it, her fingers on my face lightly stroking me. I slid my hand down her stomach, feeling the soft, feminine, gentle curve of it. As I went lower, she tightened her muscles.

"Relax," I said, like a schmuck.

I frowned, watching her face. There it was the slightest gloss over her eyes.

My entire night was in real trouble of turning into a complete and utter fuck-up. Jenna's too, if her expression was anything to go by. I couldn't read it, but she had shut down, that much I got.

"Right," I said. "This ends now."

I shifted away from her slightly and she looked surprised. "It does?"

"Yeah. Get dressed. I'm driving you home." *Yep, as soon as my hard-on comes down, that's the plan.*

"You changed your mind?" She sat up, her tits looking amazing, and it shocked me that she wasn't covering them up.

"Nope, you did. Last I checked I wasn't a rapist." I got off the bed and she continued to gawk at me. "Jenna, babe, we doing this?"

"But I thought…"

I spun and watched her. My turn to be amazed. "You thought what?"

"That we were…"

"Going to fuck, yeah, that was the plan. Now I have no fucking clue." I ran my hands through my hair and picked her jeans up from where she had thrown them onto the floor.

Then Jenna's eyes went to my dick. Not really helping to get the thing to go down, her doing that. "You look like you still want to."

I threw my hands in the air. "That obvious, huh?"

"Um, it's not exactly hard to miss." She blushed pink on her cheeks. I fucking loved it when she did that. "It's big."

"Jesus. Do not tell me my dick is big when you clearly do not want it anywhere near you. Jenna, that's fucking-un-fucking-fair."

The problem remained that she still examined my cock with her eyes. She looked curious, interested, and I wanted to tell her that it weirded me the hell out that she did that, because it did. But it also further jacked me up. There was something beguiling about her. Something that made this entire putting the brakes on wrench at my gut.

"Um, babe, you've seen one before, right? You're looking at it like it's an alien bloody concept." I frowned.

"Yes, of course," she snapped. "I've just never seen yours before. It's nice, kind of pretty."

"You need to talk to me now," I said, walking back to the bed.

"Can we talk later?" She scrambled backward—not away from me, I realized—she'd made a space for me.

"You got something else in mind?"

"Can we start again?" She met my eyes. "Please, it's just a bit overwhelming, me being here. I got a little nervous, but I'm good now."

"I don't know if I can stop this time," I said, putting one knee, then the other on the bed. I could stop, of course, but I wasn't going to like it.

I reached down, hooking my finger in the edge of the lace that still covered her, tugging it, and Jenna shifted so that it pulled down over her hip. I grinned as she became exposed to me while I slid her underwear down her thighs, over her knees to her ankles.

I was about to discard them when I felt something. I held them to her instead. "These are wet."

Jenna's cheeks were already pink, so that didn't increase, but she lowered her eyes.

"I'm very fucking relieved about that," I said. "I really thought for a moment that I've been reading you all wrong."

I placed my hands on her knees and pressed down. As her legs straightened out I made my way farther up the bed and she lowered under me. Girl still tensed, but I had a solution for that, one that worked for most people.

My cock suffered through a painful throb that had the thing moving of its own accord. But that was not my real issue. That particular problem was where I placed my fingers, no hesitation for me to slide them in her pussy. But her initial gasp when I touched her was apprehension before she let out her breath slowly. I stilled, and knowing that my face was way too serious, I met her eyes. She gave me a tiny, encouraging nod and I knew that it was now or definitely fucking never. I needed to do this, stop this hesitating shit that was not like me.

First, I stroked her folds, not drenched, but definitely things were happening for her and I slid a finger inside, my thumb pressing down on her clit and manipulating it.

She bucked her hips, punching upward as I slid in and out of her. "That's it," I said. "Let it happen."

She moaned, "Ali."

Saying my name didn't help with my hard-on problem, and when she reached out, I pulled back. Hardest thing ever, but necessary. Jenna wasn't used to me, she was probably more into dating starched-shirt yuppie types who didn't have a clue how to fuck properly. So warming things up was definitely in the cards, then it was game on.

She squirmed, but her eyes totally locked on mine. I liked that, liked it a lot. Watching her face while I made the girl feel good got me off big time.

"Is that good?"

"Oh, yeah."

I slid another finger inside her as she parted her thighs, rocking against my hand a lot more enthusiastically than I'd even hoped for. I grinned at her as her eyes rolled back before returning to mine.

"Yeah, it is, isn't it?" I got a little faster, my thumb swirling over her. She became wetter, her breathing going back to the heavier panting she'd started earlier.

Without breaking our eye lock, I reached over to the drawer beside the bed and slid it open. The sound was barely audible above Jenna's, and my own for that matter, breathing. I put the foil pack to her mouth after showing it to her and she bit down, letting me pull it back as it tore open.

"Oh, fuck," she said, her breath hissing. "Oh, fuck, Ali."

"Yeah, that's it, come on, babe." I worked her good, those hips of hers pushing up against me. "Just let go."

As she did, I slid on the condom and moved so I was over her. "You ready?"

She nodded, lost for words for a moment as I pushed inside her.

"Fuck," I muttered. She near strangled my dick.

Chapter Sixteen

Jenna

Ali took hold of my wrists, pushing them up and over my head as he drove into me. I hadn't expected that. But it felt so good. Like the way he stretched me wide open. Maybe that hurt a little, understandable since it had been many, many years since this had happened for me. And seeing I had no recollection, being drugged at the time, the sensation was new.

His eyes had been on me when he'd entered me, but he swore and shut them tight for a second as he sank inside. But they flew open when he pulled back, only to come straight into me again.

After our shaky and awkward start, this wasn't what I'd expected to happen. Our joining was the most natural, wonderful thing in the world. Ali wasn't being gentle at all. I hadn't expected him to be, but I hadn't counted on him being so damn good at this, either. Just when I thought I'd be able to show some restraint, Ali changed his angle somehow and hit a spot deep inside that had me biting down on my lip.

"Jesus, oh, fuck, Ali."

He grinned, pushing harder. I met him back, finding a rhythm that I didn't know I knew, my knees bent and I put my legs around his hips in order for him to get inside me as far as he could go. This was beyond amazing. What the hell had I been waiting for?

He'd made me come on his fingers and I hadn't even been embarrassed despite the fact that he'd watched my face the entire time. I couldn't have been, I'd been so completely turned on the moment he'd touched me that any sense of shame entirely obliterated. If anyone had told me I'd react like that, I'd have laughed in their face.

I wasn't laughing as Ali pounded against me. The bed, which had been so sturdy earlier, was moving with his relentless driving force. He was without any restraint. Even the way he held me down was intoxicating. I tested his grip on my wrists. He grunted and squeezed even harder. But when I tried the second time, he loosened his fingers.

Moving my hands to his shoulders, I pushed him, not off me, but encouragingly. He responded by sliding a palm under my thigh and gripping it, changing the angle again.

I had no time to register this even better sensation. All my muscles pulsed like they'd been hit with some kind of circuit breaker. I blew apart, my body shattering in a beautiful sensation that had me sinking my teeth into Ali's shoulder to stop from screaming.

He pulled out immediately, but before I could focus on anything remotely like confusion, he spun my body, tugging my hands forward to the headboard.

"You need to hold on," he said, his voice cutting through me. "Tight."

With that, he was back inside, his hands on my hips, fingers digging in. The first thrust sent me forward and I did as he suggested, and held tight, white-knuckling the timber. I was going to leave marks there, but so what, he was going to leave his prints on my skin.

Ali who had been pretty silent, at least as far as coherent verbalization was concerned, changed that up with our new position.

"Jesus, Jenna, your fucking cunt was built for me." He was pushing against me in shorter but deep jerks that had me struggling to keep up.

Just when I did, he gripped a handful of my hair and yanked my head back, his mouth finding my neck. I expected teeth, but the lips that landed there were more than welcome.

"I wouldn't care if you were the last woman I fucked, I'm gonna die a happy man."

He kept his fingers woven through my hair, pulling it firmly as I gave over to my senses. The sound of our skin slapping together was unexpected — it had been background noise up until then, but I let it fill my ears, heard even over the panting of our mingled breaths and Ali's short, sharp words. Sentences were no longer possible for me, and I guess him, either.

Ali released the grip on my hair, only to sit back on his heels, taking me with him. My hands suddenly free to do whatever I wanted. I wrapped one behind me, going around his neck. The other I placed over the hand he had on my stomach as he held me to him, our fingers locking together.

I was working harder now — as exhausted as I felt, I couldn't help it, moving up and down on him as he came at me from underneath. Stopping was not an option as I began to build again.

"I'm going to come, babe," he said in my ear, words barely above a whisper.

He placed his free hand to my clit, dancing against the sensitive bud and sending me off again. Ridiculous that I could do that, I could repeat myself, but I was not complaining. This time, however, I had nothing to bite down on and I screamed his name as I came.

When I learned that my dick had more uses than just pissing out of, I thought coming about as amazing as it got. Then I learned there were ways to make that even better. Then I learned there was Jenna.

If that didn't blow my fucking mind, then I don't know what those cracking synapses were doing in my head. For a moment there, I worried I'd had an aneurysm. Thank God, I didn't, because this dying a happy man with her could be improved on, or at least stretched out a bit.

To make the woman even more adorable, she tucked herself into me and passed out. Actually fell into sleep as I pulled her closer against my body. A pity really, because even though I'd come like a rogue bull, I was still hard as iron.

Swiping her damp hair from her face, I settled my chin on the top of her head and tried real hard not to think. But that was impossible as I cupped her breast and played with her nipple.

Earlier that night I'd started to resign myself to the fact that the sexy-as-hell woman in my arms wasn't into sex. A crime. Still, it happened. But when the fucking started she went off like a grenade with the pin pulled. No way I'd mistaken that kind of response. None of it could have been faked. She'd been too unguarded, too receptive.

I grazed the top of her head with my lips as I tried to work her out. Shy, conservative and given to little bouts of temper that I thought were cute as all get out. And with the biggest walls from anyone I'd met outside of my MC.

Not to mention that she liked it with the lights on and stared at my cock like it was lunch, calling it pretty of all fucking things.

Then get her naked, and bam, all bets were off. Still, I had the feeling she'd been a while in between bouts in the ring. What I'd first mistaken as skillful muscle control was not that at all. Maybe nerves initially, even though I'd gotten her off with a hand job to start things up. No, this woman had some mysteries happening. Didn't matter, we all had our secrets and things came out eventually.

She slept heavy, her breathing even and deep. She looked so damn sweet lying there that I left her alone for half an hour, content to watch her. Thoughts of that perfect pussy had me moving.

I eased her on her back, pushing her legs apart and bending her knees up. Putting her feet on my shoulder, I dipped my head. I knew she'd taste good, honey and spices, and totally Jenna. I glided my tongue through her and she lazily opened her eyes.

For the tiniest moments, she looked as if she was a very happy woman, but then she scrambled back and out of my way. I reached up, returning her to me.

"This is happening," I said.

"Ali, no." She had her hands on either side of my face.

I put my head up and frowned. "You don't like this? 'Cause I sure as hell do."

"Why?"

Fair question. "Because you taste like fucking heaven and I'm up and close to your pussy. Good enough?" I growled at her, putting my head back down and letting the vibrations filter through her.

"Oh," Jenna said, her hips bucking up. "Carry on then."

I chuckled, couldn't help it. I'd almost forgotten her sense of humor, a real bonus as far as I was concerned. Mostly I acted like a serious prick. I needed that. Needed her.

Needed her?

That should have been a scary thought, only it wasn't. I slid my tongue in a circle around her clit, before sucking it into my mouth. I wondered how fast I could make this, simply out of a need to know. Drawing her in farther and using the tip of my tongue to press against her, she lasted only seconds more, coming at a satisfying, leg-shivering rate. That was gold. We'd only just fucked and already I felt like I knew her on some fucking level. Her body, at least. But there was nothing routine about hearing her again cry out my name.

When I climbed up her body her eyes were wet. Jenna turned all emotional and, for once, I loved that shit. If women did that or got clingy, I was up and going while thanking them and bolting while still doing up my pants. Not with her, though. I kissed her, forgetting that I had only recently been down on her. Didn't seem to concern Jenna, she kissed me back. Normally I left most of what I took on their thighs and stomach, but seeing she didn't worry, I wasn't going to, but it felt right to apologize for disturbing her.

"Sorry," I said.

"For what?" She looked confused.

"Waking you up like that."

She arched her brows and I did the same back at her. "What time is it?"

I glanced at the clock beside the bed that I blocked from her. "Still early, eleven-thirty."

"Do you think we're missed?"

"Nah, if you wanna go downstairs, we can." I didn't want to. I wanted to call it a night and hunker down in my bed with her.

I wasn't a complete asshole, I had no objections to women sleeping over. I just normally didn't give a shit one way or the other. But there wasn't a chance this side of hell that Jenna would be sleeping alone.

"I'm supposed to go at midnight."

"You can stay," I said, stretching out beside her. "Or take me home."

That sounded like an even better option, getting her out of here and having her to myself in the morning. Hopefully my wakeup call gave her some ideas for a payback blow job first thing in the morning.

When Jenna got out of the bed and started to get dressed, I joined her. No way was she getting out of my sight, but she hadn't argued about me going home with her, not that I wouldn't win there.

She used my bathroom for a quick clean-up, coming out while applying lip gloss over her mouth. Pointless really, I'd only kiss that shit off.

I stretched my hand out, wiggling my fingers at her.

"You want to hold my hand? Down there, with all those macho brothers of yours?"

"Yep, soft as fuck," I said, shrugging my shoulders. "But seeing at one stage you fucked me while holding my hand, I'm thinking that evens it out."

She grinned, looking pleased at herself. "I did, didn't I?"

She took my damn hand.

Out in the hall we ran into Cage and two chicks who looked familiar. The pair as attractive as Eastern European supermodels. Both tall and cat-eyed pretty. Two weeks ago, I'd have probably had one of them on my own arm and later, under me in my bed. But now they were about as appealing as the dildo show the pair were about to go and perform down in the bar. That was if this visit was anything like the last one.

I took Cage in, he'd most likely fucked them both, and my boy also appeared stoned. Cage tended to do his alcohol and drugs in moderation. The last few years I had to say, the latter very rarely. He didn't fuck around with what he put in his body. A fitness freak and clean-food eating asshole, like Jenna, Cage could be described as an enigma.

He took one look at my woman, slowly running his eyes over her, a smirk forming over his face. "About fucking time. He do you right, princess?"

I expected her to go bright red, most chicks who weren't club would. But she met his gaze. "You have no idea."

I stifled my laugh. And the two girls giggled. Jenna just smiled at them politely. It wouldn't have surprised me if she'd introduced herself and shaken their hands. But she didn't, her eyes going to the end of the hall. *That's right, we are supposed to be leaving.*

Reaching out, I swiped my finger under Cage's nose for nonexistent powder residue. "Don't let Wraith see you. Your pupils are fucking pricks."

He nodded once. "Righto. Keep away from Daddy."

Jenna frowned at that. I'd fill her in later. Or not.

When we reached the car park, Jenna looked back at the clubhouse. "Should we have said goodbye to Jack?"

"No, babe, we're not that formal around here."

She pulled her keys out and pointed them at her car. "If you say so."

"You know, your car is a shitbox." It wasn't that bad, but it could have been better. It was about a decade old, one of

119

those dumb little hatches some women drove.

"Well, it's my shitbox," she said, getting in behind the wheel. "Are you coming?"

Didn't need to be told twice with this woman. I clambered in beside her. The vehicle, was of course, way too small for me, and her smile when I sat beside her came out as pure smartass. I just hoped she had a decent-sized bed. There was a reason I didn't normally do sleepovers outside my room at the club.

Her house was a small rental in a nice part of town. Filled with pale-colored furniture and bright bits and pieces scattered about. But there were no photos on the wall or the bookshelves. Nothing to tell me more about the woman who had brought me to her home.

A weird, sleek, brown cat appeared and made a horrendous excuse for a meow before it rubbed against my legs.

She looked at it like it was her firstborn. "Careful, he bites."

"Really?" I scooped it up and rubbed under its chin. The animal started purring immediately. "Like his mum."

She gave me a rueful smile. "Make a liar out of me, Hammer, why don't you? Funny, he liked Cage, too."

Yeah, about that. It had seemed a good idea at the time to get my brother to keep an eye on her while I had been out of town, but I'd be full of shit if I'd thought I wanted to do it again. A lot like putting a fox in charge of a hen house. Not that I didn't trust and love him, but this was Jenna, I didn't plan on taking chances with her.

"You want some tea?" she said over her shoulder as she led me to her kitchen.

I got the feeling this was her favorite room. There were a lot of cookbooks around, some open on the table, and shiny pots hung from a rack in the center of the room over a huge table that appeared solid. On one of the benches sat a raised stand with a clear dome — a cake that looked professional under the glass.

She switched on a kettle and gave me a questioning look. *Tea, right.* "No thanks. Take a beer if you've got one."

She opened the fridge and handed me one as she set about making herself some drink that when she added water smelled like flowers.

"He really likes you." She smiled. Unfortunately it was at the cat, not me.

"He won't when he finds out what I plan to do to you next." I leered at her. "Drink your tea then you can show me your bedroom."

Jenna held her mug with two hands and leaned back against the bench. She'd gone shy again, but I wasn't as worried as I had been.

I nodded at the cake. "You make that?"

"It's a hobby. I can't eat it all, of course. I'll pass it off to Casey and she can take it into work. The nursing home doesn't mind me dropping the odd one off, either." Fuck, she was such a citizen, but then, I knew that. "Would you like some?"

I shook my head and held up my beer. "Maybe another time. They don't exactly mix."

"Suit yourself." She took out a plate and knife, cutting a slice for herself. It actually did look great, especially with her eating it with her fingers.

It was refreshing the way Jenna had a healthy appetite. It got way old when women picked at lettuce, pinched their thighs and told me they were fat. I never got that, didn't they realize that I was just happy that they were naked?

She broke some off and pressed it to my mouth. I took it in, licking the icing from her finger. It was good, more than good.

I raised shocked brows. "Serious? She cooks?" Yeah, I'd heard all about Jack's cake, but I wasn't expecting this.

"She does. You should try my roast."

"I plan to."

I watched silently as she sipped her tea and decided to check out her house. She didn't seem to mind as I wandered around, staying back in the kitchen while I explored with the cat at my heels.

I found her room and switched on the light. What I had been looking for. There were photos on the dresser and the bed appeared big enough.

Sensing her behind me, I picked up one of the frames. She was beautiful even then. Two girls, one of them clearly Jenna, the other close enough in looks to be her sister. Only real difference being, both of the teenagers had jet-black hair.

"I used to dye it. We both did."

"Those your parents?" The other frame held a normal-looking couple who appeared to be in their late thirties, or early forties. Not recent, the same vintage as the one of her and her sister.

"Yes, we don't speak."

That shocked me. Jenna didn't seem the type to not get on with her family. But maybe her parents were assholes.

"What's your sister's name?"

"S-Susan."

She lied. The tells were clear, the eyes darting and the heat to her face. I didn't pick her up on it, but I wanted to. It was strange, her bullshitting about something as benign as the name of her sister.

I could check it out, of course, but in all honesty, I'd prefer it if she told me herself. Seeing we didn't know each other yet, not that well, anyway, I decided to let her get there in her own time. I doubted she was being treacherous in her motive and it was stupid of me to even assume I had earned her trust.

Jenna scooped up a silver chain with a heart dangling from it off the floor. "Damn cat," she said. "This is why he never comes in here, he steals shiny things. He must have slipped in earlier."

I went back to the photo of Jenna and her sister — they were both wearing matching necklaces like the one she replaced carefully beside the frame.

I glanced around the rest of the room. More pale furniture, all matching with white linen on the bed. Yeah, mechanics didn't do white real well. But at least there was not one single stuffed animal. I could have hugged her for that. I did in fact, dragging her over to me and wrapping my arms around her again. The scent of her had changed, she smelled like sex now, I wondered if she realized.

"Mind if I use your shower?" I'd already found the bathroom.

"Go right ahead." She pressed her cheek against my chest. "You wanna join me?"

I loved shower sex, loved having her against the tiles with water cascading down us, and I loved climbing naked and still damp into her sheets with her. But Jenna pulled back when I decided one more time before shut-eye.

Her hand was on my chest as I loomed over her. "I just can't," she said.

"Hey, I'm happy to do all the work this time. You've more than kept your end up." The woman was not passive.

"It's not that." She winced when I cupped my hand between her legs.

"Oh, right." I rubbed lightly. "Wear you out."

I should have felt a hell of a lot more guilty about that than I did.

"You could say that." She smiled up at me. "Do you mind?"

Her hand strayed down to my cock, her fingers not making it completely around me. As she began to run them up and down, I sighed and rolled off her. Yeah, her hand on my dick was fucking awesome, but if it was all the same with Jenna, I really wanted her mouth there. Not one to like a servicing, I covered her fingers, stilling them.

"We'll wait until morning. Feel free to wake me up with a blow job." I climbed off her.

"I don't mind," she said, her hand attempting to move to me again.

"I do. Get over here." Without waiting for a response, I

slid her closer, turning her so her back was to me, and found myself spooning her. *Yeah, I don't do that, but a funny thing was, I wanted to.* I even put my leg over her thigh, getting her in there real close and good.

"Now shut those damn fucking gorgeous eyes of yours and don't forget my morning blow job." I closed my own then, the last thing I remember of that night.

Chapter Seventeen

Jenna

I hadn't shut the blinds the night before, and after sliding out from under Ali, I turned as he moved to his back. The stark reality of my situation hit me full on as the covers hovered dangerously around his hips, the vee there pointing to a reminder of what we'd been up to back at his clubhouse and later in my shower.

His torso was a tawny color that I just knew would tan deep in the summer, his lashes dark and long against his cheeks. But I took that moment to study some of his ink work. Pictures and written passages mostly.

I reached out and traced my finger along the edges of an eagle that disappeared on the other side of his stomach. So engrossed, I didn't know he had woken until a powerful hand clamped down over mine.

"Where's my blow job?"

I looked up and he grinned, his hair messily falling in soft spikes over his brows.

He had mentioned that the night before and I grazed my bottom lip with my teeth. After how things had worked out, it seemed a shame that I was going to ruin all that with some clumsy moves.

"You don't want coffee?" Stall tactics. I used them out of desperation.

He shook his head and pulled me up into his arms. The movement made me shudder as a painful sensation hit me between the legs. I nearly rocketed out of the bed, the intensity so great.

Ali sat up, alarmed. "You all right?"

I put on a smile. *Not really.* I was sore as hell, nearly as bad as last night after the pounding he'd given me. I wasn't used to it, and now I felt the full effects.

"I'll be back." He got out of the bed and walked stark naked across my carpet. With his back to me, I got why women went on about men's asses. *Damn, it shouldn't be legal to look that good.*

Ali looked amazing as his muscles bunched and rippled when he moved. I guess he'd overwhelmed me the first time I'd seen him naked to take it all in. But his shoulders were even wider when uncovered, his waist nipped in narrow. He disappeared, returning soon after, showing me an impressive morning erection that I didn't have the energy to do much about.

I realized I could hear water running. "Are you making me a bath?"

"If you can believe I'm bathing you as opposed to getting head, then yes, that's exactly what I'm doing." He seemed surprised himself. "I'm sorry, Jenna, didn't mean..." He frowned.

"It's fine. I wasn't complaining at the time."

"No," he said. "You were all, 'fuck me harder, Ali', screaming down my damn room. Paying for it now, though?" He tried to hide the smirk on his face.

"Asshole."

All my muscles were stiff and sore, but it was a nice kind of pain in a way, like after a workout. But the sensation between my legs was not. I knew it would go away.

"Can't help it if my cock is ridiculous." He made for the door, dodging the pillow I threw at him. "And let's not forget pretty."

If he hadn't moved so fast, the next one would have gotten him for sure.

He redeemed himself a short while later when he came back, scooped me up, and carried me to the bathroom. After Ali deposited me in the gloriously hot water, he stood back.

"You want anything?"

Coffee, but not in the bath. "Juice?"

"Sounds good." He turned and started to leave, pausing in the doorway. "You're going to have to shove over when I get back. Who knew a midget like you would have such a big tub. It's like fucking *Scarface* in here."

"You want me to say hello to your little friend?" I couldn't help that as the water went somewhere to ease out my aches.

He raised both brows. "Cheeky girl."

I settled back and waited, but when he returned he had dressed, held one juice, and wore a downcast expression.

"Sorry, babe, I got called in."

This had to be his exit strategy and I'd almost been fooled.

"Okay, I guess I'll see you around." I sank farther in the water, glad he'd thought to put in some of my bubble bath, making me a little less exposed.

He frowned, the hand not holding the glass squeezing into a fist that he released before repeating the process. The tendons on his forearms stood out. A tension had set into his shoulders and his brows drew close.

"Fucking club," he said. "I'm real sorry about this, babe. I know how it looks."

"I should be used to it. Duty calls and all that."

"Yeah." He raked his hand through his hair. "If Cage didn't get too fucked up last night, he can go instead."

"I saw, remember? He was wasted." *Drugs, of course. Why it hadn't hit me when I first saw him I have no idea. Guess I'd been all post-orgasmic brain dead or something.*

"Which means he should be good now." He bent, ignoring my ducked head. He kissed me, tilting my chin up with his fingers to hit dead center. "I'll call."

I nodded and with a sigh he left me.

* * * *

Pony was smart enough not to open his mouth as I

climbed in beside him and slammed the door shut. The drive out to the club took only ten minutes but it seemed like forever while my brain thudded in my head, full of the shit I planned to let fly at Wraith the minute I got in his face.

Man didn't even have a chance to greet me. I was all up in his shit. "What the fuck, brother? One day the fuck off."

"Sorry, Ali." Yeah, a lot of damn people saying sorry this morning, not that Wraith sounded real sincere. "I would have gotten Cage to go, but he's fucked up."

"What did he have to say for himself?"

"Nothing coherent." Wraith frowned. "Not impressed."

"Well, sometimes the brother needs an outlet. Can you blame him?" I glared. I might have been pissed at Cage but this club made him and they had no fucking right to call him out when he lost his shit on the rare occasions he did. So he did some blow. Big fucking deal. Not like we never sold the shit. *Fucking hypocritical much?*

I chose to ignore the fact that Wraith wanted out of that game. It wasn't the time to see the president in a good light.

"You wanted to stay with Jenna?" Wraith had an amused look on his face. "Well, I'll be damned. You're serious about her."

"Of course I am. I made that clear at church a week ago." I shook my head.

"I thought that was you telling your brothers to not get in there while you were away." He grinned at me. *Very discon-fucking-certing.*

I grunted and landed in the chair opposite the desk he sat behind. "How long?"

Strangely, he seemed to still be contemplating me and Jenna. Not like Wraith—our personal shit, as long as it didn't interfere or cause issues in the club, was of no interest to him. He hated drama. It made him pop more antacids than even the heaviest deals and stresses.

"This is good," he said, finally. "About time you grew up."

I didn't even bother to dignify that with an answer.

Wraith cleared his throat and gave me my instructions.

Just some run-of-the-mill leg work. Any bastard could have been doing that shit. But I'd been putting my hand up for so long, I guessed I was just the first name that had come to the president.

It wasn't like I didn't enjoy my work for the club, and this feeling of wanting to stay home was bugging the shit out of me.

Added to that, Jenna had clearly thought I had run out on her, and my mood didn't improve. I planned on making things up to her as soon as I returned. Which meant that whatever roadblocks I ran into while I was away, I'd be riding right over them.

"You good there, brother?" Wraith said. "I don't want you cutting corners."

It was like he read my damn mind sometimes. I should be used to it. Between him and Cage, they thought they had my number.

"I'm good. I'll see you in a couple of days." I got out of the chair.

"Just don't take any stupid risks. It's one thing to want to get home to a woman, another to not make it."

My eyes narrowed. "You doubting my abilities now, boss?"

"Not at all. I just want you focused."

"You got no worries there." Again, I went to leave. The sooner I left, the quicker I'd be back.

"Ali," Wraith said, stopping me. "Shit will change. When this sale goes through, and we get out from under Dixie, it's going to be a whole new world. It'll take a while. Nothing worth doing comes easy. But you'll have plenty of time for her then."

I turned back to him. "I've just met the woman, Pres, don't have me married off yet, hey."

He chuckled. "My own home life might be fucked up, but I'll never regret Paige. There's nothing wrong with wanting home and family. Not everyone makes a mess of it, and like

I said, things will be different. Smoother."

"Yeah, right, whatever."

Then I was out of there, on my bike and heading away from the clubhouse, and from Jenna, to do more stupid shit for the MC.

Chapter Eighteen

Jenna

I was not disappointed that Ali left. More like I had a guilty conscience about having gone so far to keep him interested. I wasn't supposed to enjoy that, at least not as much as I had.

As soon as he'd left, I'd climbed out of the tub and, wearing my robe, sat at my kitchen table trying to make sense of the mess I'd made of things. The problem with not having close friends was not having someone to bounce these kinds of situations off of. I'd sat in enough break rooms in my time to know that women had a knack for sorting out each other's lives, or at least giving decent direction. I had none of that.

All I could do was list pros and cons. So far, I'd scratched out most of what I'd written, the paper in front of me a scribbled mess. I balled it up and tossed it to Hammer. That was another thing — Ali had not only let him out of the laundry, he'd fed him. It made no sense. He'd used the club as an excuse to get away from me, and he'd given my cat breakfast. He'd even put the food away.

My phone chimed and I picked it up. Casey.

How was last night?

Before I had a chance to answer, it sounded again.

Sorry for the intrusion, I just wanted to make sure you were home safe.

I smiled and replied.

Thanks, and yes, I am. What are you up to today?

Hanging by myself. Is he there? Or are you there?

I frowned, but tapped another text.

I'm an idiot. He made some bullshit excuse about club business and lit out as soon as he could this morning. I feel like an idiot. A whorey idiot.

Seriously, did you just slut shame yourself? I'll be there in fifteen.

Casey arrived a few minutes under her estimated time, breezing in wearing morning track pants and Ugg boots. She greeted me with a kiss on my cheek before divesting herself of her coat and hanging it up on a peg. "I don't want to hear bullshit from you," she said.

I raised my brows in amusement. "You don't?"

"No. If Ali left, that's his loss. Asshole."

"Yes, he is an asshole. But it takes two, right? I shouldn't have slept with him, Casey. I really shouldn't have." I noticed she had takeout coffees and a bag that looked suspiciously like it could contain warm donuts. The cinnamon scent curled up my nostrils, confirming my assumption. The girl was priceless. "You brought food."

"Of course I did. Fuel to fell said asshole." She plonked the pastries and caffeine down on the table and took a seat.

"Thanks." I sat opposite her. "I made such a mistake."

"Was it that bad?"

"No. I mean, it was good, then it was bad, good again, greater still, and then good, then bad."

She nodded, like she got that completely. "So you and Ali…"

"That was the greater still part. I really messed up, though. I got to the clubhouse and all those bikers… It was scary. I mean, how embarrassing. It's not like I'm not around them all day." I shuddered, remembering how I'd basically put my face against Ali's chest to block it all out.

"Bikers are scary," she said. "It's kind of the point."

"Especially when they're drinking and loud. I see them all week, but in overalls, not cuts. It was like a big reality smack to my head." Not to mention the uninhibited displays of public sex I'd witnessed.

In the end, it hadn't felt like much of a birthday party. My not being there for most of it hadn't caused me guilt. After all, I'd already celebrated Jack's actual day with him. I never should have gone.

"So Ali acted like a drunken pig, then?" She accepted the plates I handed her and divvied up the donuts.

"No, he was just nursing a beer when I got there." I decided to leave out Cage pretty much delivering me to him and what Ali's friend had said to me just before my arrival at the bar. "He was kind of subdued."

"But then he groped all over you?"

"No, he was nice, put his arms around me and got me a drink. When he knew I felt uncomfortable, he offered to get me out of there." I frowned, so far so good. "Well, there was some groping, it went with the kissing."

"You like Ali kissing you," she said, a wicked smile forming. "So we can move on from there."

I recounted everything right up until Ali threw me over his shoulder and took me upstairs. She started to frown by then, her coffee the only thing she touched. Neither of us seemed interested in the donuts.

"Did he get heavy?" She sucked in her bottom lip, her jaw set tight.

"Oh, no, nothing like that." I could see how all that could be taken out of context. "He offered me an out, but then he kissed me again."

She let out a relieved sigh. "Okay, I don't need details, maybe just tell me on a scale of one to ten how he measured up."

"I froze."

"Happens."

"I wanted to, I really did, but my head was not in the game. Body yes, but I… Anyway, it came good, and then, well, I'll say eleven." I'm not sure why I talked so openly. That wasn't like me. But getting everything off my chest did feel better. My stomach flipped as our conversation brought back all the details of the night before. I might have been inexperienced, but even I knew the sex had been off the chain.

Yet, he'd left me. I needed to remember that. More importantly, it was not supposed to upset me.

She pushed my plate to me. "Eat that," she said as she looked deep in thought.

"He stayed over after I had sex with him. Then this morning he made some club bullshit excuse that he needed to go." How stupid I'd been. It would have been better to simply leave the clubhouse and put it down to a fun night. But I had to take him home, had to wake up with him in the morning and feel good about what I'd done. Even if for a brief time, my happiness, as undeserved as it was, ate at me the most.

"It was a big deal to you, wasn't it? Having sex, I mean?" She still looked pensive.

"It's not to you?" Of course not, Casey likely had a lot more experience than me about these things.

But she surprised me. "Oh, like you'd never believe. I don't do casual. I mean, I had a short time when I started university, a couple of one-night stands. But really, I prefer sex with someone I love, or at least have the potential to. My younger, much cooler sister calls me a serial monogamist. So, I understand a little of what you're feeling."

"So, you don't think I'm simply a filthy slut who is getting what she deserved?"

She chuckled. "No, that description we can give to Ali. If it makes you feel better. After you tensed up, what did he do?"

134

"Offered to take me home, he thought I wasn't into it anymore. He didn't say much, I think I confused the hell out of him. I mean, it's not like I wasn't giving signals when I took my clothes off." I laughed then, too, but it sounded sad.

Dancing around my past was as natural as breathing to me. I never shared. I never had anyone to share with since I'd had Jack. I kept my friends distant and my thoughts close. Right up until that moment with Casey in my kitchen, it had suited me fine.

But the compassion she showed me encouraged me a little. The way her eyes looked upset for me as she worked things out for herself. Guess it didn't take a genius to realize at least some of my past.

"How long ago was it?" She reached out and squeezed my hand.

"A long time. I was fourteen."

"Ah, shit, Jenna."

Opening up to Casey, on at least some of my past, wasn't as hard as I'd expected it to be. It helped that she didn't ask for details and simply listened without much interjection. I kept so much from her. Hellion and Jack weren't anything I was ready, if ever, to discuss.

"I remember it being rife at college," Casey said when I stopped talking. "Drink spiking was a huge problem."

"It was when I went, too," I said. "But I never went out much, so it wasn't like it was an issue for me."

Casey gave me a curious look. "*Breakfast Club*?"

"Oh, yes, please."

I'd resigned myself that Casey would want to keep talking. But after the previous night and Ali's leaving, my finally opening up to someone about some of my past, I was emotionally spent. A couple of hours with one of my favorite old movies sounded a lot more appealing.

When my message tone chimed at the end of the DVD, we both jumped.

"Well check it." She gave the phone a pointed look.

It was Ali. For a moment, I hesitated. Why would he text, unless it was to say thanks for the memories? Probably making sure that I knew it had just been for fun.

But I had to do it, had to see what he wrote.

Sorry about the runner, I'll catch you in a few days. Also sorry that I won't be able to call.

I showed the screen to Casey, who shrugged. "Talkative, isn't he? You wanna watch another movie?"

"Why not?"

Anything to put my mind off Ali and what we'd done.

Chapter Nineteen

Jenna

Chrissie wasn't in the office on Monday morning when I arrived, but I didn't think much of it until Wraith came in and dropped off the banking.

"Chrissie not here?" Wraith's gaze fell to the pile of papers on my desk and the even bigger one stacked on Chrissie's, and his mouth formed a hard line.

"No, not yet." I paused in my typing, my fingers shaking too hard to continue. "I'm sure she's just late."

He grunted. "Guess we haven't met formally. I thought we'd have caught up Saturday night."

He stood in the middle of the office. The president wasn't as large as Ali, coming in around six feet. Yet he seemed to fill the room. Dressed like most of them, in leather and faded, worn denim, he wore the clothes like an Armani suit.

"No, I suppose not. Chrissie has pointed you out to me, though." My hands grew warm, the back of my neck prickling.

"So, you know that I have final say here," he said, glancing around the office before landing his eyes back on me. They were a strange shade of violet. I had to wonder if they were the last thing Sophie had seen before she died. I knew that Wraith wasn't one hundred percent certain as her murderer, but that didn't make me more comfortable. Nor did the fact that no one had called me out yet.

"Yes," I said.

"I have simple rules, Jenna," he said and stepped forward. "We'll get along if you follow them. I'm sure Chrissie has run through them with you. I'm just going to reiterate so there's no confusion. Do you understand?"

"I do." Oh, God, he made me want to pee my pants worse than my run-in with Cage and Pony.

"One, no club business discussed outside of the club. Two, no trouble caused between the brothers. Though you have that covered, that was one pissed-off man I sent out today." He chuckled. "Three, I don't tolerate liars, always remember that."

My heart jumped about in my chest. Shit. Was he telling me he knew I'd lied? I bit down on the inside of my cheek. "I understand."

Then he reached his hand inside his jacket. I froze. *This is it. It's happening.* But like the time Cage did the same move, he pulled out keys. These were smaller with an Audi fob. He tossed them onto the desk.

"Work vehicle."

"I have a car."

"Yeah, we run a garage, Jenna. This is more suitable." He stared me down. "I've had your things transferred to your new vehicle."

"Why?"

"Think of it as part of your package. A reward for the work you've done."

I started to think he was luring me in, giving me a false sense of security. The car was likely bugged, probably some sort of tracking device in case I made a run for it. I thought of my phone, Ali's messaging me, the fact that he'd had hold of it the other day. I didn't think he'd had a chance to put a tracker on it, but seeing I had no idea how those things were done, I couldn't be sure.

Swallowing, I tried to play along. "Thank you."

With a final glance around the office, Wraith turned on his heel and left. When I looked out of the window, he was dialing his phone. By the time he'd made it to the end of the workshop he'd jammed it into his back pocket, clearly not making any connection with whoever he had called.

Even though I was still alive, I jumped when Cage bounded into the office. He looked fresh and bright-eyed, completely different to the dopey creature he'd been at the party. All sexed-up and stoned when I'd last seen him.

"I guess I have to apologize," he said, his eyes downcast when he looked over at me. But the corner of his mouth twitched a little.

"Don't bother," I said. "I can tell it's bullshit."

He cracked a grin. "Well, I do feel a little bad. I could've gone in Ali's place if I wasn't so fucked up."

"Well, you know what they say, Cage? Just say no." I stood, realizing that I'd have to launder the money. Or, as they called it, 'do the banking' that morning. I didn't have a choice. Now was not the time to shirk my responsibilities.

I'd already split it in three lots, making out deposits for three different banks, glad there wasn't a casino in town. I had no idea how I knew it, most likely reading or movies, but I knew it was how criminals cleaned money, as well.

"Well come on, princess," he said, holding open the door. "Road trip. You gotta be looking forward to that at least."

We took one of the white SUVs from the parking lot, Cage driving and me sitting beside him with thousands of dollars of dirty money at my feet. *Just another day at work.*

I waited for him to offer up some crude remarks, but when they didn't come I realized that Ali and me disappearing as we had wasn't that big of a deal to anyone but Ali and me. It made me relax against the expensive leather upholstery.

Cage had hit the music, heavy rap on low volume as we slid out the gate. "You want something different?"

I shook my head. "I don't mind Tupac."

His brow shot up as he glanced over at me. "Classic. But I've already checked out your music."

"I like anything. Hate country mostly, though."

"Fuck, me too." He grinned.

"And people who over sing." I kept my eyes straight ahead. I was starting to relax and I was sure that was not a good thing.

"Yeah, fucking making one word into a hundred syllables while sounding like a strangled cat. Makes the hairs on the back of your neck stand up." He leaned over and turned the volume up as Nelly started. Not so loud we couldn't talk, though.

"How long have you been in the club, Cage?" I assumed his father was a member. Because after studying the pictures on the office wall, I knew that Cage had been around a long time. It hadn't been hard to make out the small dark-haired child as the pierced, tattooed man beside me. He'd been adorable, changing around twelve to looking harder, but even that seemed too young. "Was your dad a member?"

"Yep, mother was a club whore so any one of them could be my old man." He made it sound so blunt that my head snapped to him. "It's cool, princess, I'm not hung up about it. She left when she found out she was having me, but didn't cope and I ended up back here when I was five."

Cage was twenty-three, which meant his arrival would have been around the same time as Jack's. Not that a small child would have known what the adults in the club had been up to.

"Did you go to school in town?"

He shook his head. "Nah, I was educated in the clubhouse. A brother called Teacher because he was one. A regular home-schooled mud bricker."

"That's disgusting," I said. "You should have had a proper education." That horrified me. Hellion would have been in charge of that decision, of that I had no doubt. But all those brothers had let it happen. It boggled my mind.

"I did. I'm very well educated." He glanced at me. "Not like I'd be looking for work outside of the club, so formality wasn't exactly a problem for me."

"I'm sorry, I'm not judging you."

"You are, but that's cool. Only to be expected." He shifted in his seat, holding the wheel in a light, comfortable grip. "Not all of us are from behind white picket fences, princess."

"I'm not judging you," I repeated, emphasizing every

word.

He shot me a quick glance. "Okay."

"Do you see your mother?" A really personal question, but it was occurring to me that Cage might have been taken too.

"No, I leave her alone."

It was a strange way to put it, but I accepted what he said. It sounded as if he knew her location, but chose not to see her. Made me wonder about the woman herself.

"So, you and Ali finally fucked."

Aaaand, Cage comes back.

"You mind if we don't talk about that? It's personal." Heat rushed to my cheeks. Damn these men. There was no way I could be casual talking about what I did when I got naked.

He gave me a look that told me he thought I was being ridiculous and shrugged. "Okay, Jenna's pussy is a secret, whatever."

I slapped his arm. "If we're going to be friends, we need boundaries."

"Friends?" He looked highly amused. "It's okay, just because you and Ali…you and Ali are doing unmentionable things behind closed doors, doesn't mean you and I need to be friends, princess."

My face fell. Of course, he didn't want to be friends. I was simply a woman, and the men in the club had only one use for women. Friendship wasn't it. I slumped back in the seat.

"I'm messing with you," he said, a smirk on his face.

"You are?"

"I am." He nodded. "We can be friends, and I will not mention your pussy…too often. At least until you get used to me."

"What would Ali do to you if he knew you were talking to me like this?" I raised both brows at him wishing I could do that single brow raise that he did so well. I didn't think Cage was flirting with me. This had to be some kind of test.

He let out a small chuckle. "Nothing. Because Ali knows that the only interest I have in your pussy is keeping out anyone who isn't Ali. I don't touch anything, or anyone, that belongs to my brothers."

"Cage?"

"Yeah, princess?"

"You mentioned it again."

"Yeah, I did, didn't I?" He grinned, the asshole.

Dangerous asshole, I reminded myself.

Chapter Twenty

Jenna

Jack had left earlier in the day and hadn't returned. Chrissie hadn't come in, either. That left me alone with my thoughts and a pile of work. At least it kept me occupied, and I convinced myself that I was in no more danger than I had been the day I had walked into the Devil's Prophets compound.

I was so involved in my work that it was only when I glanced up and noticed that the garage had become empty did I shut down the computer. I filed a few things and picked up my bag to leave.

The lights were still on, however, and I pulled the door shut behind me, locking the office.

"Hey, you!" I heard a female voice and looked around. I didn't recognize the woman heading for me. She was taller than me, with long thin limbs. Despite the chill in the air she wore a strappy tank top. Her hair had that blue sheen that dyed black hair got after it had been freshly done, her makeup too thick. Her face and exposed skin was artificially tan. She might have been attractive, but had a hard edge to her. I couldn't determine her age — anywhere between early to late twenties.

There was something familiar about her as she came closer. I realized she was the woman that the other ladies had pointed out to me at the party. Leanne, the one who, according to them, wanted Ali.

"There's no one around," I said, injecting some friendly into my voice. "You're not really supposed to be in here."

The rules to the workshop were strict. No customers or unauthorized personal on the premises unattended, especially after hours.

"Is that so?" she said. "I've been here plenty of times before. I don't need the bitch secretary telling me where I can go."

I decided to play dumb. "Do I know you?" I said, feeling wary with all the animosity and anger rolling off her. She got closer to me now and there seemed to be more than hostility coming from her. I realized she appeared high, the drugs fueling her aggression.

"We have a mutual acquaintance, one you need to keep away from. I'm back now, and no fucking citizen chick is getting in my way."

"Look, if you have issues with Ali then you discuss them with him. I don't even know you." I went to walk past and she stepped in to block me.

Footfalls sounded and relief washed over me as Pony came into view to the side of us. He held a wrench in his hand, wiping the grease from it with a dirty rag.

"Oh, I will be talking to Ali, not that he'll want to talk much." She flashed a sneer. "Not his strong point."

I almost smiled at that — she had no idea who Ali was. To her, he was just a brother who she wanted to make her old man, a way into the club. I wasn't putting Ali down at all with my thoughts, but I read this two-dimensional creature like a fully charged Kindle.

"Let me pass," I said as her hand lashed out and clasped around my arm. Artificial nails, some I noticed had broken away, pinched into my flesh. I tried unsuccessfully to shake her off.

She yanked me closer, my body spinning so that my back pressed to her front. Pony stayed still, a small amused smile on his face. If this was what the prospect called entertainment, I'd be giving him a piece of my mind as soon as Leanne had finished kicking my ass.

She went to turn me back around and I brought my foot

up, slamming it down into her instep as a class I took in self-defense years ago came back to me. My elbow came up and hit her in the center of her chest. I spun back then, the heel of my hand smashing against her face.

Leanne let out a groan type of a squeal, her hands going to her nose, cupping it as blood flowed between her fingers. I stepped back, shocked at my reaction. I hadn't even thought about what to do, I'd just done it.

"I'm, oh, shit," I said, and turned to Pony.

He grinned like an idiot. "Hot damn," he said. "Remind me not to get on your bad side." He already was, not that I wasn't on his.

"Pony, she attacked me. Why didn't you stop it?" I trembled. By then, Leanne's face became covered in blood, her fingers doing little to staunch the flow. This all could have been prevented.

"You broke my nose, you fucking bitch," she said in a nasally whine.

"You shouldn't have let her in here, Pony," I said as he threw the blackened rag to her.

He looked a little concerned then at my calling him out on his slack enforcement of the basic security.

"Jesus, don't tell Ali," he said, worry wiping any semblance of a smile off his face completely.

"Don't *you* tell Ali," I said and stormed off.

If I had any brains, I'd have gone home and packed my bags, fleeing this place. As it was, my original goal of being here was starting to go to the back burner. Not that I'd forgotten my son, not in the slightest. But I needed to get back on track of getting to know him.

Otherwise, what was the point?

Chapter Twenty-One

Ali

The ride to Jenna's house from the club only lasted a few minutes. I needed more time to process what I'd just heard. *Fucking Leanne.* I'd seen that bitch early on Saturday night and managed to avoid her. In hindsight, I should have made it loud and clear that I was still not interested.

She'd laid hands on my woman and the only reason I wasn't breaking my normally hard and fast rule of not hitting females was because Jenna had turned tables on her and broken the bitch's nose. She was, at that moment, either at the ER or getting the fuck out of town. Either way, she was not important.

But I had had some luck. The meet I had planned had fallen through. The dickhead had been MIA, and the general consensus was that he now lay buried out in bush land, feeding maggots. Not my work, although if I'd known it would mean I got back to town Monday night, I'd have considered it.

The house was lit up. I'd shot Jenna a text saying I was home early and she'd replied in typical Jenna fashion and offered to make me dinner. I was hungry all right, but not for food.

I pulled into her driveway and parked under her carport. The Audi was most likely in the garage, making me smile that she'd tried not to accept the car. Bad luck, it was hers.

A guy owed me money and, not having the cash, had given me the overpriced grocery grabber instead of payment. Said it suited him as his wife was divorcing his ass and he didn't want her having the satisfaction of getting the vehicle as well as half the house. It was of no use to me. I had a truck when I needed four wheels and I just hadn't gotten around to selling it.

I liked the idea that Jenna was in something safe and reliable that I wasn't going to spend every second weekend fixing for her when I could have been fucking her. So overall, it worked out well.

Her door wasn't locked, pissing me off a little as I entered. She needed to be more vigilant when it came to her security. I'd talk to her about that.

But thoughts of lectures died away when I saw her. She was at the end of the short hall, her arms folded, wearing pink and white checked flannel PJ pants and a tank top with thin straps and a bit of lace in the center. *No fucking bra.*

Her hair was piled up loosely on top of her head and the first thing I did when I reached her was pull out the elastic that held it and let it tumble down around her shoulders.

"Fuck, you're beautiful," I said, claiming her mouth and pressing my hand into the small of her back so she could feel just how much I meant that.

She was into it. She pressed her body up hard against me and put her legs around my waist when I lifted her. The fear I'd been carrying that she was going to go catatonic on me again went out of the window as she ground against me. She'd missed me, too.

Spotting the kitchen bench, I walked with her and sat her on it, not breaking lip contact as I devoured her mouth. She tasted so fucking good, her mouth hot and desperate against mine.

I pulled the straps on her tank, her tits spilling out, hard pink buds just waiting for my attention.

I went down there, sucking one in and nipping her with my teeth. Not enough, I bit down harder.

She gasped, pulling back.

"You can take this," I growled against her. For emphasis, I moved to the other one, getting it inside my mouth and paying equal attention to it.

I looked up as her head rolled back, her ass squirming on the counter top. She was loving it, which was a good thing. I wasn't the slow and gentle type. If that was what Jenna wanted then she was shit out of luck. But it wasn't looking that way, her thighs parted wider as I rubbed my still covered cock against her pussy.

Clothes, yeah, bit of a problem that. Not mine, hers. I stepped back and started pulling off her pants. No underwear, she was catching my habit as her pussy came into view. I dipped my finger into her, pressing deep as she gripped it.

"You been having dirty thoughts, Jenna. Thinking about me fucking you?" I stared her down.

"Yes," she said, voice all breathy and hot.

"Fucking you hard?" I kissed her mouth, pulling her bottom lip with my teeth as I broke away. "Jenna?"

"I was." She put her arms around my neck.

"Babe, I'm torn here, wanna eat that pussy all up, but need to fuck you like I need to breathe. We good here?" I was already reaching into my back pocket for the condom. I was pretty sure Jenna wasn't on the pill. *Yeah, I'd snooped, what can I say?*

She nodded, her hands going from around my neck to the front of my pants where she undid the belt and yanked hard on my zipper. She was in there, pulling out my cock with both hands, holding it firm. She pushed my jeans down my hips and gave my balls a firm grip, making my dick even harder when she met my eyes.

"You can take it," she said, a cheeky expression on her face.

I hissed a breath. *Oh, yeah, I can more than take a bit of rough handling.*

She moved her hands away and put one on each shoulder as I got the condom out and on in one quick motion. Then I was inside her, driving in smoothly and pulling back out as I punched my hips against her.

Jenna looked down, watching my dick fuck her cunt with

the hottest look I'd seen on her yet. I had to smile, couldn't fucking help it as I grabbed her ass, sliding her along with me. She took the hint and started to move against me, jacking things up even further.

I was not going to last like this, but I didn't think she was, either. Didn't matter if it was fast, as long as I got my girl off, I was happy.

"Ali, God, harder, Ali."

No argument from me. I took things up a notch, feeling my balls looking to explode. I moved my hand on her ass farther, finger prodding against her. She wriggled and I slid inside, using her dripping juices to assist entry.

Her eyes widened, and I grinned like the prick I was. That was a first for her, I'd bet any money. But she wasn't exactly complaining as I matched the rhythm my dick was making with my finger play.

"You like that, babe?" I could barely speak, but needed to hear from her.

"Um, oh, God." She started pulsing around my cock, waves crashing over her as she bit down hard on my shoulder. That was becoming a habit, I realized. She either cut loose with a fucking amazing scream or she rode things out silently. Whatever turned her on, I was good with both.

I fucking blew then, shoved real hard against her and let loose.

I had to leave her for a second to take care of the condom, but I was back real quick, gathering her into my arms and kissing the top of her head.

"Thought I'd imagined how good you feel," I said. "Looks like I played things down. Did you miss me?"

She nodded against me, her arms around me. It was good holding her — damn woman had turned me into a cuddler.

"Your phone is ringing."

Jenna's words had me digging inside my cut. I was still wearing the fucking thing as I did up my pants one-handed. It was Jack.

"I gotta take this." She nodded, her mouth forming a

straight line. I guess she thought it was Wraith. "What's up, little dude?"

I turned from Jenna, hearing her pull her clothes back on. Which of course was kind of pointless but cute at the same time.

"Chrissie," he said.

I let out a hard breath. I knew what was coming. Funny, but I hadn't seen any signs and there was usually something. But then again, I'd hardly been around much.

"Fuck. Hospital?"

"Yeah, I'm just leaving now. You wanna catch up for a drink?"

"I'm at Jenna's, you know where that is?"

"Yeah, see you there."

When I turned back, Jenna looked worried instead of pissed off. "What's wrong?"

Pretty much fucking everything except the freshly fucked woman in front of me.

Chapter Twenty-Two

Jenna

So, Chrissie had a habit of taking copious amounts of pills when life got too tough. Guilt will do that. I didn't feel sorry for her and if that made me a bad person, I could live with it.

But I did feel terrible for Jack. What a big burden for an eighteen year old to carry around with him. It angered me that Chrissie would place that responsibility on his young shoulders.

I knew that suicide wasn't a selfish act in itself, but from what Ali told me, it might have been calculated on Chrissie's part. Attention seeking at its most dangerous.

Jack arrived with bourbon and Ali found shot glasses in a cupboard while I went off to change into something less nipple-baring.

When I returned, they had set themselves up at my kitchen table. Jack didn't look too bad. They were talking low and I started to get dinner going. I had promised Ali I'd cook for him, but making a meal that my son would eat gave me the warm fuzzies.

"You don't have to do that," Jack said. "We can send out for something."

"It's fine. I like to cook. It's nice to have someone to cook for." I turned and smiled at him while he tilted back his glass. "Besides, you should have proper food in your stomach if you're going to be drinking that."

He gave me a grin.

I'd managed a quick shower and was pretty sure that

I looked okay, but Ali's hair was messed up. Not that I remembered doing that. He had the disheveled 'I've just had sex' thing going on. I was embarrassed but figured Jack's mind was elsewhere and not on what we'd been up to.

I started to slice vegetables for a stir-fry. I'd already prepared the beef. I'd chosen simple food, but I'd already known that Ali and I would have been otherwise occupied, so fast seemed a good idea.

When I turned back to them, Ali watched me, a strange look on his face.

"Hope you like spicy," I said.

"Spicy's good," Jack replied. "Smells great already. "

I'd put sesame oil and garlic into the wok and tossed in chilies as I went to fetch the meat.

"Brother moves fast," Jack said. "He's already got you cooking for him."

"I earned it," Ali said.

I shot him a warning look and something devilish came over his face.

"Really?" said Jack, grinning wide. "Interesting."

"And private," I said, watching Ali.

He had both hands on the table, playing with his empty glass. At my words, they both cracked up laughing.

"Shit, you make him laugh, too." Jack shook his head. "Woman, you're a triple threat. Fucking, cooking and making my brother laugh."

My mouth dropped open and when my cheeks burned, I turned back to the stove. Really didn't need to hear that from my son.

"Ali laughs all the time," I said, my back still to them while I regained my composure.

Jack is a biker, I told myself, *he's freer with some things than other people.* He doesn't know I am his mother. *What he says cannot affect me.*

When I spun back around, Jack watched me and Ali frowned. He was serious out in the garage when he worked.

But the few times, the shamefully few times, we'd been together talking, Ali had an easy way about him. But now as I watched him with Jack, I could see the tension across his shoulders. And since I knew he was close with my son, like he was with Cage, this had me thinking.

I wasn't special. Far from it. Ali liked me, I knew that much. How much, though, I was clueless about. He liked having sex with me. Hell, I liked having sex with him, but so what? He could very easily find another woman to pass the time with. The man was gorgeous. But there was more to him than that. I shook off the thought. Ali was a means to an end. The very reason for his presence was seated with him at my table. I had to remember that.

The sound of the meat sizzling filled the silent void that overtook the room. When Ali's phone rang, I flinched.

He dug it out of his cut, glanced at the screen and stood.

With that, he left the room and a moment later I heard him talking on his phone but couldn't make out a word of the conversation.

It had to be the club, of course, and I assumed that he'd be leaving again.

"I'm sorry about Chrissie," I said, tossing the food around in the wok.

"Yeah, thanks. She's not trying to kill herself." Ali had said similar, but hearing it from Jack made me angrier.

"Are you sure?"

He nodded. "I'm worried, though, that she might go too far. She's playing a dangerous game, least that's what the old man used to say."

"Does she have a doctor?"

Jack shrugged. "A shrink, yeah. She doesn't see her regularly."

"Perhaps she should." I turned off the gas burner and went and sat at the table.

As much as I told myself that I didn't feel sorry for Chrissie, my stomach tightened. Living with a man like Hellion couldn't have been easy. I knew what he could do. I had to wonder how well Chrissie had known her late husband. Pretty well, if they'd been together for more than two decades, was the logical answer.

"I thought it would be better when he died." Jack's words were quiet. "Not that I wanted that, but I thought after... I just thought it would be different. Easier."

"She lost someone she loved, Jack." I reached out and covered his hand. "It's only been a couple of months, you need to give her time."

He blinked and downed his shot. "Don't get me wrong, I loved my old man. But he had his faults. I told you he cheated on her. More than with the woman who had me."

Something like sympathy tugged at my heart. I ignored it as best as I could. Easy when Jack was in front of me, eighteen years too late. They had stolen him. They'd killed Sophie and neither the dead man nor his widow deserved anything less than my hatred.

I thought of Anna, the wife of the current president. How Wraith's girlfriend resided at the clubhouse. That had to hurt. Not only the betrayal of the marriage, but having it blatantly rubbed in her face.

"Don't worry," Jack said. "Ali's not like that. He's loyal, you know?"

No, I didn't. I didn't know anything.

"That was the club," Ali said, and came back into the room.

"You're going again?"

He bent and brushed his lips over my forehead. "No, someone else can."

Jack's brows shot up and he gave me a knowing look before he splashed liquor into their glasses, pausing over a third one. "Jenna, you in?"

That sounded like a good idea.

Chapter Twenty-Three

Jenna

"Now as I recall, you and I were in the middle of something when we got interrupted. You remember that?" Ali grinned, getting on the bed and stalking over to me on all fours. He was so damn sexy that I couldn't help but stare. Good thing he wasn't in the least bit shy.

"Oh," I said, and bit my lip. "That."

He grinned. "Yeah, that. Christ, you're not one of those women who doesn't like sucking cock? I find that hard to believe."

He moved fast, landing on his back, his arm stretched up and his palm went behind my head. He didn't pull me down, just rubbed gently. With his free hand, he scratched under his chin.

He was naked, erect and waiting for me. I was still wearing the jeans and a long-sleeved top I'd changed into. Clothing that was turning his expression to one of disappointment.

"Jenna, you're sucking the fun out of the room instead of sucking my —"

"Just a second," I said, and put up my hand. "I just need a minute."

I moved to my knees and knelt beside him, staring down at his dick. It was a nice dick, didn't need to see a whole bunch of them to know that I liked Ali's. But I hadn't really had that much of a chance to examine him properly. I thought perhaps if I did, I'd have more confidence in what he wanted me to do. What I actually wanted to do to him. Only problem, I was scared of looking like an idiot.

I moved so that I was between his legs. He watched me with some amusement on his face. But there was heat in his eyes as I got closer. Under all the ink, Ali's skin was a nice shade of olive. But his cock was pink, the head part darker, almost purple. It held a little moisture at the tip.

His hair was dark, his balls quite large, bigger than I thought they'd be. I dipped a little lower and contemplated picking them up to see how heavy they were. They'd slapped against my thighs and ass before, so I knew they wouldn't be light.

"Are you okay there?" he said.

"Hmm, fine." I reached out and cupped his balls, lifting my hand a little. They were heavy, full and warm. "I'm just trying to work out the best way to go about this."

I sat back, pulling off my top before wiggling out of my pants and leaving on my underwear. Why not? It was the new black lace that I'd bought on the weekend.

"Don't overthink, babe." His face had grown serious and he was studying me, too. "All it wants is your lips on it. But I'll warn you, he spits when he's angry."

There was more to it than that. I knew that much and I didn't want to mess this up. I hunkered down some more, stretching out, stomach on the bed. I took hold of his balls again, wrapping my free hand around his shaft, sliding my thumb over the head and spreading the fluid.

He seemed to like that. His breath hissed. I slowly bent him back, lifting his cock from where it was running along his stomach. I didn't look at him at first, just tasted the tip of him with my tongue, my eyes closed as his skin slid under me. He tasted nice and he felt amazing.

"Look at me," he said.

I opened my eyes. Ali's face had changed. His own eyes were heavy-lidded and one hand was gripped the sheet, the other rested on his thigh.

I enclosed the head in my mouth, and ran my hand up and down his shaft. I contemplated putting both hands on him, but his balls were so comforting in my palm that

I just played with them instead. I kept looking up at him as I sucked gently at first, getting the feel of him. He was so hard, like steel covered in the softest velvet. And warm. The heat this man carried was better than an open fireplace.

But I got a little gamer, sucking harder, working him with my hands a little rougher. He liked that, liked it a lot. I could tell from the way his hips moved with me and the look of pure pleasure on his face.

I'd heard of deep-throating, but had no idea how anyone did that. I pushed as much of Ali as I could into my mouth, but when he hit the back of my throat, I had to pull away. I learned my limits and stuck with them.

Yet, as I gained confidence, and as Ali's hand went into my hair, tangling his fingers in it, I pushed myself a little further.

"Fuck, Jenna, slow the fuck down." He was sounding out of breath, on the verge of coming.

I slowed a little, wanting to prolong things. I liked giving head. I liked being in control of how Ali felt, and I loved how he was loving it. Basically, I treated Ali's cock like the most delicious ice cream on the planet. I licked, sucked and scraped my teeth over him.

And when I took his balls into my mouth he tugged at my hair in appreciation. But it was my tongue running under them as my hand continued to jerk him off that got Ali's attention.

"You need to get up here. I need to fuck you."

I ignored him, instead taking him back into my mouth, pressing my fingers below his balls, grazing his ass a little as I got more game.

"I'm serious, Jenna, I'm going to come in your mouth if you don't…" He gave up, he had to know I had an idea what I was in for.

I sucked hard, my cheeks hurting as I pumped my hand on him. When he came, I took it, drinking him down, raising my head up a little so that I could taste him on my tongue. Some slipped out when he'd finished and I looked back up at him, licking the slight spillage off my bottom lip.

"Jesus, don't you fucking dare do that." He was staring at me.

I gave a final lick up his shaft, a little swirl over the opening to take anything that remained, then I climbed up the bed and nestled under a very grateful Ali's arms.

"You didn't lie," I said. "He really does spit when he's angry."

* * * *

"You know," I said into Jenna's ear as I caught her from behind, dragging her back to me, "you suck dick like a fucking champion."

"Good to know," Jack said as we stumbled into the kitchen. Kid was up early and looking like hell. "I made coffee."

Sure enough, he'd come through with the right stuff. Jenna was blushing up a storm, but fuck, I hadn't known he was there. I'd forgotten that I'd suggested he crash on Jenna's couch when she'd gone to get ready for bed. Didn't matter, he'd heard the compliment, not seen the reason behind it.

Jenna was wriggling against me, trying to get away, and I was having none of that. "Settle down," I said, giving her a swat on her ass.

"I need to make breakfast." She sounded pissed off, and of course, I kept pushing.

"We can eat at the club," I said. "You leaving, Jack?"

"On my way." The kid chuckled a dirty laugh and Jenna wrenched out of my arms.

I didn't like that one bit. She danced backward and pulled two cups down from the cupboard. Whatever, Jack would be gone soon enough and I'd try again.

As usual, I was impatient. Couldn't help it around her. I guess this constant horny state would slow a little later on, but right now it was code red and I made another attempt to pull her to me.

This time she slapped hard at my hands. "Jesus, Ali."

"Yeah, you said that enough last night. Your tone was different, however."

She glared at me. For fuck's sake. I wasn't getting her naked, just touching her.

"I'm going around to Casey's tonight," she said, not looking at me. "So I won't be home."

"Ditch her, she'll understand." I lifted the mug and took a drink.

"I will not," she said. "You wouldn't ditch your brothers."

True. "No worries, we can hook up later." This was going downhill fast. I was glad when Jack put his cup in the sink, thanked Jenna for the couch and headed off.

She was no more relaxed when he left.

"What's going on here?" I said. "You were fine before."

"Some things are private, at least for me." She wasn't touching her coffee.

"You're saying that you and Casey didn't dissect Saturday night in infinite detail?" *Fuck, I know that had to have happened.*

"I told her we slept together, but no, no details." She had her mouth in that hard line.

"Too busy being shitty I left, huh?" I understood that, seeing I wasn't too happy with the situation myself.

"Yeah, as a matter of fact, yes. But that's not the reason she didn't get a blow-by-blow account." Jenna sipped from her cup. Good, hopefully that would make her happy.

"If you think I'm going to be filling the boys in, think again." My mouth quirked a little. "I'll play that your way."

Her brows rose. "Really?"

Christ, is this all it was? Her wanting to keep our fucking to ourselves? That's nothing. I'm not one to brag, but yeah, we talk shit about women we screw. But I got where Jenna was coming from, there was more than sex there, and no way was I going to be discussing that part of things.

She wasn't falling into my arms in forgiveness, but at least she wasn't glaring at me, either. Jenna downed the rest of her mug and placed it beside the one Jack had left behind.

"Babe?" Christ, it was becoming real obvious that until she got through the day with no word on what had gone down with us, she wasn't going to be happy.

"Not even Cage. Actually, especially not Cage."

I let a breath out of my nose about that. Brother was important to me. "You don't like him?"

"Actually, he's growing on me." Jenna let a small smile escape.

"Not too much, I hope."

Women loved Cage — they were either trying to fuck him or fix him or some combination of the two things. Man was not above using that to his advantage. Loved the bastard more than my own life, but he was a total deviant.

"No, you have no problems there. So, you still wanna get food at the club or here?" At least now she seemed a little more chilled.

"Depends. We gonna argue some more?"

"I'm seeing Casey after work still. We've got Pilates."

"I figured you would be. Wanna move on to the makeup sex part?"

She eyed me ruefully. She was down with that.

Chapter Twenty-Four

Jenna

I found Ali asleep on my couch when I got home from Pilates. Stretched out with his socked feet over the edge, he looked sweet and tempting. Not for the first time, I wondered what the hell was wrong with me. I shouldn't be seeing him as anything other than what he was, or his purpose. He was my key to the club and my link to Jack. Nothing else.

"Hey," I said, sitting down on the coffee table as he cracked first one, then the other eyelid. "I could have been a burglar."

"A very beautiful one."

"Did you eat?"

"I was waiting for you. You wanna go out?"

"It's nearly nine, and I grabbed a quick bite with Casey. I can fix you something."

He reached out and pulled me down onto him, trapping me in his arms and legs. "How about I just eat you?"

"Is that what you think?" Maybe if I just didn't look at him.

"Or we could talk?" He gave me his serious face. "About what happened the other night in my room."

I froze in his arms, probably reminding him. "I told you, I was overwhelmed. I get that way when I'm surrounded by bikers."

"I'm going to work out what's going on in here," he said, tapping his finger to the side of my head. "But it's okay, we got time. I plan to be spending some time here, might even say I'm going to move in by stealth."

"Um, if you say it, it's kind of defeating the whole sneaky thing." I grinned, despite everything.

"You got your secrets." He kissed me, tugging on my bottom lip. "We all do."

"Well, you're one to talk." I tried to smile up at him and, when that failed, let my hand trail over the front of his jeans.

"Nah, not working," he said.

That was not actually true. "Did you bring some stuff with you — clothes and things I mean?"

He nodded at me. "I get the feeling you'd rather do this here than back at the clubhouse."

He was right about that. "If it's okay with you?"

"I don't care where we are to be honest." He kissed the tip of my nose. This was a different Ali, softer. "Long as I'm with you, it doesn't matter."

The kisses were slower, gentle and his hands pushed my hair back from my face, not tugging it. I liked this. Not that I didn't enjoy him any other time. But this sweetness was something I needed and he seemed to get that.

His phone rang, making my chest constrict. He checked the number and tossed it to the other side of the room.

"Was it Jack?" I asked.

"Nope, not the kid. Just club shit."

"Shouldn't you answer it?" It was ringing again.

He pressed his forehead against mine and rocked both our heads side to side. "No, I don't think I should."

"You're getting called out again?"

"No, I'm going to make out with you on this couch until you're in a frenzy and grabbing at my dick again."

I grinned under him. That sounded like a very good plan.

I was well past the frenzied state when a hard pounding sounded on my front door. Wriggling like a fish on a river bank under Ali, who was teasing me without mercy, I jerked my head up.

"Fuck me," he said.

"If we're real quiet, they might go away."

"Not Cage," he said.

"What's he doing here?"

"Wraith would have sent him." He climbed off me and scratched his head as he made his way to the door.

Sure enough, Cage was behind Ali, looking annoyed as he came into my living room.

"Seriously, couldn't you just answer him?" Cage flopped down beside me on the couch. "Hey, princess."

"What did he want?" Ali sat on the couch opposite us.

"Just to tell you that they found the thing you lost the other day. Seems there was some assumption that he had to clean up and that you were the one that lost it in the first place."

"Oh, right. Yeah, should have answered that."

"Did you," Cage said, "lose it?"

"Nah, wasn't me. I would've told you if I was that careless."

They were talking in some kind of code. My head went between them as if I was watching a tennis match. But I stopped myself from asking them to speak plain English. Ali had not been able to find something that someone else had lost. I had no idea why that was important.

"Right," I said, slapping my hands on my thighs as I stood.

"Don't worry, princess, you don't have to lose your girl hard-on, I'm going."

"We're going to eat anyway. You can stay if you want."

I nearly rescinded the invite when he snickered. "Nah, I've done that already."

"What Cage means to say is that unless the food you offer him is kale or some shit, then he probably won't eat it." Ali laughed low himself.

Cage wasn't as big as Ali, yet, though Ali didn't carry any fat, his friend had a leanness about him that emphasized his muscles. *Actually, he has a great body,* I noted. *Athletic.* I caught Ali watching me check out Cage and pulled my eyes away.

It wasn't like that, but what did he expect? He had me heated up in the first place.

Cage got to his feet and gave me a slow wink that didn't help things. Ali was looking rather pissed off by then, drawn brows, his eyes narrowing further as he continued to watch me.

I put on my best innocent expression and looked up to the ceiling. It was all his own fault.

"Yeah, should go right about now." Cage fist bumped Ali who I was sure only offered his hand out of habit as he passed by.

When the door clicked shut, Ali continued to look at me. But something flickered behind his eyes. Something that had my chest constricting.

"I should put you over my knee and spank that beautiful ass of yours," he said, a low growl behind his words. "Before I fuck it."

My eyes widened and immediately flew to his. "Um, not sure about that."

He moved cat quick and straddled me, pushing me back against the couch, catching my wrists in his hands, holding me there. The first time he'd done that, he let me go on the second attempt to push up on him.

So, I struggled once, then twice. But he held fast. My third attempt had him pushing harder against me.

"Oh, I'm real sure about that." He bent down, his lips close to my ear. "Run!"

With that, he got off me as quick as he'd gotten on. I hesitated for a second then took off, planning on locking him out of the bedroom. But he had me before I even left the room, jumping over the couch and scooping me up around the waist.

He got me down on the floor, my stomach to the carpet. One hand held my wrists above my head, the other pulled my pants down, baring my backside. He slapped hard and sharp—he'd have had to have left a mark.

Still holding my hands above my head, he pulled my

pants down farther. I was so shocked, I didn't even cry out. He slapped again, harder this time. He was serious.

I squeezed my eyes shut as he chuckled, bringing his hand down for the third time. This time, I did yell. That hurt, even if it did ratchet up my adrenaline levels.

His fingers grazed over my skin, sliding between my ass cheeks. I sucked in my breath, bracing myself. *Oh, God, this is happening.*

I started to tremble, first just a bit, my breath hitching, but then my entire body vibrated in fear. My teeth chattered together and it was Ali's turn to suck in a breath.

"Oh, hell, baby, I'm playing. Jesus, Jenna, talk to me." He lifted off me, standing up. "Fucking hell. I'm so sorry."

Falling to his knees beside me I could see him from the corner of my eye. The big man was blinking fast, running his hands through his hair. But I couldn't move. Apart from the shaking, I was immobilized.

He put out his hand, only to draw it back.

"I'm just gonna..." He reached out again, this time with both hands as he eased my pants back up. Then, very carefully as if I was going to break, he picked me up and pulled me onto his lap. He adjusted himself, unbending his knees and stretching his legs out in front of him.

He was rocking me slowly, his big arms around me. I wanted to speak, to tell him I'd been silly and overreacted, but I was beyond words.

"I'll never hurt you," he said, his words thick. "You gotta know that. Please, babe, talk to me."

"I know," I said.

"But you thought— For a second there, you thought I was going to."

No, not once, but for a moment there, I forgot who I was with. I couldn't explain that to him. It wasn't going to make any sense.

It wasn't the spanking, I realized, my mind racing. It was something else, the position, not him behind me, but the way he held me, with my face down to the ground, my hands above my head, trapped there with one hand.

I blinked, trying to pull myself together. "Ali?"

"Yeah," he sounded distant.

"I was being silly. I know you were only playing."

"Didn't seem like that to me," he said, kissing the top of my head. "You want to talk about this?"

"No, I don't."

"I don't want to fuck up again." His words were whispered, heartfelt and no lie. "I'm not used to boundaries, but I wanna put some down for us. Okay?"

I nodded. That sounded reasonable. He'd turned off the light in the room when he'd let Cage in, probably thinking I didn't want Cage seeing me all dilated pupils and flushed. The lamps still burned, but it was too dark. That had no doubt added to things.

"All right."

"Lights on," he said. "That one I know. If I'm behind you, not flat out like that."

I nodded against his chest. I think that was right, I just wasn't sure.

"Spanking, well that's out."

"No," I said, surprising myself. But I had to give him some honesty — so far, I hadn't been very forthcoming. "And not at the club. Not until I get used to it."

"Yeah, that's cool. I can see how that might be intimidating." He was still rocking me. "And?"

"I think that's it." I frowned.

"What about what I told you I'd do?"

"I might need to work up to that. I've never tried it."

"But you want to? I mean to try it, not just to make me happy. I'm not down with that shit, no favors." He kissed the top of my head. "But right now, I wanna try something different."

"You do?" A nervous jolt shot through me.

"Yeah, you might like it."

He stood, me still in his arms, and took me to my room, hitting the switch with his elbow as we entered.

Laying me down, he carefully took my clothes from me before standing and shrugging out of his own, locking down on me with just his eyes this time.

When Ali came to the bed, he took my breath. The kisses were the soft, lazy ones from earlier, but this time there was no sense that they were leading anywhere, or were a tease. They held their own weight, whether on my mouth, my breasts or between my legs. Everything slowed down, intense, but with a foggy edge that warmed me as much as it turned me on.

As for eye contact, that was never a problem for Ali, he seemed to prefer it. When he entered me, it was unlike anything I'd ever experienced with him.

I arched under him as he stroked slowly in and out. It built some, but there was none of the pounding I had come to expect from this man. This contradictory man.

Even when I came it was different, longer maybe, but also something we shared together, seeing his own release was at the same time.

Ali seemed to like cuddling behind me when we slept, his leg over mine, his arms around me. But that night he rolled to his back and put me on top of him. He was all hard muscle but it was the most comfortable place in the world.

Chapter Twenty-Five

Jenna

Jack arrived a little late for work the following morning. Before he had a chance to start, I went to him where the overalls hung from pegs in the back of the room. All the other men were working and out of earshot.

"How's Chrissie?" I asked as I crossed the floor closer to him.

"She's good." He didn't look happy and I wondered if things had taken a turn for the worse.

"Tell her I said hello and that things are going smoothly around here."

My son turned his back to me and kicked off his boots. "Yeah, I'll be sure to do that."

"Is anything wrong?" Apart from the obvious, earlier he'd seemed to take Chrissie's predicament in his stride.

"Nah, all good, princess," he said, facing me and pulling on the protective gear. "Why don't you head back to work? That's what you're here for. And from what I've heard, you'd do anything, or anyone, to keep your job."

"Excuse me?" My cheeks heated.

"Ma told me. She thought she was playing shit smart, giving you the push you needed. What she failed to take into account was that fucking my brother so you can keep your job makes you no better than the sweetbutts in the clubhouse. Good one."

"That's not what I'm doing." That was exactly what I was doing. And I was okay with the entire scenario. What I had trouble with was Jack's finding out and his attitude.

He snapped the buttons shut and sat down on the bench to put his boots back on. "Don't even know why I'm pissed off. You and every other woman who comes here does so for the same reason. Why should you be any better?"

"Jack, I think you're misinterpreting the situation."

He stood, jerking a finger to me. "No, I know exactly what's going on here. Good luck to you, and for what it's worth, I won't go giving your game away. Ali's not some dumb jerk who won't work it out for himself. Fuck, he's used to it like the rest of us."

He shouldered past me, causing me to stumble, and went to join his brothers. When it came to Jack, I hadn't been able to do right by him since the night he was conceived. It didn't look like that was going to change any time soon.

Jenna was hunched over her computer, her hair in an untidy ponytail and her glasses on. I stood for a moment, drinking in my adorable woman.

"Hey, sexy," I said from the doorway. "You want to grab lunch?"

I winced as I recalled how I'd fucked up last night, wondering if that had anything to do with the utter misery on her face.

"I'm not hungry."

"Babe, what's wrong? I know I was a dick last night. If you want to kick my ass over it, go ahead." Anything to get that look off her face.

"We've discussed that, Ali. I'm okay, I know you meant no harm." Her fingers were poised over her keyboard. "Maybe we can catch dinner or something?"

"If you want." I parked on the edge of her desk. "But maybe you tell me what's got you so down. Is it the workload? 'Cause we can get some help in here. Bel said she used to work in some office somewhere, maybe she could help."

"No, it's okay. I'm getting on top of this. I'm just having an off day." She bit her lip. "But it would be nice to go out for dinner."

That sounded like lip service, like the last thing Jenna wanted was to be anywhere, especially with me. If her mood wasn't down to what I did, then I reasoned it had to do with whatever she was keeping from me. She had to know I was thinking along those lines.

"Ali, I found a gun in the bedside drawer. Were you going to tell me about that?"

Christ, is that all?

"Babe, it's legit." *Well, untraceable.* "There's another in the kitchen. Sorry, non-negotiable. Are you one of those anti-gun psychos?"

"You could have warned me, that's all."

"You're right. Hammer might have found it or some shit. We really need to be careful."

A ghost of a smile formed on her mouth. "Casey can shoot. Her dad taught her. He's a detective."

I hid my grin at that. I had an inkling that Cage might have been interested there, and he'd blow a gasket if he thought he was scoping out a cop's daughter. Couldn't wait to tell him, but right now, I was more interested in lifting Jenna's mood.

"Well, if Casey says it's all right…"

"Ha ha. Why do you need a gun?"

"I don't need a gun, I just have guns, plural." I tapped her head. "Spill."

"I already told you, just a bad mood. The guns didn't help."

"Would it make a difference if I showed you how to use them? Don't want to sound all cliché and shit, but chicks and firearms are hot."

"You are impossible."

"That I agree with. Well?"

"Maybe one day." I got the feeling from her tone that one day wasn't going to come. I just hoped it was in reference to the Glocks.

I managed to get through most of the week without

pissing her off too much. She even seemed like her old self, but a sadness had crept over her that she was trying to hide from me. She still liked fucking me, and once that would have been my only concern. Not with Jenna. It might have been a priority, but shit ran deeper than that.

Jack still spoke to me, but the friendly tone he'd been using had changed. He talked more smartass teenager to me after our altercation in the garage. No one seemed to notice, although I certainly felt it. I stopped asking him about Chrissie, getting my information from Ali instead.

The real problem besides Jack's changed attitude to me was Ali. We were growing closer, and fighting it was proving hard. Once I was back on track with Jack I'd leave, and that wasn't something I was looking forward to.

Ali was a lot of things—rough, crude—but he had an undercurrent of sweetness that he didn't bother to hide from me. Even around his brothers he was always tucking my hair behind my ears, holding my hand, stroking my arm, stealing small kisses. I couldn't even enjoy that, because once in front of Jack, when he'd tangled his fingers in my hair and kissed the top of my head, my son had caught my eye and rolled his own.

So between avoiding Wraith, pining for Jack and trying not to let my feelings for Ali get carried away, the only good thing I had going was my friendship with Casey. Her coming to visit me at the garage was a welcome interruption for the day.

The boys were all up in the clubhouse having lunch when she arrived, complete with takeout for us. I was always invited along with the members, but so far had managed to stick to my desk.

"Thought I'd better check out your work," Casey said, tossing me a water. "It seems...civilized."

"They lock the monkeys up whenever anyone comes out here," I said.

She giggled. "So, Ali not about?"

Ali and I seemed to amuse Casey. Whenever I denied we were serious, she'd laugh in my face. Not cruelly, but in a way that made me think it was how she treated her sister, whom she talked about a lot, or any of her other friends. Casey was just a nice, happy, well-adjusted woman who didn't tolerate bullshit.

"Lunch with his boys. Brothers, whatever."

"Well, I guess you have to share."

"I warn you, they'll be back any second." Even as I spoke, some of the mechanics were filtering in through the door. "I'll escort you out later. They can be full-on when they're showing off."

Casey took a drink from her bottle and shrugged. "I'll be right."

"I'm not sure about that, Cage is heading this way. He's kind of the worst."

"You ready to do the banking, princess?" Cage said as he flung open the door and turned to Casey. "Hey, nurse, are you ready to—"

"Cage," I said, standing. "I'll catch up with you after lunch."

Casey just raised her brows and took a bite of her sandwich. "What were you going to say?"

Before Cage could answer, Ali and Jack walked in.

Casey gave him a little wave around her chewing, speaking after she swallowed. "Hey, Ali."

"Casey," Ali said, nodding.

"This is Jack," I said.

"Oh, hi, Jack. Heard your party was pretty good." Casey stood and offered her hand.

Jack took it and said. "Another one."

"Another what?" Ali didn't look impressed.

"Hot citizen," Cage said, stepping between them. "Why don't you take princess banking instead? Come on, Jack, you need to get back to work."

I sent a silent thanks to Cage, forgiving him for his cheek to Casey, not that she seemed offended.

Ali watched them leave, Cage's hand in the center of Jack's back, pushing him out of the door. Ali shrugged and landed on the couch.

"Day off?" Ali said to Casey.

"A couple actually. Oh, the joys of shift work. I guess I should leave you both to it." She gathered up her food.

"You just got here," I said.

"Yeah, hang with Jenna." Ali closed his eyes. "I'll wait for you both to finish lunch, then me and my girl can play hooky for the rest of the day."

"He's not bad, Mitchell. I'd take him up on that offer."

After Jack's comment, I decided to do just that.

Chapter Twenty-Six

Ali

Cage fired off and exploded a few zombies with a hideous accuracy. Made a man think, if Jack's predictions of an undead apocalypse as to how the world ended came true, he might come in handy. At Jack's juvenile ways, I smiled to myself.

"Check you out, fucking contented old man." Cage rolled his eyes so high he was in danger of not letting them back down.

"Aw, you miss me. I still got time for you." I reached out and rubbed his head. He was keeping me company while Jenna was out shopping with Casey. She'd been so excited, like it was a new gig for her. I'd always thought women did that shit constantly.

Cage pulled away and killed me on screen. "Fucker," he said.

"So, you don't approve then?" He seemed to like Jenna well enough, but sometimes things went weird when brothers stopped screwing whores and got serious. Sounded fucked up, but I'd seen shit go down that even I couldn't believe. I never saw that with Cage, though, but I had to ask.

"Princess? Nah, love her to bits. Just never thought you'd take this route with that kind of chick. Thought you'd get someone a little more into fucking."

"You think Jenna's straight?" Dangerous territory — the respect I had for that woman made it real easy to honor her wish, discussion with Anna aside, that I keep our private business locked down.

"I know she is. That's cool—missionary and birthday blow jobs are probably okay for some." He grinned wider. "Just don't come crying to me next time I got a party going on in my room that you're not invited to."

"Right," I said, firing shots over at him.

"You know, they teach them to fake orgasms along with tennis."

I chuckled. "Uh-huh."

"Can you tell the difference?" He cocked his head to the side.

I rolled my own eyes. "Jenna wouldn't fake it."

"She's very polite. Manners are important to her."

"She's not that polite," I said.

"Keep telling yourself that brother," he said, and went back to the screen.

I didn't reply, I'd heard the front door and got up to greet Jenna. Cage made a whipping sound as I left the room.

"Have fun?" I said, when Jenna put the bags she was carrying down on to the floor. At least one of them was from a lingerie shop.

"I might have to slow down in the office. I'm going to need the overtime to cover this lot." She smiled up at me. "You have a good time on your play date with Cage?"

"I missed you." Ignoring the smartass comment, I pulled her close, breathing in that sweet sexy scent of hers. "You're wearing too many clothes again."

"Am I?" She smiled, not an ounce of coyness on her face. "You going to do something about that?"

It occurred to me then that Jenna couldn't tell the bikes apart. Mine was similar to Cage's that he'd parked out the front, but not so much she shouldn't have been able to tell the difference by then. My ride was in the garage. Jenna was about to learn a valuable lesson. If she'd made the effort to recognize my bike, then she'd have known we weren't alone.

Pressing her up against the wall, covering her body with mine, I started rubbing myself against her. She was wearing a dress, another mistake. Bunching up the material to expose those shapely legs of hers, I took hold of her underwear and tore it from her. I ignored her gasp — after all, she'd bought more — and I plunged my hand between her legs.

"No, but I am going to make you come." I worked my fingers deftly inside her.

"Ali, we're in the hallway."

"Do you care?"

She parted her legs, showing she didn't. Turning her so that her back was against the wall, I dropped to my knees and pushed my face between her thighs. Jenna helped out, lifting one leg and putting it over my shoulder, her hands tangling in my hair.

"Holy fuck," she gasped as my tongue slid between her folds. I kept moving at the steady pace she loved. With my free hand, I played with her ass, gripping her cheek tightly. "Christ, Ali. Don't you fucking stop."

Grinning, I removed my fingers, meeting her eyes.

"Put them back." Her words were loud.

"Where?" I said, relentless with my tongue.

"Inside me, put them inside me."

I did, but very, very slowly. Her hands twisted in my hair, pulling sharply. She felt like heaven and I needed more.

I had my jeans undone in seconds, standing and pushing inside her in one smooth move. My mouth crushed down on hers as Jenna pulled at the loose neck of her knitted dress, exposing her bra. She shoved the cup aside, finding her own nipple and pinching hard.

Holy fuck was right. Slamming home because she was so close, I took my mouth from hers and bit into her neck.

"Jesus," she gasped. "Fuck me, fuck."

I came at the same time, not able to wait it out.

Jenna's legs were unsteady as I brushed her skirt down and fixed up her dress so that she was covered.

"I thought you liked to look." She was damp-eyed and her cheeks glowed.

"They're only for me," I said, "and we have company."

Her face was priceless, running through from confusion, to shock, and finally to pissed off. "What?"

"Cage's here. Babe, his bike is right out the front. I admit, I was a little shocked you were so into it with him just in the next room."

"Oh, fuck," she said, her face growing redder. "Um, shit. I'm just going to shower. I'll be in the bedroom. Come and tell me when he's gone." With that she took off down the hall.

I did my pants up and sauntered into the living room. Cage was still playing the game. He glanced up at me.

"Were you making a point?" he said, without missing a beat. "If so, then you made it. But still not convinced enough to get one myself."

I reached over and picked up the controller. Jenna would need a moment to herself.

"You smell like pussy, man," Cage said, frowning at me. "Kind of finding you attractive myself at the moment."

"Oh, fuck," I said as a thought smashed through my post fuck-happy haze.

"I'm joking, man," Cage said, and chuckled. "I'm still not doing you, no matter how good you smell."

"It's not that," I said. "I need to talk to Jenna. Can you bail?"

"Sure." Cage stood and headed for the door, no questions asked.

No condom, Jenna not on the pill. Shit. Shit. Shit.

Ali's feet skidded to a stop just inside the bedroom door. "I'm sorry about that."

"Are you?" I'd been lying on my back on my bed, staring at my ceiling, torn between just having had wonderful, intense sex, and the fact that someone had heard me having wonderful, intense sex.

"I wasn't thinking, I should have used protection." He landed next to me as his words found their target and hit home.

"Shit, I never even thought. That was both of us, Ali." At least the lack of condom was a joint effort.

"I'm clean, okay." He moved to his stomach, his head resting on his folded arms. "We give blood, so they test us regularly."

I wasn't sure what to say to that—all I knew was that I was supposed to make a similar reassurance. "Me too," I said. "I mean, I don't have any diseases. I guess I should give blood, it's a duty, right? I'm not even sure why I don't. Maybe I can go with you next time you do that. What do you think?"

He chuckled. "And I always wear a condom. You're rambling. If this is about Cage, I wouldn't worry too much. He's probably forgotten about us already. The brother's not shockable. Believe me, I've tried."

"You're rambling, too," I said. "You know it's been a while for me. I just have to make sure that you didn't make me pregnant."

"Would that be so bad?"

"You're joking, right? It's a little soon for that kind of talk." I sat up. "I should put my shopping away."

He reached an arm out and pulled me into him. "Stay here for a while."

"I was actually planning on going into the office," I said, snuggling closer to him. "With Chrissie out, I don't want to get too far behind."

"It's Saturday, and you are not going into work." His leg came over mine. "That ain't happening. What you can do is tell me why it's been so long for you. A woman like you doesn't stay on the shelf."

I stiffened against him. "Not now, Ali. Please, not now."

"Then when? Jenna, you have all these secrets and they're doing my head in." He sighed against me. "What was it, some asshole break your heart, scare you off for a while?"

That was logical. I could have lied, told him that was my case. But I was dishonest enough with this man that I couldn't actually outright deceive him.

"I got hurt. It was a long time ago."

"He cheat? Because I gotta tell you, I have no plans for that." He kissed the top of my head. "I won't do that to you, babe."

"There was no relationship," I said, and he held me even tighter. "I was hurt. I've been alone ever since."

He didn't say a word, just pulled me closer.

Chapter Twenty-Seven

Ali

I knew that Jenna deciding to invite her girl around was just another way for her to put off us talking. The bomb she'd dropped on me earlier that day had stopped me from digging further, but I still needed answers. I retaliated by calling Cage back, the brother turning up to meet me out in the garage. With the likelihood of my brothers stopping by unannounced, I figured I'd make a space away from Jenna's house.

He lifted the door and sauntered inside. "She over what went down earlier?" he asked, continuing over to the fridge and helping himself to a beer. "That the nurse's car out there?"

Two yeses that I didn't bother to say out loud. "Have a beer."

"Fine, thanks, already on it." He popped the top and slammed down on the couch beside me. "This what boring couples do on a Saturday night?"

"Well you're here, aren't you?"

"It's either drink with you, or drink at the club." Cage shrugged. "Miss your ugly face."

"Jealous?" I took a sip of my own beer. "Knew you had a thing for me."

"Caught me. Make the nurse come out, I need reforming." He indicated to the door that separated the main house. "Well?"

"I think Jenna wants girl time."

"Then come out to the club." He leaned forward. "What

180

have you done?"

"Nothing, she just wants to hang with Casey." I slouched back against the head rest.

"So, why are you looking like a miserable prick, then?"

"I don't get Jenna," I said.

"You're not supposed to, she's female." He eyed me speculatively. "What exactly don't you get?"

Telling Jenna's personal circumstances, even to Cage, wasn't sitting comfortably with me. But I was drifting. I needed to anchor back down and since I'd known him, my brother had always been able to help with that.

"She doesn't trust me, not fully."

"Fuck, bro, it's early days. Stop rushing things." He pointed to me with his beer. "Just keep enjoying it like you were earlier."

"There's more to us than that," I said.

"Understand. But you gotta pull your head in a bit. Jenna's flighty, you don't want her running just because you want answers to questions that she needs time to give."

He was right, of course. "Still pisses me off, though."

"Well, you should have another beer. Find that helps."

He got up and tossed me one. *Why the hell not?*

"Should I call them in?" Casey set my kitchen table, placing silverware for four around the wooden surface.

The roasted lamb sizzled as I pulled it from the oven. "I want to rest this for a while before I carve. Would you like another wine?"

"What do you think?" She poured out two generous glasses of Shiraz, handing one to me. "Can't believe he made himself a man cave out there. He doesn't muck around, does he?"

"I think it's sweet, he doesn't want his brothers messing up my house." Taking a sip of the excellent red that Casey had brought with her, I leaned back against the bench. Ali wasn't perfect, not by a long shot, but I was finding more and more that his good outweighed his bad. Unfortunately,

I couldn't simply enjoy what was growing between us. The guilt that tugged at me prevented that.

Casey pulled one of the chairs from the table and took a seat. "For a woman who's been avoiding men and relationships for so long, you've moved fast. I'm not knocking it, sometimes you just know."

"We're not that serious. Ali will move on when he's done."

Casey coughed around her wine. "You are kidding me, right? That man is crazy about you. He worships you."

"He's having fun. We haven't been together very long."

"Ah, Jenna, he's moved in."

"He still has his room at the club and most of his stuff is there. This is just more convenient." Frowning, I set my glass aside. "I went to pay the rent yesterday. I discovered I'm two months ahead."

Casey grinned. "At least he's not a freeloader."

"Groceries, too, but I'm pretty sure he sent Spice out to buy those. I don't think he's ever stepped foot in a supermarket."

I wondered if she'd find the guns he'd strategically placed around my house so domestic. But considering her father was a detective, she was probably used to them. Besides, I'd only used the guns as an excuse for my mood.

The door between the house and the garage opened, and Ali and Cage came in with beers in hand. Casey's eyes landed on Cage. She saw me notice and flicked her gaze away.

Smiling to myself, I said, "Dinner won't be long, do either of you want wine?"

Ali shook his head. "I'll stick with beer, thanks." He nuzzled my hair, pulling me close to his side. "How long are they staying?"

"Yeah, heard that," Casey said.

"He's joking," I said, swatting Ali playfully in the side.

Cage had taken the chair beside Casey, moving it closer. She didn't pull back, but she was giving him a greasy look.

"You wear more jewelry than my grandmother," she said, examining the thick silver rings on Cage's hands.

"Do you want to see the rest of it?" Cage smirked over at her. "I could show you if you like."

"Careful, Casey," Ali said. "This will involve Cage getting naked. I haven't eaten yet."

"Oh, God, you haven't." Casey turned her attention briefly to Cage's crotch. "Gross, you have no idea what happens when one of those gets infected."

"You'll take care of me," he said, more grinning.

"I think it would take more than that to shock Casey," I said, looking up when a knock sounded on the door. "Excuse me."

But Ali was already off to answer it. I had no idea who it could be, and assumed it had to be a member of the club. Everyone I knew well enough to be in my house was already there.

"Look who smelled Jenna's cooking." Ali returned, Jack with him.

Now my night was either going to go to hell, or heaven. But at least my son was there. He might hate me, think I'm no better than some biker groupie, but I loved him above all else. Just his presence was enough to lighten my mood.

"I'll set another place."

Jack glanced at me. "Don't bother, I'm just here to see Cage."

"You could've rang, brother. Sit your ass down." Cage glared at Jack, who took a seat without a place setting.

Casey was up and remedying that situation immediately. I turned my attention to the meat and started carving, my back to everyone while I reeled in my emotions.

Dinner was rowdy. Only Jack was quiet, his eyes down on his plate. No one seemed to notice, or so I thought.

"What's going on there?" Cage asked.

Ali had decided that we could all drink in his man cave. Casey and he had already headed out, Jack as well. That left me alone with Cage.

"Nothing."

"I mean with Jack? There was that crack he made when Casey was in the office."

I sighed. "Just drop it, Cage, okay? It's no big deal."

Cage shot up a single brow. "You're full of shit. Jack's a sweet kid, but he's also spoiled rotten by Chrissie. Not to mention that his old man was a sociopath who cheated on his old lady at every given opportunity."

We both turned as Jack came back into the kitchen. "That was Wraith. He's got a computer issue and needs you to come down to the clubhouse."

"Can't it wait?"

"No," Jack said, avoiding looking at me. That hurt, seeing there were only three of us in the room and his boots were of more interest than me.

"It sounds serious," I said. "Maybe you should go."

"Nah, he's probably fucked up his shit looking at porn or something." But Cage swung his cut off the chair and shrugged it on. Leaning down, he kissed my cheek, surprising me. "Thanks for dinner, princess. Sorry, I gotta bounce."

"Yeah, Jenna," Jack said, paying me some attention. "It was good. Sorry to run out on you."

Well that was *something.*

After Cage left, I scored the job of driving Casey home. The woman wasn't lit, but she'd had a couple. Surprisingly, she was comfortable with the idea of being locked up for a few minutes in a car with me. I find women in the citizen world either wanted to fuck or flee when it came to the MC. Casey just didn't appear to give a shit.

"Which way?" I said as we pulled out of the drive in Jenna's car.

"Albert Street. Do you know where that is?" She looked over at me, a smile playing on the corners of her mouth. "Or do you already know where my house is?"

I laughed. Actually I did. "A lightweight and a smartass."

"I'll take the second," she said. "Give me a break on the first, I've just come off two night shifts. Did you and Cage have fun out in your man cave earlier?"

"About as much as you and Jenna, I guess." I looked over at her as she slouched comfortably in her seat.

"It's funny, isn't it?"

"What?"

"Jenna. Why now?"

"Why now what?" But I knew exactly what she was talking about. Still, I played dumb, it was the best way to extract information. Make them talk, keep your own mouth shut.

"She's kept to herself for so long, and now, well, she's making up for lost time, that's for sure." She swiveled a little toward me. *Yeah, the woman wants to talk.*

It occurred to me that Casey might have known things about Jenna that I didn't. Women talked, it was different for them. I frowned. She probably wouldn't give up much. Besides, if I wanted anything real from Jenna, I needed for her to be the one who parted with the information herself. Anything else and it would be pointless. I needed trust in this situation, otherwise I'd just have gotten Cage to do a more detailed background check.

"It's my winning personality," I said. "Plus, I'm a pushy bastard. She didn't stand a chance."

"I just wonder what the trigger was, that's all." She started looking out of the windscreen, her question only putting more of them in my head.

Casey was right, something had changed for Jenna. Something made her want to put herself out there. Open up to friends, a man in her life. What it was, though, was anyone's fucking guess.

"This is you," I said.

"Thanks for the ride, Ali," she said, getting out of the car. But she leaned back in, looking at me carefully. "It's not just because you're pushy. She really does like you, Ali. Show a bit of patience. It'll be worth it."

I basically grunted at her. I hated that she was right, and I hated that I didn't want to take her advice.

Chapter Twenty-Eight

Jenna

Ali's kisses were heated and hard and all over me. He was whipping me into a frenzy that had me aching for him. His tongue dampened my skin and I was wet and ready.

"Now, Ali," I said. "Now, please."

He gave me that dark laugh and dove between my legs, his hands on my ass cheeks, his tongue buried deep. I loved when he went down on me, but I wanted his cock more.

"Ali, for God's sake, I can't wait."

He flipped me, getting behind me as I came to my knees, his cock teasing my entrance. God, the man was cruel.

"You want me inside you, babe." He pulled me up and back against me. "But I wanna finish eating your pussy."

He reached down, his fingers playing with my backside and I fell forward. "Ali, fuck me now."

He pressed a finger into my ass and my breath caught as I pushed against it, walking my knees out farther.

"How about there?"

"Later," I said and he pulled his finger in and out of me.

"Don't make me promises, Jenna."

"I'm serious." I was. I was that turned on by him. He could take me anywhere, but first, I needed him the regular way or I was going to start taking care of myself.

Ali pushed on the middle of my back and sent me down to the mattress. He dragged my body to the edge of the bed, my legs dangling off the side.

"How much do you want my cock in your pussy?"

"A lot." I was panting now and his fingers were teasing

my opening.

"How hard?"

"Hard as you can give me."

Ali pushed inside me. Getting traction from the floor, he slammed home. I fell back as he started to pound. He was fucking me hard, showing no mercy, and I gritted my teeth as the pleasure built. At this pace I was not going to last.

"Oh, God, Ali." I came almost humiliatingly quick. My stomach pulsed along with my sex as it squeezed him. He'd stopped thrusting and I pushed my hips against him.

Ali pulled out, still hard and staring at me with intent. Oh, Christ, I'd promised, hadn't I? Gulping, I looked back at him.

"It's okay." He touched my face. "I won't do it like that."

Good, I thought scrambling up onto the bed, my anxiety at an all-time high.

"Belly down, honey." He reached forward and took a couple of the pillows, before placing them under my hips. "You'll be fine."

His hand stroked my butt cheek. Then he leaned down and kissed it. "Love this ass."

"Ali, I'm terrified."

He kissed the other cheek. "We'll start small."

I heard my bedside drawer open. I knew he was getting out the lube. It had been there for a few days now and I hadn't mentioned it. But that was nothing. There was a gun in there, as well. Yeah, I was living the life.

He warmed the lube, so romantic my Ali. But when he rubbed it on me I was shocked at how good it felt. I let out a sigh, relaxing under his hands. When a finger pressed inside, I actually shuddered with pleasure. Lubrication made a hell of a difference. Maybe I could do this, after all.

Another finger joined, slowly moving in and out of me.

"Like that, babe?" He kissed my ass cheek again.

"It's…um…yeah, okay, I think I'm good."

He spread his fingers apart, stretching me. It stung a little, but nothing I couldn't handle. With the hand not at my backside, Ali started on my pussy, gentle teasing as he made a fist and ran his knuckles across my opening. *Damn, that feels great.*

He kept up the motion, fingers in and out, knuckles grazing me. It was possible that I could come like that. I was relaxed and concentrating on the pleasant sensations I was experiencing.

After a while, he withdrew his fingers, but his knuckles kept up their sweeping motion. He shifted and the head of his cock was at my ass.

"Brace, Jenna, but don't tense." His voice was smoky, hypnotic.

The force of him caused a burning sensation as he moved forward. Ali had said that we'd take it at my pace, but this was Ali. He wouldn't stop now.

"Hurts a little." But there was also a new sensation and new nerves waking up.

"Too much?" He pushed more in me.

"No, but don't go fast."

At least he wasn't telling me to shut up so he could fuck me. Ali was showing a great amount of patience.

"Fuck, you feel good, Jenna. Not going on the run, staying home with you."

I laughed at that and he pushed more in me and withdrew a little straight after. He started a slow pace, pushing and withdrawing, going a little deeper each time.

The knuckles at my pussy pressed harder, inching toward my clit. I concentrated on that as he got deeper in my ass. It wasn't half as painful as I expected, given the size of him. But I had the inkling that had a lot to do with Ali being skilled in the area. He was a sex god and I decided to tell him as much.

"Ali, you know you're like a fucking god, don't you?" He upped his pace a bit and I moaned.

"Fuck, Jenna, I'm fucking obsessed with you."

Then Ali let me have it. He fucked me, not as hard as normal, but he didn't let me out of the experience.

When he came, he pulled out instead of releasing inside me. I reveled in the heat of his cum on my ass cheeks as I lay panting, sore and satiated from his clever fingers on my clit. I think despite the shock of it all I had come at least three times. No one could call my man selfish.

"Hot bath?" he asked, kissing my cheek. On my face, this time. "By the way, that was fucking the best I've had. You're never getting rid of me, Jenna. I'll fucking lock you up in a cupboard rather than let you go."

I guess that should have scared me. Instead it made me feel a strange kind of security.

Later, as I leaned back against him in the warm bath and he stroked my stomach and breasts, I sighed with utter content.

"I'm glad I only remember you."

He kissed the top of my head. "Funny, I'm pretty sure I was a virgin before you, too. Fucked if I can think or picture any other woman I've been with."

I laughed against him. "We're kind of perfect together. Both a little crazy."

"I hear you. We don't have to do that all the time." He tweaked my nipple. "Ah, I need here, too."

"Seriously." I wasn't sure about that, it seemed kind of deviant. *Yeah, I know, just took him in the ass, but I'm weird like that.*

"Tit fucking's the bomb."

"How do you know? We've never done it, and you were a virgin, remember?"

Ali lost it, laughing so hard he made water splash out of the tub. "Fuck, I love you, Jenna. Hope I made you pregnant."

I laughed myself. "Ali, that isn't how you do that."

Water covered my bathroom as we cracked up together, happy in each other's arms. I needed to stay like this forever. I wanted this to never end.

Of course, that was never going to happen for me and Ali. The universe hadn't gotten through with us just yet.

Chapter Twenty-Nine

Jenna

I was surprised to see Kitty in the office seated at Chrissie's desk the following morning. He looked up when I came in.

"Well good morning, Jenna," he said, his charming accent in contrast with his rough looks. "Early as usual."

"Not as much as you." I placed my bag on my desk and dug through it, extracting my glasses. "When did you get back?"

"A couple of hours ago. I'm starting to think I'm not even needed here. You're doing a great job." He beamed over at me.

"Coffee?"

"Like I said, great job."

I started the pot and fired up my computer while it dripped. "I guess Chrissie will be back soon," I said.

"Not sure." Kitty picked up his phone and read a text on it, the smile disappearing from his face before returning with a vengeance. "How's that coffee coming?"

"About done." I poured us both a mug, pausing while he instructed me on the two sugars he required. I added some to my own, as well as a healthy dash of milk.

"How are you and Ali doing?"

I blushed a little, remembering the night before. "Okay, I think. Everyone seems to have us married off, but really…"

"Take it as it comes," he said, rising. "Don't listen to all the interfering busy bodies around here. Shit, I swear sometimes they're a bunch of old ladies, my brothers."

Chuckling, he left the office, cup in hand.

* * * *

Ali had been asking me to have lunch with him in the clubhouse constantly. I always had an excuse, but that day, he was having none of it.

Taking my hand, he led me out from behind my desk, down the steps, and through the workshop. It was deserted, all of them taking a lunch break.

"The phones... I need to man them."

Ali rolled his eyes. "There are plenty of phones, babe. Let's do this."

In the daylight, the foyer seemed darker without the lights. But it was clean, and when we entered the bar, it was like going to a small pub. Not as crowded as the night of the party, it was also less intimidating. Mags was buzzing around like a hybrid mother and waitress, passing out huge plates of sandwiches and bottles of Coke. We found a small table with four chairs in the corner. To my horror, Wraith took a seat with us. A pretty girl with pale blonde hair, all of fifteen, took the other vacant chair.

"Hanging with your dad?" Ali said to her.

It dawned on me that she was the young girl that Anna had sent to fetch me a drink at the party. She smiled over at me. "I'm Paige. We kind of met at Jack's thing."

"Of course. Jenna."

"I know." She picked up a sandwich, biting the corner delicately. "How are you finding working here?"

"She's doing well," Wraith said. "Very well."

"That's good," Paige said. "Dad, did you think about what I asked you?"

"Yes, and it's no. You're not going to an unsupervised party, and I don't want any argument."

"Mom said the same," Paige said. "Oh, well, I tried. Besides, Mel and Gretchen can't go, either."

"Why don't you do something with them?" Wraith asked around a mouthful of food. "I don't know, a spa day or something?"

Watching him interact with a girl, his daughter, was disturbing. That he seemed like a normal parent confused me. Wraith was a murderer, a kidnapper, nothing but Hellion's henchman. This was some act I was witnessing.

"We'll just do a sleepover. Gretchen's mom's hours have been cut back at work. I don't think she can afford a mani-pedi session."

Jack walked in, and she gave him a wave. Wraith frowned at that.

"Tell you what, my treat. Mel too. We don't want Gretchen feeling like she's getting charity. I don't think she's forgiven me for that netball disaster last year."

Ali gave me a smile and squeezed my hand while I tried to school my expression of shock.

Paige giggled and turned to me. "Dad knew that Gretchen needed trainers and a new uniform, so he bought them for her. He was discreet, but she was embarrassed. Still, he meant well."

"And she came and mowed my lawns for the entire season to pay me back," Wraith said. "I didn't want her to, but she's a good kid, and it was better than her losing face."

His phone rang and he pushed back from the table. "Duty calls."

As he walked away, Paige gathered up his lunch. "He'll not bother eating now he's back in business mode. Excuse me, guys. It was good to meet you properly, Jenna."

Ali started laughing when she left. "You can close your mouth now."

"Who was that man?"

"Wraith's a hard ass, I'll grant you, but when it comes to his kid, he's a soft cock."

"But he was helping her friend, too, I don't get it." I shook my head.

"Paige has had the same friends since preschool. They hang out here enough that he probably considers them part of his family. You look rattled, babe."

That was because rattled was an understatement.

* * * *

"So, what's this in aid of?" I sauntered into the meeting room to find Cage and Jack lounging around. Neither of them had their happy face on. The prez was the same, but for him that was hardly groundbreaking. But what drew my attention was the man standing in the corner. I'd had no idea that Kitty had returned. He nodded at me. He looked more pissed off than Wraith. I crossed the room and greeted him.

"Sit down," Wraith said.

I landed in a seat opposite him

"Okay, spit it out." I folded my arms across my chest.

"First of all, Ali, I kept this from you because I didn't want you going off half-cocked." Wraith threw a glance to Kitty.

I nodded. "Right, but whatever it is, you're going to tell me now."

"Pony stood by while Leanne attacked Jenna."

This I already knew, the stupid prick. Good thing for him Jenna handled herself or else he'd be still trying to get his teeth out of the back of his fucking throat.

"And?"

"Leanne called here the next day, bitch was armed. Spice confiscated a knife from her at the gates before she left. He didn't know at the time what had gone down and Pony somehow talked him into keeping it quiet."

I started to boil. Fucking rage was blowing up inside of me. "She. Had. A. Knife."

"Yeah," Cage said. "Another thing, I thought the cameras were playing up again in the garage, but after that nugget, I checked more carefully. They were wiped. "

"He doesn't like her," Jack said. I had the feeling that he was just learning this news, too. "Gives her greasy looks all the time when he thinks we're not looking. I figure it's over that spare parts bullshit."

"She never said." I glanced to Wraith, and finally over to Kitty. "Not a word."

194

"That could be my doing," Wraith said. "I mentioned to her that she's not to cause trouble with the brothers. I never thought for a minute she would take that to include prospects."

"Bring them both in here," I said.

"Spice isn't getting away with this," Kitty said, joining us around the desk. "But I'm fully aware that my nephew likes to use my name to lord it over the prospects and hang rounds. I think it's only fair that he's disciplined and warned. As for Pony, I'd like to take care of that myself."

Wraith stood and picked up his phone, firing off a message.

"I'm going to kill him. You know that right?" I stared over at Kitty. "I don't give a fuck that he's your nephew."

"Ali, I'm getting you," Wraith said, tucking away his phone and sighing. "We have kids here, and that could have been a nasty fucking situation. But you don't get to make the decision. You can go to town on him, and as far as I'm concerned, he's out."

"Wraith's right," Cage said, an apologetic look on his face. "Doesn't mean you can't make him hurt."

Kitty remained silent, getting up and moving closer this time to the meeting table. He cocked his hip against it and watched us all.

I looked up as Pony came in and glanced around the room. His stupid face was blank as he took us in, stopping on me and finally having some kind of reaction.

I stood. "Take off your cut."

He did, faster than I'd ever seen him move. He held it out to me and I took it before tossing the thing onto the table, where a still quiet Kitty barely gave it a glance.

"You're never wearing that again. You understand me?" I was unarmed. Not that I needed a weapon to take care of this piece of shit.

I cracked my neck from side to side. Behind me, I heard the scrape of a chair leg. Cage would be called to stop me, so I had to get in as much as I could before he did.

Pony started to shake. I advanced.

"Hang on." He put up both hands. "This has gone too far. I never—"

What he never got to do was finish that sentence. The laser-like sound of a gun fitted with a silencer discharging cut him short. Pony fell like the sack of shit he was to the floor. More chairs shoved back, and I discovered that, unlike me, Wraith and Cage were armed, their guns trained to Kitty who placed his 9mm on the floor and stepped back.

"It had to be done," he said.

"You just shot…" Jack shook his head. "You just shot your nephew."

Kitty's ruthlessness didn't surprise me. It wasn't the first time I'd seen him act like a sociopath. Not to mention the old rumors about how his family had died. If he hadn't had a tight alibi from Hellion, I might have believed them. I walked over to Pony and nudged him with my foot. "Dead."

"Jesus fucking Christ." Wraith holstered his gun. "You wanna explain yourself? You got ten seconds."

"It was a mistake, him joining the club," Kitty said. "Letting him go wasn't a safe option either."

"He was a fucking prospect," Wraith said, his voice thunder. "He hardly knew shit."

"He's been around long enough to know enough," Kitty said. "We both know that. Chances are, he'd talk. The minute the pigs saw him without a cut, they'd be on him. We both know he was weak. He would've talked. Then all your work, all your progress of digging the club out of the shit would've been for nothing. I did this for the club."

I wasn't sad to see Pony go. Would have liked to have at least done half the job myself. But killing your family like that was some cold shit. Jack had paled. He'd seen enough in his life to cope, but this was different.

He looked over at Kitty. "Are you planning to stay around?"

"I think I might," Kitty said.

"What about your sister? What are you going to say to her?" Jack crossed his arms over his chest. "This is going to take some explaining, don't you think?"

"I tell her he never made club, that he took off when he learned that. She knows he'd run."

"Because this was all he ever wanted," Jack said. "I know he wasn't brother material. This is on you, Kitty. You should never have put him up."

"You're right. I made a mistake. And I fixed it. You're all carrying on like a bunch of women. He betrayed the club. He risked Ali's old lady." At that, Jack snorted. "Like Wraith said, we got families around here. Just that none of you had the balls to do it."

Seeing I'd offered, I nearly took him out on that, but refrained. Pony was dead. Not much anyone could do about that now.

Chapter Thirty

Jenna

Jack entered the office. The air around him appeared to crackle. "Day's over," he said. "All citizens off the compound."

I glanced up from my typing. "Is there a problem?"

"Club business, you need to leave." He leaned in the doorway. "Now."

"That's a bit harsh, Jack." Cage bounded up the steps and entered the room. "But he's right, princess, you get an early day. Don't worry, you won't get docked."

"Where's Ali?" Worry clamped at my chest.

"He's fine, he's just in a meeting," Cage said, pushing closed my laptop.

"Can I speak to him?"

Jack said, "I'm sure he'll catch up with you later. I'm not joking, Jenna. You need to go home."

I looked out into the workshop. The men were downing tools, speaking in huddled groups, some of them already heading out.

"What the hell is going on here?" Cage looked between me and Jack. "Well?"

"Nothing," I said, rising and gathering my things. "Can you ask Ali to call me when he can?"

"Sure, no problem. But before you go, what's got Jack's jocks in a twist?"

Jack smirked. "It don't matter, brother. But for what it's worth, she's no different than the others that come here. Are you, Jenna?"

When I didn't answer, Jack did for me. "Chrissie told Jenna about Wraith not keen on her working here. She told her that if she hooked up with Ali, then she'd have a better chance."

"Since when did Wraith say that?" Cage said. "Sure, he was pissed off that Chrissie hired her without his say so, but Jenna's perfect for the job, that was never in danger."

"Not really the point," Jack said. "Jenna still only went for Ali to stay here. She's just like the rest of them. A club wh—"

"Shut the fuck up, Jack." Cage advanced on my son. "You don't want Ali to hear you talk to his old lady like that."

The real problem was, I couldn't deny what Jack was saying. It didn't matter a damn that my feelings for Ali were growing. That for a moment there, I really thought I could have it all. I knew then that I couldn't, that Jack's lack of respect for me ran deep. I was a selfish person. My sister had died at the hands of this club, and here I was, carrying on like I had a right to a life when she never had a chance.

"He's right," I said, not able to meet Cage's eye. "I needed the job, and…"

"Who cares? Seriously. I'm pretty sure that Ali didn't want you because he thought you and him would have great conversations together. Most likely he checked out your tits to begin with." He shook his head, chuckling. "We all probably did that. Point is, you're his old lady now, and Jack needs to shut it the fuck down."

"Do I?" Jack balled his hands into fists.

"Yeah, you do. You're a kid. You got no clue what it means to get serious."

"And you do?" Jack cocked his head.

"Hell, no," Cage laughed. "But Ali does, and so does our princess here. Now pull your head in, apologize to the woman, and she can get going like she's supposed to."

But Jack didn't say sorry, he simply left.

Cage waited for me to gather my things, then escorted me to my car. I could see that something was going on. The compound had a deserted feel, all the brothers presumably inside the clubhouse.

Secret squirrel stuff, and I doubted anyone would enlighten me. I had to wonder if I even wanted to know.

* * * *

"Pony was derelict of duty," Wraith said, addressing the room of assembled brothers. "He fucked up at work, too. The punishment would have been the removal of his patch, and giving Ali some alone time with him. Not a bullet, Kitty, you went too far."

Truth be told, I might have as well, but the point was moot now.

"Ali's woman could've been killed," Kitty said.

"All due respect, brother," Cage said. "But since when do you give a shit about Ali's old lady?"

The corner of Kitty's mouth kicked up and his head turned carefully in Cage's directions. "She's a good secretary. I'd hate to lose her."

"Over your nephew?" I said, my eyes glancing briefly to the box where our phones were stored. Jenna had to have been calling me after her ejection from the premises.

"I do what I do for the club. Always have, always will. No man here can doubt that." Pushing his chair back, Kitty crossed his arms over his chest. "Pony was a liability. I took care of that. I brought him in—it was my job to take him out."

"So, you think if someone fucks up, or you judge them to fuck up, you'll just shoot them?" Jack shook his head. He and Pony weren't close, but they'd grown up together in a way. Pony had been older than Jack, but only by two years.

"Of course not," Kitty said. "These were exceptional circumstances."

"It goes to vote," Wraith said.

"Hang on." Dusty clasped his hands in front of him on the table. "Kitty is a lifer, we're not taking his cut."

"Will you let me finish?" Wraith sighed. "I want you back on the road, keep reaching out to the Diamonds, see what you can do with that. It's either that, or hand over your cut now, club's choice."

I wasn't sure what Wraith was playing out. Way I saw it, there was no choice. Kitty should have been out. He was a loose cannon. Hellion had always given him too much free rein. My thoughts were going in the direction that our prez didn't want our own club imploding the way the Diamonds were looking to. He had too much tied up in our business aspirations to let that happen. Cage raised a brow at me. In the next minute, Kitty was going to be very aware of where he stood with each and every member of the club.

"Prez," Kitty said, his words low, "I wanna call in a favor. I'm owed."

"Being?" Wraith grunted impatiently.

"No vote, I get the choice. I'll continue my liaisons with Geezer's crew. If nothing comes from it, I'll hand my cut in."

"Confident," Cage said, smirking.

"Very," Kitty said. "Well?"

"You got two weeks. You step foot in town before that, then you hand in your cut." Wraith banged his gavel.

* * * *

Jack circled his beer with his hands, elbows on the bar, his neck bent. I read through Jenna's messages. She seemed worried, and I shot back one that I wouldn't be coming home that night, but I'd see her in the morning. It was time to hang with my brothers.

On the other side of me, Cage leaned closer. "She sus?"

"No idea," I said, pocketing my phone. "Guess I'll find out tomorrow."

Spice placed a shot of bourbon in front of me. He'd been quiet since the meeting, having been allowed to attend. He was nine months into prospecting and it was doubtless he'd be patched soon. "Might as well get wasted then," he said.

Not a bad plan. "You in, Jack?"

As an answer, Jack sculled his beer, then slammed the bottle down on the mat. Spice poured him a shot and he drank that too.

"Good boy," Cage said, reaching behind me and patting his back.

"She's not who you thinks she is, you know?" Jack's words slurred as he knocked the empty beer bottle over. "Shit."

"Who?" I asked. I wasn't quite where he was, but getting close. The women had returned half an hour ago, Ruby settling close by Cage.

"Jenna."

At that, Cage turned his attention from the redhead to us. "Careful, brother."

"No," I said, waving Cage down. "I wanna hear this."

"She's only with you to keep her job," Jack said. "She's no better than the rest of them. All about hooking a brother to get their own way."

"Hey," Ruby said. "I resent that."

Jack focused on her. "Yeah, if Cage took some other chick upstairs, you wouldn't be sitting here crying about it, you'd spread your legs for the next available brother."

"Fuck you," Ruby said.

"Precisely," Jack said.

But I wasn't thinking about what they were saying, Jack's words were filtering through the alcohol haze, pissing me off.

"Stop thinking, Ali," Cage said. "Kid's full of shit."

"No, I'm not, she didn't even deny it." Jack started on another beer. "Sorry, but it's true."

"She didn't need me to keep her job," I said.

"Well, she thought she did," Jack said. "Same difference, really. It might not have been about the patch, but she wanted an end result. I thought she was different."

So did I.

"Brother," Cage said. "She chose you, remember that. She had twenty brothers to pick from if that was her game, and she chose you."

Wish that meant something.

Jack ended up passed out on a couch, snoring, his head in Ruby's lap. Seemed they'd made up. Cage had indeed disappeared with one of the other girls, a favorite of his called Nicky, and I was left at the bar.

"Another?" Spice stopped wiping down the surface when he got to where I'd propped.

"Grab some keys," I said. "You're taking me somewhere."

I needed answers. I was sick of the questions piling higher and higher.

Chapter Thirty-One

Jenna

As much as I told myself it was good to have some distance from Ali, sleep was eluding me. I still had no idea about what had happened earlier in the day when I'd been sent home. It might have been about them discovering me, and at first I was convinced of that, but it made so little sense that I was simply let go.

There was no car parked outside my house, and I'd gone to the store for milk, and although no expert, I'm sure I wasn't followed. Leaving town would have been easy — going to the police even easier. I hadn't, of course, but as I lay in my bed staring at the ceiling, I started to consider the options. It was never too late.

But the sound of a pounding on my front door had me sitting up and pulling the covers from me. Grabbing a robe, I headed out to find who was calling in the middle of the night.

Halfway to the door, I realized it could be a hit man, or whatever they called them, from the club. If he wanted in, not much was going to stop him, but I had the choice of making a run for it through the back.

"Open up, Jenna," Ali's voice boomed through the timber.

"You have a key," I said, as he stumbled over the threshold.

He said nothing, just put his arms around me and staggered with us both into the hallway wall. His breath smelled like bourbon. His mussed-up hair had fallen to partly cover his eyes, eyes that were bloodshot. Ali who was normally so effortlessly pulled together looked like a mess.

He wasn't wearing his cut, just a T-shirt. It was a cold night but his skin burned hotter than normal. He lifted one of his arms from my waist, and, making a fist, pressed it against the wall.

"What the hell, Ali?" I pushed against his chest. Normally he moved back when I did that, despite the fact that I had no hope of physically besting him. This time my forcefulness just had him grinding his groin into my stomach. He might have been so drunk he could hardly stand, but something was working for him.

The hand that was on the wall slid down, coming on to my body as he bent and let it run under my thigh, lifting it and pushing harder against me.

"Ali, no," I said. I didn't like this. He was neither talking to me nor looking at me.

Ali could be rough, but there was always intimacy with us. Ever since the first time he acted very aware that he was with me, but I didn't like the lack of connection that was happening, the way he was keeping his eyes from my face.

I placed my hands flat on his chest and pushed as hard as I could. He still wouldn't budge, the hand holding my thigh gripping tight to the point of pain. With his other hand, he bunched up my robe, pulling it to my hip, his fingers digging into my skin.

"Ali!" My voice sounded throughout the house. "Get the fuck off me."

His hands dropped away, both of them going back to the wall where he heaved himself off, shaking his head to clear it. He stood there, neck bent forward breathing heavily. I ducked and slid out from under him, moving so I was a few feet away.

"You need to go to bed," I said quietly, already planning to surf my own couch. "Ali, are you listening?"

He nodded slowly. "Yep, I heard you. We need to go to bed. That's a very good idea."

"No, you're going to take the bed and I'm going to sleep

in the living room." I took a few steps and placed my hand on his back. "You need a shower, but I think that can wait until morning."

"Nuh-uh," he said and moved startlingly fast and grabbed me again, this time lifting me off my feet.

"Put me down," I said. He wasn't real steady and the thought of us crashing to the carpet was a very real fear.

It was one that eventuated. Ali dropped to his knees, his hold on me still too firm for me to escape. In slow motion, he came forward and started to lower himself. I had no choice but to go with him, and I ended up underneath six and a half feet of biker muscle in the middle of my hall.

He'd been holding out, keeping a lot of his weight from crushing me when we were together. But not this time. This time I was feeling the full brunt of him, and I could barely breathe. I was lucky he'd put us down slowly, otherwise I'd have had the wind knocked out of me.

I poked the one hand that was free into his side. "Ali?"

He was out cold, his breathing even, a slight snore coming from him. I rocked side to side, trying to move him over. It didn't work, he was immobile. I poked again and still nothing. I yelled right in his ear, slapped his face, gentle at first, then with more force. Nothing worked, even tugging at his hair and pinching his earlobe. He was basically unconscious and I was most likely going to suffocate underneath him before the sun rose.

I reached around him and started to feel his back pockets. Sometimes his phone was in his cut, other times he put it in the back of his jeans. I was lucky, he had it tucked in there and I managed to pull it out. Even better luck, it was his own phone and not one of the burners he sometimes had.

Of course, it was locked. But there were three numbers that could be called without entering the code. One was the emergency services number, another was Wraith's and the third was Cage's. Given the choice, I nearly dialed the emergency number, but settled on Cage as the lesser of the two club evils.

It took a few rings for him to answer. When he did, it sounded like I'd woken him. "The fuck, brother?"

"It's me, Jenna." I was aware my voice sounded strained. Lying under nearly a quarter ton will do that for a girl.

"What do you mean?" Cage sounded like he'd been deeply asleep, making me realize it was most likely someone else that had dumped Ali at my door. "Jenna?"

"Someone brought Ali home," I said. "He's really smashed."

"He's not an angry drunk, just let him sleep it off. You're safe."

"He's right here," I said. "He's passed out."

"That's good, just go back to bed yourself." Cage yawned. "I'll see you in the morning. Just don't worry about him."

"Cage, he's right here."

"So you said, princess. You're safe, okay?" He sounded patient. "Goodnight."

"No, wait."

"What's going on, Jenna?" he said, sounding more alert.

"He fell on me. I can't get him off."

To Cage's credit, he didn't start laughing right away, not in an obvious way, anyway. "I'll be there in ten. In the meantime, give him a few belts. He might move."

I didn't bother telling him that I'd already tried that.

* * * *

Cage arrived with Jack in tow. Both of them looked no better than Ali. But at least I hadn't heard bikes, and the sound of an engine idling in my driveway made me think they'd been driven. I was totally embarrassed not only to have Cage help me out, but my son, as well. It was mortifying, but seeing it took two of them to lift him I had to wear it. Jack hated me enough—this was going to make it so much worse.

They managed to get him into my room and onto the bed. I came in and pulled his boots off, but still planned to sleep on the couch. I could smell the alcohol coming out of his pores. Gross was an understatement. But even I could see the funny side of things when Jack and Cage could no longer keep it together.

"I'm not even going to ask how that happened," Jack said as I walked them both to the door.

Cage was looking down at my legs. Somehow, probably during our struggle against the wall, Ali had managed to get my robe off. I was only wearing my white tank and a pair of white boxers with pink hearts on them. He wasn't checking me out as such, I realized when I looked down – a hand print that would no doubt bruise was at the top of my thigh.

"It was an accident," I said, reaching to the floor and retrieving my robe. I pulled it on and wrapped it tightly around me. "He wasn't even aware that he did it."

Cage said, "He wouldn't have meant it. I know him, he won't feel too good about marking you up like that. Do you want me to stay?"

When I shook my head, Cage opened the front door, gave me a one-armed hug and exited, muttering to himself about killing the idiot who Ali had convinced to drive him to my house.

That left me alone with my son.

"Thanks for coming, Jack. I know you're not my biggest fan." An understatement.

"It's none of my business," he said. "I shouldn't have said anything."

"You care about Ali, I understand that." I stepped closer.

"I was disappointed." He sighed. "Guess I had you on some kind of pedestal. Whatever."

A small, dry chuckle escaped me. "I'm sorry I didn't measure up."

"I should go," he said, his eyes catching mine. "You'll be okay. I don't really know what's going on between you two, but sometimes Ali... Just give him a chance, okay?"

His hand landed on my upper arm and I glanced down at

it before looking back at him.

"I will."

Jack gave me a small smile then slipped out of my house.

My mind scrambled to catch up with what might have been a step forward for Jack and me, but it shattered when I heard Ali emerge from my room.

"Did you fuck him?" He stood at the end of the hall. "You getting something out of him too?"

Chapter Thirty-Two

Jenna

Ali's face clouded over, becoming dark, but he appeared very alert for someone who had been passed out on my bed just moments earlier.

"Don't be stupid," I said, shaking out my limbs. I didn't feel any pain. "You passed out, fell on me and I had to call Cage to come and help get you off me."

He looked annoyed at that, like he didn't believe me. "That wasn't fucking Cage."

"He brought Jack with him. You're kind of heavy, Ali. Go back to bed, we'll talk in the morning." The couch beckoned me, exhaustion invading my body as all I wanted to do was lie down and sleep.

Ali clenched his fists, his entire body tensed and readied. He pressed his balled hands into the side of his head. "Fuck," he said. "Why was he here?"

"I've already told you." I tied the belt on my robe tighter and let out a sigh. "You're drunk, I don't want to deal with you right now."

I found myself pressed against the wall again, Ali leaning his body into mine. It was all too familiar, and there was no way I was prepared to end up stuck underneath him again and having to call his brothers in for another rescue attempt.

"Ali, leave me the fuck alone." I turned my head to the side.

"I want some answers. I want to know what's going on with you and Jack." His knee went between my thighs.

"Jenna, fucking tell me."

"There's nothing going on. He's a kid, for God's sake. You should listen to yourself, that sounds sick." I went to move, but he held me firmly.

His fist crashed into the wall, going right through the plaster with a cracking sound. I looked to where the impact had occurred. Dust fell down around the hole he'd created.

Right up until that moment, even with Ali's body pinning me to the floor, I'd felt safe. Despite his size, and the menace that sometimes surrounded him, I was not afraid of Ali. That changed with the damage he'd caused my wall.

"Please go," I said, hating how weak and defeated I sounded. I'd brought one arm up to shield my face, but I could see him still, looking startled and regretful.

He stepped back, his eyes on me full of concern. "Jenna," he said. "I wouldn't hurt you. I promise I won't hurt you, no matter what."

I glanced to the wall and back at him. "You need to go."

"No, I want to explain. I need to talk to you." He was still standing back from me, desperation emitting from his being. "Please, babe, we can talk."

"I'm not carrying on with Jack," I said. "That you think that, changes things."

He turned from me, walking a few paces away. "I don't know what it is, but it's something. That first time I saw you with him, you looked at Jack like he was the second coming. Every day I've seen you since then, it's been Jack."

My heart squeezed in my chest. He was right about that. It wasn't something I could deny.

"It's not what you think," I said.

"And then I find out we started as a lie. Is it still that, babe? Still bullshit?" His eyes squeezed shut, springing open and looking clearer. "I fucking love you. Now I find out you were using me to keep a damn job."

"Ali, no." *But it* was *true, wasn't it?*

"Then tell me. Tell me what it is that you've been hiding from me." Leaning back against the wall, he sank down, his legs sprawled out in front of him. "Please."

I lowered myself, sitting at his feet with my legs crossed. I reached forward and put my hand on his ankle, just wanting an anchor. I had used him. It didn't matter that my feelings had grown. I'd hurt Ali. And I couldn't say it wasn't intentional.

"This isn't the time," I said.

"Excuses."

"You're drunk. You just told me you loved me, and now you want to fight?"

"Is that where it's going to lead? 'Cause the way I look at it, nothing you can say to me is going to change..."

"You need to trust me on this," I said.

He rubbed at his eyes with the heels of his hand. Watching Ali come undone was breaking my heart, but I couldn't tell him. Even if he got up and left me, it was too soon. I wasn't ready to talk and I knew he wasn't ready for the truth of my situation.

"Okay," he said, and reached out both hands to me. "We'll do this in your time."

I went to him, curling up in his lap, my head on his chest. He pushed up from the floor, still holding me. That he'd been too drunk to stand not long ago, and now he carried me steadily down the hall, blew my mind. He still smelled of alcohol and sweat, but I no longer cared about that. I just wanted him. I wanted this to all be okay.

He lowered me to the bed and left me. Confused, I lay waiting to hear the front door slam, for him to leave. Instead I heard the bathroom door and ten minutes later he came to me, clean, still damp and naked from the shower.

* * * *

I sneaked out of the house the next morning, leaving Ali to sleep off his over-indulgence.

"You look a little flat, princess?" Cage said, seated behind my desk with his feet crossed at the ankles resting on the top.

"Really, Cage? You've had all night and that's the best you can come up with?" I tossed my bag onto my desk and unbuttoned my jacket. "Do you need anything, or are you just here to annoy me?"

"Things work out last night?"

"You sound almost concerned." I took a seat behind Chrissie's desk. "I wish you'd told me that Jack had spoken to Ali."

"None of that shit matters, and you know it." Cage raised one pierced brow to me.

"It did to Ali."

He chuckled. "I'm pretty sure when Ali first decided he was having you, he was thinking with his dick. People end up together for all kinds of reasons. Who gives a shit, long as you love him?"

My turn to raise brows, only I couldn't do the single one like Cage. "I don't love Ali."

He laughed again and got to his feet, exiting the office.

"I don't love Ali," I repeated but I doubted he heard me.

When I returned, this time, to my rightful desk, I slumped forward, resting my head on my arms.

Shit, I love Ali.

* * * *

It wasn't as if I'd avoided him for the entire day, we were both genuinely busy. After I finished up my work, I found Ali still in the garage, rubbing his hand at the back of his neck.

"Hey," I said, sidling up to him. "You want to grab a drink with your boys before we go home?"

"You really don't want to spend time with me, huh? Can't say I blame you after last night." His hand hovered around my shoulder before he dropped it down. Despite it being covered in grease, I didn't mind. There was always dry cleaning.

"It's not that. Casey called and I asked her to drive over here. Least I can do is meet her when she shows up."

"Right," he said. "Your shield."

I punched him lightly in the ribs. "We're going to talk, Ali."

"Tonight?"

I nodded. God, this might be it, the last time I spent with him. I should have simply gone home, got it over with. If Ali was going to dump me, or the club was going to bury me out in the bush, it was best just to get on with it.

"It'll be good," he said, kissing the top of my head. "But we should go have that drink. But first I need a shower."

Casey drove through the gates and Ali and I headed across the compound to meet her.

"Hey, you two," she said, climbing out of her car. I had to laugh because she was dressed in clean, fresh, blue scrubs. "I'm only having one drink, I'm knackered."

"Nice outfit," I said.

Casey rolled her eyes. "If I'd went home and changed, I swear I wouldn't have moved from my couch. This was the best I could do. All I had in my locker were clean undies, not even any gym gear."

"Clean undies are good," I said.

She linked her arm through mine and we proceeded to the club house.

"You're at an MC, lightweight, you don't need 'em." Ali moved his hip out of the way when I tried to land my elbow on it.

"Phht," she said. "Is that what you reckon?"

But even in the baggy hospital attire, Casey looked great. Her lack of care was what I thought was most appealing about her. It also made her an unlikely target for the bikers. They'd have women in there with their sexy gear more off than on.

Loud music and laughter greeted us when we entered the darkened bar. I was right about the women, but Bel lifted her hand and waved us over to where she sat with Cage and Jase. I already knew that Jack wasn't there. He'd ridden off earlier, presumably to see Chrissie.

"Hey, guys." She smiled as I introduced Casey and the two of them seemed to hit it off.

Lucky for that, because Ali pulled me around the corner of the bar and got me between his legs. He spun me, pressing me up against his chest.

"I've wanted to do that all day." He forked a hand through my hair at the back of my neck, tilting my head back and kissing me.

"I thought you wanted to talk," I said against his mouth.

"We can do both. You keeping that pussy of yours warm for me?"

He was whispering and I was sure no one was bothering to listen to us.

"I guess you'll find out later," I said into his neck as I kissed it.

Ali sometimes lacked patience. He slid his hand down the front of my pants, working his fingers into my underwear and yes, sliding two inside me. I froze. If I moved, it was going to become obvious he wasn't just feeling me up on the outside of my clothes while I leaned between his legs.

I sensed movement behind me and glanced over my shoulder. Cage had slid from his bar stool and put his back to us as he started talking to Casey and Bel. He was wide enough to block what was happening if he stayed where he was. I was hoping like hell he did, because what Ali was doing felt pretty great, the tension I carried sliding from me.

"I'll make it quick," Ali said, his fingers speeding up. "Just go with it, Jenna, relax into me."

My breath hitched at this unexpected turn of events and my thighs parted more for him. The hand on the back of my head pulled me even closer to his mouth, his tongue running along the seam of my lips before pushing inside and exploring. The kiss was too hot for public consumption, let alone what his hand was doing inside my pants.

I was vaguely aware that the faster he was getting, the more his arm was obviously moving. Despite Cage as a wall in front of us, anyone who cared to look would have known exactly what was going on. It didn't stop me. In a way, it made it all the hotter.

I was building fast like he promised. "Come on, Jenna," he said against my mouth. "Come for me, baby."

When I did, it was silent, his kisses taking anything I would have cried out into him. He pulled me even closer, giving me a final small peck.

"You want more?" he asked.

My legs turned to jelly. Ali's arm around my waist was all that steadied me. He had to half carry me through a side door, but alone in the hallway, I came to my senses.

"I can't leave Casey in there."

"You heard her, she's wearing underwear. Something you should definitely not be doing." He slid his arms more firmly around me. "We fuck then we talk." He kissed my ear. "Then we fuck some more."

"I'm not sure. I shouldn't."

"She's perfectly safe, babe. You're mine, she's your girl, and that puts her under my protection. No one will bother her unless that's what she wants. Now, come on... Oh, I get it."

"It's not that," I said, knowing that he meant taking me up to his room. "I'm fine."

But there was no way any conversation was going to happen at the club.

I glanced over to a darkened corner. Ali's gaze grew hot. "There?"

Why not? Public seemed to be one of our things. "Make it fast."

"Not a problem." He grinned and led me to the place I'd been eying.

* * * *

When we returned, things were just as we had left them. All except me and Ali—we were looking like two people who had just fucked each other senseless right outside the bar.

"You're a romantic," Cage said, his hand landing on Ali's shoulder, "I'll give you that."

"Drink, babe?" Ali took over one of the stools, pulling me onto his lap.

"Just water," I said, alcohol holding no appeal for me. The thought turned my stomach. Weird, I'd never said no to a glass of wine before. I shrugged it off as adrenaline from what we'd been doing.

Casey gave me a cheeky grin. She had a shot in front of her and I had the feeling it was not her first for the evening. So much for just one drink then leaving.

Ali reached over the bar and snagged a bottle of bourbon. He tightened his hold on me and stood. Okay, so it looked as if we weren't staying.

"I'll see you later," Casey said, laughing.

"You behave yourself," I said, pointing a warning finger at Cage as Ali manhandled me from the room.

I probably should have felt more guilty leaving my friend in the bar full of bikers. But I didn't. She was a big girl.

Chapter Thirty-Three

Ali

"What the hell was last night about?" I spun and saw Jack heading for me. Fuck, the little dude looked cut up. Jack hadn't even been in the clubhouse, but as per usual, news traveled fast among the brotherhood.

"What's up with you?" I asked, as Cage eyed him curiously.

"That's not how you treat someone like Jenna," Jack said, spitting the words at me. "What the hell were you thinking? Jenna's not some sweetbutt."

"You think I don't get that?" Funny, he seemed to have had a different opinion the other night. I folded my arms and stared him down. "Let's get this straight, Jenna is not your business."

"She's my friend."

"No, she's my woman. You don't get a say. You think she was complaining?" Kid was ruining my Jenna high. I needed the little asshole to shut this shit down.

Nobody in their right mind could have predicted Jack's next move. When I saw his fist coming for me, it took a split second to react. However, I caught the damn thing and moved closer, turning him and pinning his arm against his back. I was rough with him, but the kid had it coming.

"Fuck's sake, Jack."

The boys circled us, Cage going in to break shit up, as was his job. But I wrenched Jack's arm up and pushed him off me. I wasn't fighting the kid, despite him being out of line.

He turned and barreled back into me. He had balls, I'd

give him that. Again, I blocked him. But he danced back before sending in an unexpected gut punch that hit fucking home. I returned the favor, not hard, just sent a fist to his chin to get him to knock this shit off.

That's when Jenna appeared on the stairs, her face a mask of horror. As I looked up, Jack paid me back, but I barely felt it as my woman hurried down the steps looking like she was about to bolt.

I managed to break through the wall of brothers and go after her.

"Jenna, wait, that wasn't what it looked like. Kid came at me, that was pure defense." *Well mostly. But shit, the kid did start it.*

"Don't even." She spun on me. "He's eighteen years old, for Christ's sake. He's half your size, you fucking asshole."

That pulled me up. "It just got out of hand, Jenna, it's cool."

"No, it's not, it's not cool." She turned and started walking away. "This is not what I want, Ali. Not at all."

I raced after her, grabbing her arm and spinning her back to me. She flinched and I stepped backward. "Jenna, babe, you need to calm down."

"You're nothing but a thug," she said, her voice raising. "I don't know what I was thinking."

"I know what you're doing here, you're trying to walk away so we don't talk." I put my hand up and guided it down. I was regretting letting her out of our conversation the night before. "I get that, babe."

"I'm walking away from you period. We're done, Ali. Fucking over."

Huh? What the fuck just happened here?

"Let her go, brother." Cage was beside me. "She needs to calm down. You're only going to make this worse."

He put his hand on my arm and I shook it off, sending my palms through my hair and dragging them down my face.

Jenna never said shit for shit, she was serious.

"I have no clue what just happened," I said.

"Then you sure as hell wanna get one."
Like I didn't know that.

Chapter Thirty-Four

Ali

As my call went to Jenna's voice mail, again, I pinched the bridge of my nose and tossed the phone against the wall, shattering it.

My brothers were leaving me the fuck alone. My brothers were smart.

All except for one cunt, and he didn't bother to knock.

Cage bowled into my room and landed his ass on the armchair beneath the window.

"Should I have brought ice cream?" He grinned over at me.

"Fuck off."

"Go and talk to her. Go and explain shit. Everyone there saw Jack come at you. He was out of line and you could've beaten the shit out of him for what he said. Only you didn't. Princess will understand. She got over the shit with Pony, didn't she?"

"It's not about Jack," I said, lying there, staring up at the ceiling. "That was just an excuse. Jenna wanted an out and she took it."

"Is it about the other night, you know, when you nearly crushed her?" He snickered. Guess it must have looked hilarious to him.

Fucked up thing was, Jenna and I had joked about it the night I'd brought her up here and nailed her to the wall and every piece of furniture in this room, including the chair that Cage now occupied.

Of course, the next day, it all turned to shit. I still

couldn't pinpoint things going sideways apart from my little roughhouse with Jack. I refused to believe that Jenna walked because I didn't stand there and let the little shit pound on me. There had to be more. *Fuck if I know what it could be.*

I knew of course that the clubhouse freaked her out. But she'd been willing when I suggested taking her up to my room. It was like a door opening for her, for us. Jenna facing her fears and kicking ass. I just never thought that door would slam shut in my face.

Sure, I'd finger-fucked her in the bar, in the crowded bar. But that wasn't it. Jenna might not say it out loud, but she definitely had a kink for public sex.

"At least you're smiling."

I glanced over at Cage, pinning him down with a cold stare. "What part of fuck off don't you get?"

Cage put on a look that could be construed as hurt. The dumb prick. "It's her secrets."

"She doesn't get it. As bad as anything could be, it won't be enough to change how I feel about her." I sounded like a pussy, I just didn't give a flying fuck. "I love her, brother."

"Yeah, I know." He looked over at me. "Sad fucking thing is, she loves you, too."

Yeah, despite everything. I knew that.

"Just say the word," he said, his face growing serious. "Wouldn't take much."

I knew that, too. Still, I'd prefer Jenna to tell me shit in her own time and because she wanted to. Going behind her back was wrong.

But it was looking like I didn't have a fucking choice in the matter. When Cage hesitated at the door, I didn't give him an answer. Not yet.

Chapter Thirty-Five

Jenna

For two days Ali had been texting and calling me constantly. I ignored everything including his knocking on my door several times. I knew that he could pick the lock or break it down. After he left on his final visit I remembered that he had keys. At least he wasn't forcing his way inside.

Wraith had called, too. Him I'd answered. But my attempt to quit my job had been met with a definite hang-up. I'd been left staring at my phone, imagining his pissed-off frustration that was probably only beaten by Ali's. I'd have to talk to him, but first, I needed distance.

The only person I'd really spoken to from the club was Jack. I'd thought it was Ali at my door and had ignored him, but when I checked that he was leaving, I'd seen my son. I'd gone out to him and he'd played down the fight he'd had with Ali, admitting his own fault.

I believed him, but that was not the reason I was ending things. I was a coward, I just couldn't do it. I couldn't stand the thought of Ali learning my truths and breaking things off himself. It was better this way, better for everyone. Especially Jack, because the more I thought about it, I knew he did not need me further complicating his life.

On the third morning, I dashed to the letter box to collect the mail. Ali had messaged an hour earlier asking to meet in a public place. He wanted answers. He wasn't getting them.

"Shit," I said, as he stepped into view. "I didn't hear your bike."

"I walked." My handsome Ali was sporting dark circles beneath his beautiful blue eyes, his face drawn beneath the black scruff that covered the lower half of it. His clothes looked slept in, even if he didn't appear to have gotten any slumber.

I felt terrible, then reminded myself that this was better for him, too. "You need to go. The neighbors have threatened to call the police if you disturb the peace again."

"Then let's keep this peaceful. I just wanna talk, babe. You owe me that."

He was right. "I'm going away," I said.

"Wraith said you tried to quit." He folded his arms, toeing the cement in the driveway with his face lowered. "I love you, please don't do this."

"It was never going to last, we're too different. You need to get someone..." What? Younger? More club-life orientated? Normal? Undamaged? Who was all those things? I had nothing.

"I don't want anyone else, Jenna. I love you, and I know you love me. You don't do that easy. I never took that for granted. I fucked up. I let Jack get to me. I nearly crushed you, for fuck's sake." He folded his hands behind his neck. "Shit, I can see your point."

"Ali, it's not that. It's not really any of that." I winced — it was probably better I just let him think it was club crap that was driving me away.

"Then what?" He was so open-faced, all of his pain there for me to see. My heart exploded inside my chest. "Don't give me that we're too different shit, babe. Ain't gonna work."

I hardened inside. Forced steel throughout me. I could feel it flowing in my blood, in my organs and in my airways.

"We are too different. I don't want to be with you. Not forever." Yes forever. Forever and ever and ever.

"So, what?" He let out a dark laugh. "This was just you getting off with some rough trade? Keeping your job, the job you are damn well walking from now? The one that you were overqualified for in the first place? I don't believe that. I'm not giving up on us. You never want to tell me your secrets? Then fine, keep them. If it means I lose you by wanting to know, then I don't want to know."

I pivoted on my heel and started for my house. This was too painful. That I was causing that kind of hurt in someone I'd grown to love was making me want to cave. And I couldn't do that.

He didn't try to follow me, and when I looked out of the window a minute after I got inside, I watched him walk away.

Chapter Thirty-Six

Ali

"What's this about?" Cage slid into the seat opposite me. We were in the club bar, only two old timers, Dusty and Bleak, were in there drinking, too far away to overhear.

Mags was pouring beers. She'd never come over and butt in on two brothers talking.

"I need a favor." I fucking hated myself, but I had no choice.

"Shoot." Like he didn't know.

"I want you to run a proper check on Jenna. I want everything, parents, siblings, education, the lot. If you can dig up any past assholes in her life, then I want that, too." I looked down at my bourbon.

Cage let his breath out slowly. "On it."

"I don't want to do this... I don't have a choice. She's hiding something. She's not coming back without a fight." I looked up. Cage was watching me closely.

"What if you don't like what you find?"

"I've come up with a thousand different scenarios, brother." I spun the glass between my fingers. "There's not a one that would put me off her. If that woman has a husband tucked away somewhere...I don't give a rat's ass."

He shrugged. "I'll bury the fucker. Problem solved. Gimme a couple of days."

"Thanks."

"What about her girl, Casey, you ask her?"

"I get the feeling that she won't say a word. I don't want to push there. If I know Jenna, and fuck, I do not know

Jenna, I think heavying her friend will make her cut me out even more than she has." I snorted a laugh.

"We got a lot on her," he said. "But nothing from when she was young. I can't see that helping, brother, but I'll do it, anyway."

He stood, his chair scraping across the floor. That was typical Cage. When he said he was doing something, it was normally immediate.

I just hoped that whatever he found was of some use.

* * * *

Can we talk?

The message was one of several from Ali, but it was simple, straight to the point and fair. Not that I'd changed my mind and wanted to talk to him. But he had stuff at my house and I guess he needed to collect it.

I'd boxed up his belongings the day before, not even considering he'd come on his bike and wouldn't be able to take it all with him.

It had been days, nearly a week. I still missed him and wondered how I was going to get through the next hour or so. Not that I knew how long these things lasted, but Casey's advice had been that this needed to be done. Some crap about closure.

I had no idea. It was all too new to me.

I'm not sure why, but I took him wearing his cut as an act of defiance. He was clean-shaven, bright-eyed and looked perfectly fine. He carried himself with a cockiness that grated on my nerves as he entered my house.

"I put your things in the garage," I said, walking ahead of him and trying to look as cool as he did. "Except this." I picked up one of the guns from the lamp table and turned to face him.

He raised both hands and stepped back. It was then that I realized I was pointing it at him. *Whoops.* But the safety *was* on.

"Jesus," he said, his resolve wavering. "You're going to shoot me? You ended this, remember?"

"You helped. You pushed."

"I know that." He reached out and took the weapon. "You sure you don't want to keep this? It's a good, clean gun, untraceable."

"I'll be all right, thanks."

"Keep the smaller one—it was a gift, okay?" He shoved his hands in his pockets. "I'm sorry I accused you of lying. It was more of omission, right?"

"Same thing, I suppose." I felt uncomfortable, and even worse, heat surged inside me. Regular sex then nothing was getting to me. I wasn't sure if that was shallow. But it wasn't like I wanted it from anyone else. I wanted Ali, and him being right there, looking so good, was torture.

"Whatever it is you're carrying around with you, I can wait," he said, his voice cracking. "This stuff with Jack— it was stupid of me. I just got possessive and you were keeping shit from me."

"You keep things from me, too," I said.

"Not personal stuff. You want to know, then it's all there for the taking. As for the club, we can work that out. I get a choice there, I can tell you everything, or I tell you nothing."

"Really?" I was skeptical about that, not that it mattered.

"Sure. Course, when you take that road with your old lady, you gotta do things right. There's no fucking around, no bullshit. The feds think it's Christmas if they come across a pissed-off old lady." He chuckled. "It's a not a bad deal."

"Relationships aren't deals." That much I was sure of.

"Sure, they are, but there's more. We were good, Jenna."

"We were a couple of weeks."

"A *good* couple of weeks," he said, coming forward. "Please, babe. This is special."

"Is it? Was it?" I shook my head. "Good sex…"

"Great sex," Ali corrected.

"Doesn't a relationship make."

"Come on, it was a hell of a lot more than that. Jenna, this shit doesn't just happen, or if it does, I have no clue. But it was only going to get better. Throw me a bone here, babe. I fucking love you. I don't want this to end."

I turned from him, his hands going to my shoulders and clamping down tight. His lips on the side of my neck kissing me with quiet desperation. I was never immune to his touch, my head going back as the kisses become nips.

"Don't." I pulled away and spun back to him. "Just don't."

"Fuck." Ali's hands went to the side of his head. "You wanted that."

I went to move past, open my front door and throw him out. But he stopped me, gripping my upper arms.

"I. Don't. Want. You."

"Sick of your lies."

My hands tore at his chest. His arms shrugged out of his cut, the leather falling to the floor as his mouth hungrily possessed mine.

He lifted me, my feet dangling as he crossed the room, bringing us behind the couch. Turning me, he bent me forward, his hands ripping at my sweatpants.

"Take off your top."

I scrambled, yanking my sweater over my head as his belt jangled, the sound of his zipper going down. My hands braced down on the cushions as Ali's fingers came between my legs. He worked a little, grunting because I wasn't quite ready.

The fingers left me and I turned as he spat on them. "Ali?"

"Touch your clit."

When I didn't move, he took my hand and positioned it between my legs. He spread my fingers, pressing them against me.

Then his dampened digits started to stroke my entrance. I pulled my hand away.

"Have it your way," he said, his voice alien to me as he gripped my hip with one hand.

"Please, don't hurt me."

His entire body went rigid. The hard cock that had been

jutting against my thigh softened almost instantly.

"Hurt you?" He sounded bewildered. "We're angry, Jenna, but I'm not going to hurt you."

He pulled me up against him, his arm around my middle as he righted my pants then his own. My breathing was heavy. His was shallow.

"I thought…"

"You thought wrong." He spun me to face him. "Jenna, where's this coming from? It's not making sense, babe. Angry sex, that's all this is."

"Angry sex?"

"When you're mad at someone it's hard to admit that you still want them. Shit, it's normally pretty hot." He put his hand against my cheek. "Jenna, I wasn't going to force you, babe. You gotta know that."

I was so dumb, so damn naïve. "Maybe it's for the best that we stop."

"You never answered. What brought this on? You like being with me. The first time we got together was like a nuclear fucking explosion. Hell, babe"—he grinned wolfishly—"you had no problems with taking me in your ass."

I blushed, red and hot. "Stop it."

Something shadowed across his eyes. The smile faded. "Who hurt you?"

I sank to the carpet and he followed me down. His arms cradled me, rocking me a little as his hands swept across my forehead.

"I had a baby," I said.

No reaction, no stiffening body or sharp intake of breath. "When?"

"When I was young. A man put something in my drink. I woke up the next morning and he drove me home. I found out I was pregnant a few months later. It was my first time and I don't even remember it."

No, I only remember Ali.

"Ahh, babe, I'm so sorry, so fucking sorry. You know I'd

never do that, right?" He continued to rock me. This big man, this biker was sounding heartbroken for me.

"So, you see, I can't do this. I tried, I really did. But I can't." My eyes stung, shocking me. I never cried, not anymore. I welled up on occasions, got a little misty-eyed when I was emotional, but the tap to the waterworks had seized up a long time ago. "Please, Ali, it hurts too much. I can't do this and know that I'm going to mess it up."

"We can try. Believe it or not, I actually can be patient sometimes." He was stroking the side of my head.

"It's not the sex. I can handle that, it's…it's…"

"Shh, you don't have to explain. I know all about your walls, Jenna. I just thought I was getting over them."

His phone message sounded and I let out a dry laugh. "That'll be the club."

"No, I'm expecting something else."

"Take it, Ali, then I think you need to go."

I pulled back from him and he nodded. "Don't just leave town, okay? Don't you go without saying goodbye."

He stood—whoever was on his phone had him moving fast. He stopped long enough to kiss the top of my head before he left. But I had the feeling he was gone before he actually got outside.

Chapter Thirty-Seven

Jenna

Casey listened as I recounted my time with Ali.

"So, you told him everything and that there was a baby?" She reached out and touched my hand that rested on my leg and squeezed it. "That's huge, Jenna, you opening up like that."

So, now they were both up to speed on everything. But like Ali, Casey didn't know who my baby was, or even more deadly, who my baby's father had been.

"A little boy. I think I made him feel bad. God, that was sucky timing to say that to him."

"No, there's never a good time. Did you feel threatened by him?" She pursed her lips. "Jenna?"

"No, never. It's like he said, angry sex, only I think I was sad." I laughed, short and sharp. "Let's face it, I'm a freak. What woman wouldn't want a decent pounding from Ali?"

"Sorry, I had to ask. Stupid of me. I mean, the man backed right off. Are you sure this is not salvageable? You and Ali might seem like a strange combination, but you seem to work."

"I don't think I can do the relationship thing," I said. "It's not for me."

Not to mention Jack. I was selfish there, too. I was only assuming all this time that he needed me, or would even want me in his life. It was time to quit there too before I ruined things for him as well. Not that I could tell Casey that.

"Do you really believe that, or are you just licking your

wounds here? Because you can't keep him strung along. That's not fair to either of you."

"I love him, Casey. I wish I could work this, but I can't."

"What about some help?"

"I've been counseled," I said. "Believe me, I know what I went through."

She sucked in her bottom lip and sat back on the couch. "It's the baby, isn't it?"

She hit the nail dead-on with that one. "I don't think there's enough counseling in the world to forget that."

"You know, you can always register, find out where he is. He probably grew up knowing he was adopted, it's not too late." She put her hand back on me again. "Maybe you need to do that for some closure."

My lies, and that was what they were, were getting complicated. I had to remember that my story was that my parents made me give my child up, not that he had been taken. But with my head full of everything, it was getting harder and harder to keep up with it all.

"You and your bloody closure," I said.

"Yeah, well, I just said to talk to him." She linked her fingers through mine. "So will you think about it?"

"It's too late. I don't want to go and screw up anyone's life."

"What about your life? You're young, Jenna, but do you really want to wake up in twenty, thirty years' time and look back and wonder if you could have made something else? Honey, you're not the spinster type. Something happened, it scared you, it would anyone. But you can live now."

"I don't want you to take offense, okay? I'm not just wallowing in self-pity here. But how the hell would you know what my life is like?"

God, I am turning into a bitter bitch. I'd just been mean to the first friend I'd had in years, a woman who'd done nothing but show support and compassion for me. I really needed to leave and let these people get on without the millstone of me around their necks.

233

"You know what?" she said. "I don't. I can only imagine the pain and suffering you've been through. But I know this, you are the sweetest person I know, and how this whole thing hasn't killed your spirit, I have no idea. Don't let that happen now. If you have to leave Ali to find a new start, then do it, but don't do it because you're running away."

"I *am* running away."

"Well, run to something." She sat back. "I don't think that makes sense. Sorry."

"You mean pull my big girl pants up, pick up the pieces and try again." I couldn't do that, but I didn't want her to feel bad. "Maybe a fresh start…again. Maybe this was a starter. Remember you said that about me and Ali, that maybe he was someone to tick off my bucket list."

"I did, didn't I? But that was before he was a real person. I'm on your side here, but I don't think you really want to end things with him."

"Okay, change of subject, I'm tired of talking about me. Let's talk about you and Cage."

She covered her face with her hands and let out an exasperated moan. "There is no me and Cage."

"Uh-huh, you keep denying that."

She peeked out through her fingers. "Okay, he's cute."

Ha! Cage cute? I need to get to the bottom of this one. If I can't be happy, then she damn well is going to be.

Chapter Thirty-Eight

Ali

"Here's what I got." Cage slid into the booth, holding nothing. All the information was stored in his head, no paper trail. "Jenna had a sister."

We were at a small coffee shop in town. I couldn't do this at the MC. I didn't think it was club business and wanted no one sticking their beaks in.

"Had?"

"Dead. Misadventure is the official cause. Overdose. Fifteen." Cage let that settle.

"Irish twins," I said. "I got that from the photo that there wasn't much difference in their ages." I nodded at him to continue.

"The girl's name was Sophie, not Susan, so you were right about that. But she was survived by a sister, Jenna, so she never bullshitted her name to you." Well, that was something. "Parents' names are Daniel and Eliza Mitchell."

"Living?"

"The mother, but the old man died some thirteen years back, pancreatic cancer." He sucked in his lip rings while I mulled that part over. "As for Jenna, she was reported as running away when she was fourteen, no sign since. She never shows up until she is twenty or so. The club already had that, uni records and such."

"So she was off the grid. So much for running her background." *What the hell?* It was like the club had done a perfectly normal check-up. Work and education only. Sure, Jenna was by all appearances a typical citizen, but Hellion

235

would never have accepted such small details.

"There's nothing suspect, apart from the runaway status and the dead sister, but that's not that unusual." He shrugged.

I wrapped my hands around my still warm coffee mug. "Jenna had a kid."

Cage raised both brows at that piece of information. "Well, if she did, it was before she was twenty."

"She just said she was young. That she was drugged." My stomach was starting to sink as the possibility of Jenna's running away at such a young age because she was having a kid herself hit me.

"Oh, right," Cage said. "Well you know what we have to do." He stood, giving me an impatient look.

"What?" I glanced up.

"We go and talk to your future mother-in-law."

* * * *

The house was run-down, but in its day, it would have been a normal family home. The garden now, however, was overgrown with weeds. Everything was a chaotic mess of neglect, except for one neatly trimmed rosebush that I'd bet anything was white when in bloom.

Kneeling before the plant was a woman with graying brown hair and an emancipated build. She held a small trowel and was diligently turning the earth with slow movements.

"Mrs. Mitchell?" I said, walking across the weed-infested lawn.

She didn't bother to turn and look at us. "If it's money you're after, the check's in the mail."

Cage shot me a glance and turned up the collar of his dark windbreaker. It was fucking freezing, the afternoon having turned to shit. A slow drizzle of rain was evident in the dampness of her lank hair and the darkened cement footpath that led to the front door.

"Not after money," Cage said. "Just some information."

She turned, the movement seeming painful to her. Eliza looked nothing like either of her daughters. She might have been attractive once, but not a head turner like Jenna. Her eyes were dull and bloodshot, and her skin had the bloated look of a woman who took her wine by the boxful, and early in the day.

"About what?" She crooked her head to the side, for the first time reminding me a little of her daughter. Maybe the mouth, even with the pronounced wrinkles of a smoker surrounding her lips.

"About Sophie," I said, thinking on the fly. All the way over neither Cage nor I knew how we were going to play this. Torturing or bullying information out of a mark was one thing, but this was someone we weren't equipped to deal with.

The look of agony in her eyes was evident as she blinked at us. "She died."

"Yeah," I stepped forward. "Overdosed."

"It was an accident," Eliza said, defensively. "There were no other signs on her that she'd been using drugs. It was her first time, her…"

"Her what?" I asked as gently as possible.

"It doesn't matter." She turned to walk away. I didn't blame her. We weren't wearing our cuts, had come by car, but we towered over her and running to the safety of her home was a smart option. But I couldn't let her go.

"What if it wasn't an accident?" I asked, louder this time. "What if someone hurt your daughter, Mrs. Mitchell?"

That stopped her. She pulled up short and spun to us. "She was a little bitch, but she wouldn't have purposely hurt her sister."

"You're talking about Jenna," Cage said, gaining some ground himself. "No, you're right, she wouldn't have done that."

"But it was her fault." Eliza stared him down.

"Jenna ran away," I said.

"But she came back." The woman blinked again, wetness filming her eyes. "Two days after Sophie died, she came back."

"Why did she run away?" I asked.

Jenna's mother looked ready to leg it, and Cage moved so that he was between Eliza and the house.

"Who knows?" She threw up her hands. "I never asked."

"Really? She came home and you never found out why she left. That would have come up." I searched her face. It was almost blank, just a flicker of something going on in her head, but nothing like I'd expected.

"She left again."

"You chucked her out?" Cage had her attention.

"It was her fault Sophie died, she admitted it. I was used to Jenna being gone, she'd been gone for nearly five months." Her voice rose, not cracking. She was pissed now. At least that was some emotion.

We both must have looked stunned at that—throwing out a teenage daughter was harsh. Especially when you considered that the other child had just fucking died.

Eliza folded her arms defensively across her stomach. "I had my reasons. You have no idea."

"Tell us then," Cage spoke and I was glad. I was pretty sure my words wouldn't have been so reasonable.

"She wasn't a good girl," she said, looking down at what passed for lawn on her front yard. "I always thought that Sophie was the wild one. Turned out it was that little bitch all along."

"What makes you say that?" I asked. Even now, close to thirty-three, Jenna fucking exuded innocence from her pores.

"When she took off, I questioned Sophie. Jenna had been acting strange, not like herself. She spent more time in her room, hardly ate dinner with her family, snapped anyone's head off that talked to her, real moody."

"Sounds like a teenage girl," Cage said, glancing over at me. Wraith's daughter was fifteen. We'd seen some of her tantrums, even felt a little sorry for the poor old president when she went off.

"She was doing drugs." Eliza nodded. "She had all the signs, sick all the time, tired."

"She lose weight?" Cage said, going back to Eliza.

The woman shook her head. "Actually, she was getting a little chubby. What do they call it? The munchies, that's it. I found these things out."

"What did Sophie say?" I asked as the symptoms she described sounded like something way different to what Eliza was putting it down to. Pissed me off that I was coming to a conclusion that this woman, Jenna's so-called mother, should have come to herself.

"She said that they went to a party over at Mt. Xavier." At my hometown, I jacked up.

"What, a kid's party?"

She shook her head. "No, a biker show. They went together, all that little bitch's idea I bet, despite what Sophie said. They were separated, and the next day, some man dropped Jenna off. We were at a church retreat, so we didn't know about it at the time. But that's when Jenna changed, or showed her true colors."

"Did it ever occur to you," Cage said, looking as angry as I felt, "that your fourteen-year-old daughter was pregnant?"

"Probably, the little slut."

"Who dropped her off?" My words were bit out, full of venom.

"Sophie said he was older, maybe in his thirties. He had blond hair, tied back, and was driving…" She paused, trying to recall the details and failing, so she shrugged it off.

"A black truck," Cage finished for her.

I cut a look to him. "Let's go."

I needed away from this bitch. Even though I knew it was losing her daughters, one dead, one just out there doing god knows what to survive, I didn't have any sympathy for her. She could have chosen a different path, a different attitude. She hadn't, and walking away from her was, shit, fucking easy.

Chapter Thirty-Nine

Jenna

Single, heartbroken women still had to eat, not to mention grumpy cats. With a beanie hat pulled low over my lank unwashed hair, I rushed into the grocery store, momentarily blinded by the overheard fluorescent lights.

When I'd found my bearings, I started over to the pet food aisle and started loading tins of cat chow into my basket. A few fresh vegetables and I could be out of there.

But a high-pitched girly voice caught my attention. It appeared that Chrissie was stocking up as well.

"But you love these," she said, following her words with a giggle.

"When I was ten," Jack replied, laughing himself. "Okay, go ahead."

"Well, if I'm cooking you dinner, you're staying over and this is your breakfast."

I shut my eyes briefly and shuddered. Jack and Chrissie, the last two people I expected to run into. But I wasn't out for the count—if I moved quick enough, I could avoid them. But stupid as I was, I had to have a glimpse, just a little sighting of my son.

I crept around the corner, half-hidden by a floor stack of toilet paper, and peered in their direction. Chrissie looked great, her hair in a high ponytail, wearing sleek black pants and a tight leather jacket. Jack was not in his biker gear, just a sporty hoodie and jeans. His hair was hanging loose and he was looking at Chrissie as if she was the center of the world. He had pride in her, probably because she had picked up the pieces of her suicide attempt enough to venture out, looking like everyone's version of a MILF.

I glanced down at the coffee spill on my pants and a sense of shame engulfed me. There was no need for this. My unkempt appearance was inexcusable.

I went back to the two of them, their heads bowed together as Jack said something that had her shoulders shaking with laughter, that bloody ponytail swinging from side to side.

She touched his arm with a familiar gesture before dropping away, and linking hers through it. Jack guided her in the opposite direction.

Flashes came back to me, Jack on the football field, a skinned knee and Chrissie running out to tend to him. He had been eight. She'd been so full of concern that she'd looked about to cry.

A school play where she'd stood to applaud ten-year-old Jack's acting abilities. Despite him playing a tree, anyone would have thought he'd been up for an Oscar. She'd clapped so hard, nudging the biker who had held the video camera and filmed the entire scene.

Chrissie pushing a stroller, and Jack so small then, not even a year old. He'd woken up, his plaintive cry ripping me apart. She'd crouched beside him, cooing comfortingly while I had hidden behind a bush, watching her and, hating her.

She was his mother and he loved her. I was the interloper here, not Chrissie.

I had no right to interrupt his life. He was moving to adulthood. Maybe he'd marry one day, have children of his own. She'd be grandma, not me. All I would do was mess things up and confuse him. *Why would he want me in his life when he has her?*

Despite everything, she was pulled together and cooking him dinner. While I couldn't even have a relationship like a normal woman. In my two-day-old track pants with my dirty hair, I knew then I wasn't fit for him.

I put down the basket I was carrying and backed away,

my ass knocking into the stack of toilet rolls, sending half of them crashing to the floor. Lucky for me, Chrissie and Jack had rounded the corner and hadn't witnessed my embarrassment.

I fled then. There were other supermarkets and I could just get my cat food and go home. Maybe have a shower and clean myself the hell up.

Chapter Forty

Ali

I'd done the math before I reached the car. Seeing Cage didn't believe in coincidences any more than I did, he'd clearly been thinking the same lines.

"Jesus fucking Christ," I said, as Cage started the engine. "She's fucking Jack's mother. She must have heard about Hellion biting the big one. He gave Sophie a hotshot? Killed her?"

"That part makes no sense. He would have been able to tell the difference between the two of them. I'm thinking he had her for a while." He shook his head, like he tried to get his thoughts in order. "Fuck me."

"So, he got someone else to kill Jenna, but they got to Sophie instead." We peeled out of the street, the tires squealing before Cage reined himself in. Good thing, I was hoping to survive the ride home so that I could finish getting some answers.

"Makes sense," Cage said.

"Whoever did it, Jenna's a loose end." One that wasn't going to be tied up if I had anything to do with it. "You think Wraith would know about this?"

Cage shook his head. "Not at the time, Wraith was only recently patched fully back then. Jack came just before Hellion took me in. But I remembered his truck, he had it for a few years after."

"So Jenna and Sophie go to a party, Hellion puts something in Jenna's drink." The words were fucking painful, but I forced them out. "Gets her unconscious, rapes her and gets her pregnant. But then what?"

"He would have threatened her," Cage said. "If he drove her home the next morning he'd have worked out how young she was. That shit would have landed his ass in jail."

"You think he worried, kept an eye on her and realized she was pregnant? Her own mother didn't."

"That's something Jenna can tell us," Cage said. "The other players being dead and all. Fuck, man, this is a clusterfuck of huge proportions. That mother-fucking cold bitch."

"She's a drunk," I said, sitting back against my seat. "Probably been drowning out everything for years."

"Yeah, likely. One thing, you never let Jenna near her. If your girl feels guilty over her sister, that old bitch will only amp it up. It must have been obvious to the old girl that we know Jenna, but did you notice she never even asked if she was pregnant when I brought up the possibility?"

"She didn't care," I said.

"Probably best not to dump that piece of info on Jenna. That shit will cut deep."

"Jenna ended this, remember? I won't get the opportunity." I sank farther in my seat. "After what this club has done to her, you think she's going to take me back?"

"She was with you in the first place, brother. But she hasn't told Jack yet. It makes me wonder if she's worried about whoever it was that killed her sister." We hit the open road and Cage sank his foot down.

"Or Jack's talked to her about his mother. Jenna would take that personally," I said.

We all knew Jack's vocal thoughts about his birth mother, but most of that we put it down to bullshit. He was a kid with abandonment issues. As for the story of the junkie who birthed him, I'd taken that as true enough. Never really thought about it until then.

"What about Chrissie? You think she knew?"

"She got Jack out of it, but I can't see her being down with killing a kid like that. That shit is a special kind of evil. You know Chrissie, head's full of air more than anything, so no,

I doubt it."

He might have been correct, but Jenna's safety was more important than any assumptions of Chrissie being clueless about how Jack had actually been brought into her home.

As bad as I thought anything could be, I'd at least had the comfort that the club hadn't been what had hurt her. Now that I knew that to be a big fucking lie, I had no idea what my next move would be.

I'd planned on getting answers, of bringing the truth that Jenna kept from me and using it to fix the rip that had pulled us apart. But now, that had all blown to shit.

"I have no idea what to do," I said after we'd driven in silence for a while. "I guess I have to walk away, let Jenna decide."

"You are fucking kidding?" Cage slammed on the brakes and pointed at me. "You find who killed her sister, you punish the fucker by tearing him apart. Then you help her fucking tell Jack who she is and then you marry her and put a ton more babies in her. You hear me, Ali? You make this shit right."

I couldn't help the grin—everything might have been coal-black bleak, but Cage was right, and very detailed.

"Maybe not in that order," I said, the smile not fading. "I might have knocked her up."

Cage punched my arm and started the car again.

"Hey!"

"That's from Jack. He might not realize it yet, but you're doing his ma."

Walking away was not an option. But neither was forcing Jenna to come back to me. The only thing I could do was to lay it all out there in front of her.

Chapter Forty-One

Jenna

The knock was soft enough for me to assume it was Casey coming to check on me again. Sweet, but no one died of a broken heart, it just felt that way. I'd been planning to sleep the afternoon through, so I was tempted to ignore it.

The next rap was sharper and I dragged myself to the door, Hammer doing his noisy trot beside me, his nails a familiar tap against the tile. It wasn't so long ago that this cat had been my only company.

But it wasn't Casey. I should have checked first and now I was full of regret. Didn't matter, I looked like shit. I was sure that Ali would be able to control himself around me.

"You shouldn't answer your door without checking first," he said by way of greeting.

"How do you know I didn't?"

"The surprised look gives you away." He stepped forward, his huge frame filling my doorway, his beautiful face full of compassion that I didn't deserve. "You might as well let me in."

I moved to the side as he crossed the threshold. "I thought you were going to give me some space?"

"Shit's changed." He waited until I shut the door. "I know that Jack is your son. I know it was Hellion who raped you."

That horrible squeezing feeling jarred across my chest. "How?"

"Cage did some digging, then we did some more." He looked guilty himself then. "I couldn't let this rest. Your sister, what happened there?"

"She was going to take us home, Jack and me. I was worried. Hellion was acting strange, and I got the feeling he was going to take him from me. I don't know why, I just had an instinct, so I called her." I led Ali to my living room. He deserved the truth.

He sat opposite me, nodding for me to continue.

"It sounds stupid now, but apart from some doctor visits and the hospital, I hadn't been outside."

"You weren't locked up?" He looked relieved at that.

"Not really. He said he'd kill my family if I left or went to the police. I believed him."

"You should have. He would've gone through with it." Ali leaned forward, catching my hand. "He did, didn't he?"

"There was a bus due to leave in around an hour, but it was cold, so I told Sophie I needed to get something to put Jack in. The baby seat was in Hellion's car and I didn't have a pram or anything. So I went out. I was gone for less than half an hour and when I got back, Jack was gone and Sophie was dead with a needle in her arm." I paused. I'd never forget the sight of my sister dead and Jack's empty bassinette.

"Ah, fuck, Jenna." He gripped my other hand. "Hellion?"

"I doubt it. Hellion was keeping me a secret. I worked that much out for myself. But he knew me—he'd never have gotten me mixed up with Sophie." I sighed, unable to look Ali in the eye. "The night I met him, he'd called me Sophie. I never corrected him."

"Where?"

"A party. Sophie had a crush on this boy, I guess his dad was a hang around. I wasn't supposed to be there, but I couldn't let her go on her own, so I went."

"Did you get separated?"

I nodded as he continued.

"You were off the grid for a few years." He tightened the grip on my hands.

"Hellion gave me some fake identity things so I could get prenatal checks and have Jack in a hospital. A license and birth certificate, even a bank account. I used it to get a job eventually and just got by."

"You were on your own?"

"Not always. My dad never spoke to his sister. She was kind of a recluse, so I stayed with her for a couple of years. She died, early onset dementia just before my eighteenth birthday."

"And after a while you went back to being Jenna." He gave me a small smile. "Why?"

"I'm not sure. I got sick of it I guess. It was doing my head in. I just went back to being me one day."

"When your father passed?"

My eyes widened. "Yes." But even now, I couldn't explain my reasoning or my actions. It was what it was.

"Like Hellion dying brought you back here," Ali said. "That was dangerous, babe. The prick that killed Sophie might have recognized you. Shit, even your name, they might have thought you were Jack's aunt back for revenge. You could have been killed."

"It was my last chance," I said. "I was never really living."

"But you have been, these past few weeks, Jenna." He moved so that he was beside me, his arm going around me.

God, I didn't want this. I loved Ali, I really did, but this wasn't how it was going to play out. He had to realize this. I'd told him as much the last time. Pain gripped me, something tangible that tugged at my nerve endings, and I pulled myself to my feet.

"You need to leave," I said. "Please, Ali."

"Are you going to tell Jack?" He was on his feet too, right in front of me, crouched so his face was close to mine. "Babe, you have to."

"No." I hugged myself tightly, finding no comfort in my own touch. "And you can't either. This is not about you."

"Why not? It's why you came."

"Because I don't want to upset his life. It's here, it's with you and the club and Chrissie. I'm not part of it, I've left it too goddamn late. I'm not going to cause him pain and confusion. His father raped me. How do you think that's going to mess with him?"

"You must have considered that?" He shook his head. "Not to mention telling him about his aunt."

"I never thought that far ahead. I always saw the endgame. Just Jack getting to know me and me being a part of his life. I guess I would have said that I was with his dad willingly. I don't know, Ali. I just don't know."

I burst into tears. This was getting ridiculous. All that could have been done had been done. I hadn't thought there was any more pain to be felt. Even when Jack had said that he hated his mother, and it had resonated as hatred he had for me, I'd not spilled a single drop.

"Jenna." He went to hug me and I stepped back.

"No, don't you dare." I backed up even farther. "This is not happening. I lived this long on my own and I can do it again." But it was going to be so much harder than before, I knew that even as I said the words.

"Answer me one thing," he said, his face not hardening, but looking grim.

"Will you leave?"

He nodded. "After Hellion, after you had Jack. Was there any other man in your life? In your bed? Be honest, because I know if there was, there wasn't many."

"No, only you." I swiped angrily at my tears. "Make you happy? I was no virgin, but I might as well have been. You promised to leave."

He lifted a hand then dropped it. Ali could be very persuasive when he wanted something, he wasn't beyond forcing an issue, but he slowly backed away.

"You're under my protection still," he said. "You might not want me, Jenna, and I understand why. But you're in danger. I will find out who killed Sophie and end this. Then you're free to do whatever you need to do. But until then, you're under guard."

"If it means you'll go, then I won't argue."

"I don't want you on your own." He scrubbed his hands

over his face. "Can you call Casey?"

"She's at work," I said, not sure if she was or not, but I felt too raw to be around her at that moment. I was hoping that my secrets could be kept to a minimum amount of people. "Besides, if I'm in danger, I don't want to drag her into it."

"That won't be a problem. If someone does have you in their sights, they're going to wanna be discreet." He held up both hands to me. "Okay, I'm leaving."

"Thank you," I said. The tears were threatening again, promising to become a waterfall, and when Ali finally turned to leave, I let them flow.

Chapter Forty-Two

Jenna

I should never have answered Chrissie's call, let alone agreed to come for coffee. But the temptation of one last visit with Jack was too great. Only problem, Jack wasn't home.

Chrissie's house was full of Balinese furniture and bright green plants. The walls were painted a sunny yellow— large rooms that opened up into each other. It seems crime did pay. The house was impressive.

As for the woman herself, she'd recently had her roots done, and a red-tipped manicure. She wore black yoga pants and a white fitted zip-up top that when she put her back to me to lead me to her kitchen boasted angel wings decorated in tiny diamantes.

For someone who had not so long ago tried to kill herself, she looked damn near chipper. The only difference to the Chrissie I'd been working alongside of was her lack of heels. Instead she had her pants tucked into a black pair of Uggs.

"I've missed you," she said, going over to an espresso machine that looked like it belonged in a café.

As she set about making coffee, I tried my hardest to think of something to say. Seeing as her phone call to come for a visit had been out of the blue, I wasn't sure as to her motive. I'd accepted because to me it was part of moving on.

It had taken me ages to get my face in order, clean hair and clothes, and I almost looked presentable.

"Your home is lovely," I said. Not like I was going to tell

251

her I'd missed her, too.

"Thank you." She smiled, aerating milk. "I remember you like lattes."

"What's not to like?" *Coffee and milk.* Ali's words and I banished them quickly.

"There's nothing wrong with black. Less calories, not that you have to worry. You seem pretty happy having a few curves." She turned her back to me and finished making the drinks.

I wasn't sure if I'd been insulted or not, so I chose to ignore the comment. Ali had never complained about my body — the opposite if anything. He pretty much worshiped it. More thoughts of Ali... I wondered when that would stop.

"I'm sorry I haven't been to see you," I said. "I wasn't sure if you needed space or not."

"Well, you're here now." She brought over the coffees.

Chrissie had managed to make me feel like a lousy, neglectful friend. That she was merely my boss didn't seem to matter — despite everything, her words made me feel guilty and I resented her for that.

Spooning sugar into my cup, I noted her disapproving gaze and added an extra one. It would be too sweet to be enjoyable, but it was worth it.

"I'm coming back to work, but just part-time." Seeing Chrissie only managed to last the mornings anyway, I wondered what her idea of part-time was, but refrained from asking.

"Jack's party was great," I said. "I had fun."

"I know." She winked at me. I wondered if she'd heard Ali and I had broken up. I'd have been surprised if she hadn't, but wasn't about to enlighten her.

"It must be surreal," I said, ignoring her insinuation. "You know, Jack being grown now?"

She smiled. "Only seemed like yesterday when he was tiny. God, he was beautiful." She left the room returning with a leather-bound book that she placed on the table in front of me. "Here, look."

Of course, I recognized him in the first few photos that were probably taken soon after the day that he was stolen. He was wearing clothes that I didn't remember him ever having. I guessed she'd changed him, or Hellion did.

"He's not a newborn," I said. "He's tiny, though."

"He was six weeks old when Hellion brought him to me." She smiled and flipped a few pages. The dates were written down beside the pictures as he grew in front of me from an infant to a toddler. She had no idea what seeing these meant to me.

"He told me about his mother," I said. At the look on her face, I forced the next words out of my mouth. "Or the woman who gave birth to him, as he put it."

"I never met her. First I knew of Jack was when Hellion brought him home to me."

I looked up at that, not sure if she was lying or not. She seemed to believe what she was saying, meeting my eyes directly.

"A drug addict?" I focused back on the photos.

She returned to the start of the album and tapped the page. "Does that look like a baby that was born to a druggie? He was breastfed, too."

Well, I knew that, but I wondered how she did. She went back to the toddler photos, smiling wistfully as Jack got bigger.

"Took me all night to get him to take a bottle. He kept spitting it out, fighting me. He was very strong." She smiled sadly. "But for all I know, Hellion lied to me. Not like it was a first for him. And with my old man, you didn't ask questions."

"Then why does Jack—"

"Because that's what Hellion said and I didn't argue with Hellion. It seems pointless now to tell Jack, but I really don't know. I mean, he's pretty well-adjusted." She went forward and Jack was now age three. He was playing with a toy motorbike, Chrissie and Hellion sitting on the floor with him. It seemed so damn normal that I wanted to scream.

"He was cute," I said, instead.

"Sorry, you must be bored."

"No," I said, panicked by the idea that she wouldn't show me any more. "I mean, it's nice to see photos of him as a baby."

"Yeah, I suppose. You don't have kids, so it's hard for me to tell if you're interested." She looked at me strangely. "I don't mean that in a nasty way. You have time if you want to, but I never thought I'd have any. I guess when Jack came it was such a gift that I never questioned it. I guess I should have. Too late now. Dead men don't answer questions."

I heard a mobile phone buzz and Chrissie glanced up. She bit her lip and stared at the archway leading to the dining room briefly before going back to the book. Normally I'd wonder why she hadn't bothered to answer her phone, but in truth, I wanted to look more through the album.

"So do you think she's dead?" We were up to school photos by then. Jack dressed in a cute polo with the local primary school emblem on his left top pocket. It was so adorable that I wanted to touch it.

"I have no idea." She sighed. "I've thought about it over the years. My gut feeling is that Hellion paid her off. Makes sense."

In a way, it did. If I hadn't known better, if I was someone on the outside I would have believed that. Or if I was a wife who loved her husband and was just grateful to have a longed-for child, there was a chance that I'd have taken him at his word.

It hit me that I never would have done that. It wasn't because of my intimate knowledge of having a child taken. I just wouldn't have accepted it on face value like she had. I wouldn't allow my son to grow up thinking that he was so unloved by his mother that she endangered his life by taking drugs.

I went back to looking at the photos, no longer able to put myself in her shoes.

"Recognize him?" Chrissie spoke again, drawing me

back. She had an envelope that I hadn't noticed before. A loose packet of pictures. "I wanted to raise him, too, but Hell said I had enough to do with Jack."

She handed me the photo. It was in pristine condition, like it hadn't been handled much. The child was small, perhaps five years old. Large hazel eyes, short brown hair and the sweetest half-smile. Of course, that had grown to more of a smirk these days.

"Cage was adorable," I said.

Sure, I'd seen photos of him before, but not this young, not close up.

The very fact that these people had left him to flounder in a clubhouse full of bikers and groupies made me bristle. Any sympathy I'd started to feel for Chrissie washed clean as I looked at the tiny boy who grew up to be Cage.

Yet doubts were forming in my head. Chrissie, who I'd thought an accomplice to her old man's crimes, was starting to look innocent. Even if it was only because she turned a blind eye to Hellion's perverted ways, I could no longer hold her in my former regard. And that messed with everything I'd thought for the past eighteen years.

Chapter Forty-Three

Jenna

The next time I checked who was at my door, although I knew it wasn't Casey. The bike gave that much away, but seeing Cage on my doorstep was a surprise. After my visit with Chrissie, I was back to being low and confused. I'd been crying again, my eyes no doubt red and swollen. A visitor was the last thing I needed. Still, I opened the door.

Cage had that air about him and I could see how Casey was tempted, but hesitant. He was way too confident and too quick to offer a smartass crack. Even the way he carried himself made it clear that Cage was very comfortable with being Cage. The piercings and tattoos were no mask or disguise, the man might just have been born with them. He looked like he took one of two choices when he met someone, either fuck them or kill them. Maybe a third being both.

But despite that, I kind of liked him.

"Shit, princess, you look fucked up." He walked in like he was at home.

"Yeah, well, I have some stuff I'm dealing with. What do you want?"

Cage had done some digging. He knew things about me that I didn't want anyone else to ever find out. It was bad enough being exposed to Ali, but this was like an open wound being poked at. I shrank into myself.

"Ali didn't want you on your own," he said, sounding very unlike himself. His words were soft. "Neither do I. You don't have to talk, I get that. You want me to make some of that shitty tea you drink?"

Actually, that sounded good. I was dehydrated from all the bawling I'd been doing. I went to my kitchen, Cage behind me as I switched on the kettle.

"You want some, too?" I asked, grabbing two cups. If he thought he could hang at my house, then he was taking tea.

He took the mugs from me and placed them on the counter top. I turned from him, humiliated. My life was playing out in front of strangers, and one was in my home offering to make me tea. Bikers didn't do that, they grunted and behaved hard. Especially ones like Cage. He was probably thinking I was a silly little tart who had let herself get attacked by his late president. He was probably angry that Jack's mother had reared her head when she did and was only here out of loyalty to Ali. A man I'd lied to and deceived, even if I did love him, something Cage most likely thought was a load of more lies and bullshit.

"How did you do it?" His words were low.

Oh, right. How did I pull the wool over not only Ali's eyes, but the entire club's? I didn't answer, just fished out some teabags from the canister.

"I mean, you were so young, a fucking little girl. How did you survive out there, Jenna?" His voice cracked.

God, he's being sincere. I spun back to him. Cage looked bewildered and very awkward. His usual two expressions, a smirk or a scowl, were gone.

"For a while, barely."

"I hate the thought of it. I always had the club. All my brothers to back me up. You had no one. That mother of yours... Fuck." He reached out and massaged my shoulder. Normally, that would have had me jumping, but frankly, I knew he wasn't coming on to me.

"Mother?" I searched his face, which was fast shutting down.

"Yeah, didn't Ali tell you? He said he came and told you what we found out."

"Ali never mentioned my mother. You went to see her?"

My hand flew to my mouth. My mother hated me. I'd tried twice to talk to her since I'd left. Always after death. My sister's and my father's. She didn't want to know me. Why had they gone there?

"It doesn't matter," he said. He was right, it didn't. "What about Jack? Ali said you didn't want to tell him. He reckons you think you'll confuse him. But that's bullshit, right?"

"He hates me."

"Jesus, Jenna, the kid loves you. You need to tell him what's going on. You being single might put all kinds of twisted-up shit in his head." His eyes widened. "What do you mean, hates you?"

"He told me. He hates the woman who gave birth to him." The kettle boiled and clicked off. I poured the water. "I don't blame him. I stayed away too long, anyway."

"Princess, he's young, but he was raised by Hellion. He knows exactly what that cunt was capable of. He'll understand. So, he gives you some cock-and-bull story about his junkie mother and some whining about her abandoning him. He'll deal. Like I said, he likes you for you. Ain't gonna change."

I handed him his tea. "I wish it was that simple."

"Fuck." Cage put down the cup. "Just the thought of this stuff has me banging on like a damn woman, not drinking that shit."

I laughed, I don't know how, but I did. Cage smirked at me. "That's better. Now drink your tea and go and clean up. I have standards, you know."

* * * *

The shower, followed by a cold washcloth to my face, did something to make me look more presentable. I put a little concealer on to cover the redness and returned to my living room.

But Cage was gone. In his place, Ali.

"I didn't hear him leave," I said.

"If you prefer Cage, I can get him back."

The tears were threatening to come again. What was with all this crying? I was stronger than this. If I wasn't, I'd have given up years before now. Didn't matter that I'd finally broken, I needed to stop this.

I blinked rapidly.

Ali narrowed his eyes. "Babe?"

"It's nothing." Dizziness threatened to overcome me as Ali put his hands out to me. "Please don't."

"You don't want me to touch you?" His mouth formed a straight line.

I wanted so much more than his touch, but I stopped myself moving forward. This was for the best, not him being there, but making my point clear. Even though I thought I had.

"I'm sorry," I said.

"The crying," he said, shoving his hands in his pockets. "You keep doing that and I gotta touch you."

I swiped under my eyes with my fingers. It was like unlocking a dam. Shit. "Don't." I put up my hand.

"Don't what? Love you? I can't just turn that off, Jenna." He blew out a breath of frustration. "You trying to tell me you don't fucking love me now?"

"I don't know what's got into me," I said, frustrated with myself. "It happened so long ago. I've dealt with this. I did enough crying back then to last a lifetime. It's so silly. Even my stomach is upset now."

The tiniest of smiles formed on his face. "Are your tits kind of sore?"

"Ali!" He really didn't have to mention parts of my anatomy that he liked.

"Feeling a bit sick, crying, sore tits... Period late?"

My eyes widened. *Oh, shit.* I turned and ran. How dumb, not to even know the freaking date. I never had bothered getting the morning-after pill. I'd been busy and thought that the time had been relatively safe. What a fool I was — after all, Jack had been a one-time conception too.

Ali was on my heels as I entered my kitchen and stared hard at my calendar. It was Tuesday. I should have had my period last Monday. Eight days. I'd never, ever been late. Well, one time…

He pressed his finger on the little circle in the corner of the square and tapped it, flipping the next page up to where one was marked exactly twenty-eight days later.

He was so fucking happy I could have punched him. Hell, I did, drawing my fist back and hammering hard into his stomach. He didn't flinch—it was nothing to him as my fingers retreated from the hard muscle. *Bastard*.

Didn't stop me doing it again. I hit home. This time he caught my wrist, twisting me so that my back was to him and pulling me against his body.

"We don't do that," he said. "Not in this family. You made that clear when Jack came at me."

I struggled. "I hate you. I'm so fucking angry at you right now."

"I don't blame you, but we don't hit each other. Only a spanking and only because you like that." He dipped and kissed the side of my head. "I understand you're angry. You can be, this is crap timing for you. But you're having my kid."

"I'm not," I said, still fighting uselessly against him. "It's stress."

"Hey, you two naked?" Cage's voice sang through my house, followed by my front door shutting loudly. "You better not be."

"In the kitchen, brother. She's wailing on me." Ali's voice was laughter.

Cage pulled up in the doorway. His brow raised and he put a pharmacy bag on the counter. "So, you gonna go pee on the stick, princess?"

Ali released me and I stumbled. He steadied me. "Go."

I picked up the bag with two fingers, staring at it. "You bought a pregnancy test?"

I tried to picture Cage shopping for what I held and just

couldn't. My mind was totally discombobulated.

"Yeah, the things I do for you." Cage grinned. "You fucking owe me, brother."

"Whatever." Ali nodded. "Jenna, stop dicking around. Go and do it."

"You better not have made me pregnant," I said, throwing Ali an accusing look, letting him take the entire blame. I'd kick my own ass later. For now, this was on him.

Cage snickered. "This is gold."

"You shouldn't even be here," I said, pointing a finger at him. "This is private."

"Jenna, just go and do it." Ali started toward me. "I'm not above tickling you into wetting yourself."

"You wouldn't dare."

Oh, hell, he would. It was in his eyes as he advanced on me, flexing his hands in preparation.

Cage backed away. "Call me," he said, chuckling all the way out of my house.

In the end, I headed off to the bathroom and Ali waited in the kitchen. *Wait, oh, I am going to make him wait.* I'd stay in there an hour so he could sweat it out.

But the test worked quickly, not the five minutes it said on the instructions. The lines formed and there it was— evidence of what happened when you played with fire.

I shot out of the door, hitting a wall of Ali who wasn't hanging back after all. I held the stick up. "Look what you did."

"We did," he said, smiling down at me. "That was a team effort, babe."

"We're not together," I said as his arms circled around me and he crushed me to him. "This changes nothing."

"Right, babe," followed by an irritating chuckle.

I kept my arms by my side. Ali wasn't just going to kiss or talk or whatever else he had planned back into my life. I'd made up my mind. It was for the best.

Chapter Forty-Four

Ali

She wasn't going to get rid of me quite so easily, not now. Not that she ever would have. But Jenna had taken herself off to bed and firmly shut the door in my face. That was good — she was exhausted and needed the rest.

I found an MMA fight on cable to keep myself occupied and the cat helped, planting himself beside me on the couch, his surprisingly strong legs taking to my forearm like it was a rabbit he was skinning.

Jenna's phone was on the coffee table, catching my attention when it lit up with a message. She'd had it on silent, probably because of my own constant texts and calls. Wincing at the fact that I'd near gone into stalker territory, I continued the pattern, reading the screen.

The message was from Casey. She'd finished work and was on her way over. I took the words in as they scrolled across the screen before it blanked out.

Sure enough, a few moments later the nurse's car pulled up out front. Giving Hammer a raised brow, I headed for the door. I didn't want Jenna disturbed but I didn't want her pissed off more at me for leaving her girl hanging, either.

Her hand rose in a fist as she prepared to knock, and her face startled then grew shrewd when she took me in. "Where's Jenna?"

"I put her ass to the curb and took over the place," I said.

"Funny." She walked in past me, glancing around. "Well?"

"She's sleeping. She's beat."

"Yeah, well, emotional upheaval will do that." Casey folded her arms across her chest. "Why are you here? I'm pretty sure if she'd made up with you she'd have told me. I promised to run you off the road if I saw you."

I laughed, even though I was wanting to remind her that it was Jenna who'd ended this, not me. "No, I'm still in the doghouse. How much do you know?"

"Jenna's secrets? Her past? Unlike you, Ali, I respect her privacy. I never pushed her. She told me that she'd had a baby when she was young, that someone forced himself on her and that it messed her up. You're a man, you don't get it." She glared at me, but she was about as ferocious and menacing as Jenna.

"You really believe that? What, you some kind of feminist that thinks we're all a bunch of rapists? I don't force myself on women." I glowered back. I was all for Casey having Jenna's back, but being lumped in with the likes of Hellion pushed the friendship.

"I'm not accusing you of anything," she said.

"Good. Because I love that fucking woman and the thought of some asshole hurting her rips me to fucking pieces. You got issues with that then we got a problem." I hadn't meant to raise my voice, so I lowered it. "I just want to help."

"You want her back."

"That too," I admitted.

"She loves you, you big dickhead. I know you love her, but it's complicated." She sucked in her bottom lip. "For what it's worth, you make her happy. But she acts likes she's guilty over that. I can't work that part out. She had a baby young, it happens. And it certainly wasn't her fault."

"I know that," I said.

"Even if you are a damn biker."

My brows shot up. "Right, like you're not interested in bikers. Just so happens I know a dude. Got a little more edge than what you're used to, though."

Her look was full-on animosity, a little too strong a

reaction. "If you mean Cage, forget it. Not my type."

"Uh-huh, then you two better stop looking at each other. Jenna and I were all about the eye fucking at first. Look where that got us." I grinned at her.

"Misery, from what I can see. If she's sleeping, I'll go. Can you tell her I dropped in?" She went to leave. "Ali, I'm worried about her. She's down and tired. She says she's leaving."

"She ain't leaving," I said. "She's tired because I knocked her up."

At first, Casey looked shocked until it clearly dawned on her what my words meant. "She's pregnant? You know... Doesn't matter. Is she okay?"

"She tried to beat me up, but she got over that." I couldn't help it. The smile was back in place.

Casey, however, didn't look happy at all. Her face was drawn—she was worried like shit over Jenna.

"Maybe you should stay," I said. "Jenna needs people around her. Fuck knows I'm stuffing it up."

Casey slouched, and to my horror, tears sprang into her eyes. "I'm so worried about her, Ali. I just thought she was having some fun, but this is getting real now. A baby?"

"How many women you gonna make cry today?" Cage stood in the doorway, his hip cocked against the edge.

Shooting him a dirty look, I said, "You're giving that key back. How come I didn't hear you?"

"Your text said she was sleeping, I didn't want to wake her." He landed on the couch. "Did he knock you up, too, Casey? You going to bash the fuck out of him?"

Casey blew her nose and laughed. "You're really fucking weird, you know that, right?"

"Got a smile out of you, didn't I?"

I was about to tell Cage that he could have that pleasure, when I caught sight of Jenna in the hall. She hesitated and walked slowly into the room, tightening the belt on her robe. She had rabbits on her feet. I'd never seen her wear anything like that before. They were old and faded, like she'd washed them a hundred times.

"My house is full of people," she said, but she didn't sound unhappy about that.

"We can go," Casey said. "Me and Cage."

"No, it's okay." She sank onto the opposite end of the couch to me. "You told her?"

"Sorry." I wondered then if I should have.

But still, she didn't look too concerned about that. Her legs were tucked up but the rabbits were on display. Had to wonder if they were something from her childhood, or her teenage years at least. I found myself staring at them and when she noticed, Jenna pulled her robe to cover the slippers. But the ears stuck out still.

"Nice," I said.

She poked a leg out, twisting it mid-air. "You think?"

"Have some like that myself," Cage said, Casey giving him an incredulous look.

Jenna's vulnerability was on overdrive—it was probably lucky we weren't alone, because it was the only thing stopping me from hauling her off to her bed and covering her body with my own. I wasn't sure that was the right thing to do under the circumstances. In fact, I was sure it was the worst idea. Didn't stop the thoughts from appearing, though.

From the corner of my eye, I saw Cage lean over and whisper something to Casey. They both stood, looking like they were leaving.

Casey bent down and gave Jenna a kiss on the cheek. "You take care. Make a doctor's appointment soon, okay?"

Jenna nodded. "I will."

I walked them out, anything to put a little separation between my thoughts of what I wanted and the knowledge of what I had to do. I needed to be there for her, but it was hands off.

Casey opened her car door and hesitated while Cage walked to his bike. Brother must have coasted the entire length of the street to make that stealthy an entrance.

"I'll see ya," I said to no one in particular.

"For fuck's sake." Cage stalked over to me and grabbed my upper arms. "Get in there."

"Brother, not what she needs." I looked over to Casey for back-up.

She ducked her head to me. "You know exactly what she needs." With that, she climbed in and started her car.

"You heard the woman, go and fucking fix this mess. I'm heading back to put in some more hours on the Mac."

"I don't want to hurt her."

"Then don't get smashed and crush her," Cage said as Casey's car pulled back down the drive. "Telling you, brother, the woman is hurting. She needs you." He smacked hard on my arm. "Now, go do your duty. "

The brother was right. Not that I needed him to tell me that.

Chapter Forty-Five

Jenna

Ali's arms came under me, scooping me up against his chest. He'd thrown me over his shoulder on more than one occasion, but this was different, the gentleness from such a big man making me curl into him, my head going to his chest. It was warm, safe and wonderful.

So was the man who held me. Who lowered me onto my bed and carefully removed my clothes. He did grin as he tossed my bunny slippers one by one to the floor.

"Are you sure?" he said, soft kisses climbing down my neck.

"Very." I wanted nothing more. I pushed rational thought from my mind—never hard in Ali's presence—something of a habit, if anything. "I want this."

His elbows were on either side of me as he held himself up. He was barely touching and I bowed upward, my skin seeking his. I was sure there was a hissing noise when we finally aligned. Ali's mouth came over my lips, the kisses slow and sensual.

I parted my thighs so that I could cradle his body between them. The kissing went back to my neck, down my throat, to one nipple then the other. So fucking soft it was teasing. I sighed, content, when the kisses became sucks. He went down farther, his hands trailing along my stomach before he kissed there as well. He paid very careful attention and I wondered what he was thinking. Not that I didn't have a fair idea.

"You won't hurt the baby," I said.

"I know that." He licked slowly around my belly button. "Ali, you won't."

He jerked his head up. "You sure? I can be gentle. No rough stuff."

I propped up on my own elbows. "I'm sure it will be fine. No, I'm positive. You're ruining it, Ali."

He frowned at that. "Just want to look after you, that's all."

"Ali?"

"Yeah?"

"Shut up and—" I gasped as his mouth came down on my center, his tongue giving a long, languid lick before plunging into me. "Oh, God."

"That's right," he said, against me. "Your sex god."

I arched my back, pushing against him, my fingers gripping the bed covers as he kissed and licked and sucked. He would have known I was more than ready for him, but he stayed there, even though he knew me well enough to know what I wanted.

But I didn't have to put up with any more teasing—a final series of soft kisses and he rose, pulling my thighs around him and thrusting smoothly inside me.

His elbows were back, propping him up. Ali wasn't kissing me, he was watching my face as he stroked in and out slowly, over and over.

Two could play that game. I watched him back, his pupils dilating, his lids shutting briefly every now and then as if it felt particularly good for him.

He didn't need to get faster. The rhythm was perfect. But somehow he got deeper, shattering my former resolve, making me cling to him like he was a safety net and if I let go then I was lost.

But I wasn't lost, yet neither was I found.

She wasn't sleeping, just lying there tucked against me. I didn't bother to telling myself that we'd pulled the knife out of our relationship. A baby wasn't some magic fix to the troubles we were having.

I doubted that her feelings had changed. She was naked against me for starters, but I'd have been kidding myself if I thought that orgasms were enough. But it all should have been. We'd combined our DNA, for fuck's sake. I only wished that she'd wake the hell up and get over whatever hang-ups she had.

I knew her truths, and mine weren't anything out of the ordinary. I tapped my finger against her head.

"To be honest," she said. "Not a lot. Even the baby doesn't seem real yet."

"Jack?" I tried not to let it get to me when she rolled to the other side of the bed.

"Of course, Jack. Everything. And yet, nothing." She slammed her head face-first into the pillow and I could barely make out her mumbled words. "I've really fucked things up."

"It doesn't have to be that way." I reached out and stroked her arm. "But I'm not pushing, not yet, anyway."

Her head turned to me and her eyes narrowed. "I'm so freaking tired."

"Get some sleep." I wanted to talk, the thought making me shake my head. Who'd believe that? But the truth was, I really did. "I ran away," I said.

"Huh, sorry?" But she half sat up and rested her head on her palm. "Are you talking about how you came to the club?"

"Yeah, unless you want to get some shut-eye?"

"No, no, I wanna hear." She stared wide-eyed. "So, when you were a kid, you took off?"

"I was a shit of a kid. Bad-tempered, undisciplined and six-two by the time I was fourteen." I grinned. I was a great disappointment to my parents. Still was, to a certain extent, but I talked now and again to them on the phone. They'd retired up the coast a couple of years ago and I hadn't visited them. With any luck, I'd take Jenna up there and introduce her. I think she would gain their approval.

"And?"

"And I got into a fight, ended up in court and that's where I met Hellion. He offered me an apprenticeship, and if shit worked out, a patch. It was that simple, that ordinary, but now..." Fact was, without the club, I would probably be inside doing time. Not like the parents could keep me locked down.

"Wow," she said. "You got a better deal than me."

"You did not just say that?" I kept the laughter that rose in my chest down. "You are one sick girl, Jenna Mitchell."

"Yeah, and you, you poor bastard, you knocked me up."

I couldn't help it, the tension of the past few days, the news of our kid and her sometimes twisted mind, I lost it.

* * * *

Cage rested his chin on his hands as he sat at Jenna's kitchen table. His turning up in the middle of the night wasn't out of character—him being clueless as to which of our brother's assisted Hellion, and would therefore die soon, was.

"I can't believe she suspected Wraith," he said. "Well, actually, I kind of can."

"Blew me away that she even set foot on our property thinking that he was capable of tying up a loose end like that. Took a lot of guts. Guess she really wanted to be with Jack."

"Fucked up thing is, she could've gotten taken out at any minute. I got some names, brother, but no one concrete. Then again, after that shit Kitty pulled..."

"Kitty works for the club, not the individual," I said. "Hellion could've hired outside help."

"Maybe." Cage glanced down as Hammer rubbed himself around his legs. Picking up the cat, he said, "What have you done to yourself?"

Hammer had a silver chain tangled around his neck. I'd left the door open to the bedroom in case Jenna woke. I hadn't thought to lock the cat out.

"He does that shit, steals things."

Cage removed the chain, holding it up, the heart pendant swinging. Staring hard at it, I saw the moment of recognition hit him. I felt it at the same time.

"Son of a bitch," Cage said. "Well there you go. Sometimes it is the most obvious."

Kitty's beard normally obscured the thick metal links around his neck. But I'd caught glimpses of it over the years, as probably had Cage. Twisted around the chain link was a more delicate necklace. For some reason I always assumed it belonged to his old girl, or one of his kids. But now, I was looking at its exact copy. Common enough, I guessed, but too big a fucking coincidence.

"The sick fuck," Cage said.

"Wraith's given him two weeks—he's not to set foot in town until then."

"You reckon he'll stick to that?"

"Good chance he doesn't know who he's dealing with," I said, but even as the words were out, I knew they meant shit. "Fuck, he had Pony watching her. He was going to give him up, that's why he offed him."

"Makes sense," Cage said. "But he likely still thinks he killed the right one. Jenna turning up, not calling the cops, fuck knows what's going through his head. You ready to bring Wraith in on this?"

"Not yet. No way the prez would've condoned this shit, but chances are, he knew after the fact." Not something I wanted to believe, but right now, my priority was Jenna, not my club. First time ever, but there it was. "We keep a lid on it for now."

"Jesus, he's meeting with Geezer as a back-up plan. He's going to patch over."

"Fuck me, you're probably right." I blew out a breath. "At least we'll get a heads-up if he decides to come in, and he's in the dark with everything else."

"True," Cage said. "What about the meet with you and

Jack?"

"Fuck, guess that's slipped my mind."

"Don't worry about it, brother. I'll be on her like skin on bone and you know it."

I didn't like it, but Jack needed me with him, there was no one else. Cage had too many burned bridges with the Diamonds and the only way I'd get out of going was to unload to Wraith. I wasn't prepared to do that, not if he played dumb with me, and knew the threat that Jenna posed.

"You tell her yet?"

"No."

Fuck, that was just something else to worry about.

One thing was for sure, though, my cunt of a brother Kitty was dead.

Chapter Forty-Six

Jenna

The familiar sight of Ali standing at the end of my bed, fully dressed, with regret on his face, greeted me when I pried my eyes open.

"Are you going now?" I sat and pulled the covers up around my neck.

"I gotta, babe." Putting one knee on the mattress and both hands down beside me, he leaned in. "Jack's going to a meet, I'm not letting him go with just anyone."

That got my attention. "What do you mean?"

"Club business." He climbed off the bed. "We leave in an hour."

The timing couldn't have been worse. We may have shared a bed together, and more, but I had no clue where we stood and rational thought just wasn't coming. I leaped from the warm covers as if burned.

"That's it? I get nothing else. Just your secret squirrel crap?"

His mouth twisted up at the corners. "You got a lot more than that."

"Ali, last night, it didn't change anything." I made a grab for his arm. "Can you at least tell me if this is dangerous?"

Of course it is. I could see the worry etched on him, and his wanting to go with Jack stank of protection. One part of me felt grateful that someone as capable as Ali was accompanying my son and the other resented the hell out of him for letting Jack get so close to danger in the first place.

"We'll talk when I get back."

"We do this now, or we don't do this at all." I stepped in front of him, craning my neck to stare into his face.

"You're naked, Jenna. You know I can't think straight with your tits and pussy right there in front of me." His hand raked over his head. "You don't play fair."

"Coming from you, that's kind of rich." But I picked up my robe from where it draped across a chair and pulled it on, tying the belt securely. "Ali, we broke up."

"No, we had a fight. That shit happens, get used to it. But for what it's worth, I'm gonna try and not let that happen too often."

"You are so bloody infuriating. Too used to getting your own way. Well, not this time. Just because I'm pregnant doesn't mean that we're going to just—"

The hard kiss was nothing like the last few we shared before we finally fell asleep in each other's arms. When he broke away, it was all I could do to not punch his smug face.

"I'll be a day or so. And don't get any ideas about leaving. Cage is going to keep an eye on you." When he turned to leave, it took all I had to try to keep myself together.

My anger boiled to the point my body shook. I wasn't just mad at Ali, but with the entire situation. Why couldn't I be like everyone else and make a relationship work? It was all so unfair.

"I hate this," I said, and he spun back to me. "You can't just bully your way back into my life."

"You frustrate the fuck out of me, do you know that?" His hands flew to his face, wiping down his cheeks. "What makes you think you can't have this? Us? Your pointless fucking guilt?"

"Pointless?" I clenched my fists. "It's not pointless. I spent Jack's entire life watching from the sidelines. What kind of mother does that? And now I'm doing it all again, pregnant by a biker. You know, it's insane."

"You have this whole situation wrong. I'm not Hellion. I won't hurt you, and I won't take your kid away. I don't have time for this, Jenna. If I'm not at the club soon, then someone else will go with Jack. I'd settle for Cage, but…let's just say, the people we're meeting don't like him much."

"Okay," I said. Because when it came down to it, I wanted time to think. Even more important, I was worried about Jack, and despite how I was behaving, Ali was someone I trusted to look after my son.

Ali sighed. "I'm sorry, but I gotta go."

I walked him to the front door where he hesitated before bending and dropping a small kiss on my forehead.

"Stay safe," I said, closing the door and shutting him out.

Chapter Forty-Seven

Ali

Jack was going to wear a fucking hole in the already threadbare carpet. He was pacing up and down my room, his hands shoved into his pockets.

"I hate waiting," he said as if I wasn't already clued in on that score.

"Can you at least go and pace in your own damn room?" I fell onto my back. I was no fan of sitting on my ass, either, but these things normally ran this way and the kid was just going to have to get used to it.

"Was that Jenna you were texting before?" Jack stopped his walking and pulled up short.

"What if it was?" I frowned. Discussing Jenna with Jack could get awkward and I wanted to avoid it. As it was, I'd messaged Wraith, just a call in.

"No reason. I'm sorry, okay, for that shit I caused." The kid looked guilty. "It's not what you think."

"What isn't?" I folded my arms behind my head. *Let the awkwardness begin.*

"I shouldn't have said anything." He took the flimsy chair from behind the worn desk and sat on it backward, his arms crossed over it. "It's just that I thought she was different."

"She is," I said, covering my eyes with my forearm. "Just drop it, okay?"

"I like her," he said. "She's a nice woman. Ma was stoked when she came to work with her."

"And now?" I sat up, scooting back against the head board. "That's changed?"

276

"Not that I know of. Chrissie's just not back in her right head space yet. But Cage is right—it doesn't matter how stuff starts." He got up again, going back to his walking. "You and her okay now?"

"We will be."

"That's good. That's good." Jack's eyes flew to my phone when it buzzed. "Don't tell me, Wraith?" He grinned at me.

Checking the screen, I read Wraith's reply. He would expect me to keep an eye on things back home. My inquiry as to how Kitty was traveling was logical, seeing I needed the location of Geezer and his boys.

Still in the city.

Well, that was something. Hopefully, we could meet with Tyler, Chops and whoever else they had on side, and discuss this shit.

"What are the chances of this going smooth?"

"Dixie will just want guaranteed replacements for the muscle and the runs. We get men ready to step into our shoes, we walk. Simple." He knew this, but I think his nerves wanted the silence filled. Whatever worked for him.

"What if they're not going to overthrow Geezer? I mean that's just an idea."

I sighed. "Do you even pay attention in church? Jesus, Jack."

"I just don't want to fuck this up, it means a lot. The families, too."

Yeah, he was right there, and the idea of bringing Jenna and my kid into this world where the risks were significantly lower than before had me even more keen to do this right.

I swung my legs across the bed, planted them on the floor and braced my elbows on my knees. "You're right, Jack, nothing is certain. But maybe Chops is going to think that scoring the contract with Dixie is an even bigger incentive for taking over the club. Right now, they're hand-to-mouth selling meth and other low shit. This meeting is going to give them an extra push whether they need it or not."

"And it benefits us two ways because not only do we offload the shady shit, but we don't have to look over our shoulders wondering when Geezer's going to try and increase territory."

I put my head up, cocking to the side. "Very good, Jack."

"I try," he said, and grinned.

My phone chimed again. Showtime.

Only it wasn't Tyler that met us out on the footpath in a black van. *Fucking great, we've been set the fuck up.*

Diamond Jacks. At least six of them and not a one was Tyler. The ages were wrong.

"This is not good." Jack stood next to me, body tense. We'd just left the hotel, walked right out into an ambush.

I had no idea how anyone had made us. We'd kept a low profile the entire time. There was no need for any of the other club to know we were in town. We'd left our bikes clear on the other side of St. Lorne and neither of us had cuts. The two informants we'd used had been dealing with us for years. There was no need to suspect either of them.

Someone had ratted us out, however—Diamonds just didn't turn up with black vans on the off-chance that they'd find themselves some Devil's Prophets wandering their streets. Besides, even if they did, this kind of hostile show was not the normal behavior. Even someone as fucked up as Geezer wouldn't start a war over two interlopers.

Geezer wasn't around. I recognized Needles and Palmer. The rest were unfamiliar. Judging by two of the cuts, they were from a different charter.

"I don't normally get into strange vans without some candy first," I said to Needles, who was yet to emerge. The Diamond was sitting back against the van wall, a full-on assault rifle in his hands.

As big as the weapon was, I was more concerned with the men on the footpath. One held a much smaller gun, but fitted with a silencer. Doubtful they were prepared to shower the street in a noisy show of force, but the gentle pop of the other weapon would go unnoticed on a quiet rainy evening. Most of the shops were shut and had been for hours. Even the small café over the road was turning off its interior lights. Only the pub on the corner and the hotel we'd emerged from were showing any signs of life.

"I suggest you make an exception for me," Needles said.

"You wanna talk, we can do that out here." I glanced at Jack. The kid was smart and remained silent.

"You got the crown prince with you." Needles leaned forward. "Hellion's dead five fucking minutes and you're already fucking up."

"Who says we fucked up?" I narrowed my gaze. "We were ratted out."

"Bullshit," said Needles' friend with the gun. "We made you."

"Yeah, right," I said, laughing. "We could have rode up and down the street in our colors and you lot would have sat on the sidelines and waved like it was a parade. You could at least tell me who was your intel."

"You're such a fucking smartass, Ali," Palmer said, coming and standing in front of me. "I'm going to like spending the evening with you."

"Not without flowers first, asshole." I was tempted to headbutt the dickhead, it would be worth the gut punch I'd no doubt receive for the effort.

"Flowers, candy, it's not Valentine's Day, mate. But wasn't there some kind of massacre?" Needles pretended to think, then shrugged jovially. "Doesn't matter, we'll make one, anyway. Now in the van, boys."

I put my hands up as my weapons were stripped from me. Two guns, three knives and my brass knuckles. The knuckles were really a joke. I used them for a key ring.

I watched Palmer slip them on and flex his fingers. The last thing I remembered was them coming toward me.

Chapter Forty-Eight

Jenna

"Everyone cheats." Cage leaned forward, catching my gaze. "Even you."

"Never." I grinned at him, but felt it waver at the corners. "It's not who I am."

"You're tempted," he said, that smirk on his face. "I can tell by the look in your eyes."

"Cage, it was there all the time." I moved forward, too. "So, why not?"

"Because we're friends now and the fucking motel was not on my square."

Casey burst out laughing, tears running down her cheeks. "You lose, loser." She leaned back against her chair, trying hard to contain herself.

Cage threw his hands up in frustration. "Fine, but it's over, no way I can win now."

"So, you're just going to give up. You surprised me, Metalface. One little setback, and that's it." Casey picked up her drink and tilted it at him. "Are you sure you don't want a water or something? I have juice, Jenna."

She wasn't looking at me when she asked, but I was watching her, Cage as well. Something was going on there, it was the second time she'd called him that, Metalface, like a pet name she'd used before. His lack of reaction was giving me more cause for curiosity.

"Not giving up," Cage said, but he sat back. For him, our game of Monopoly was over. "Besides, it wasn't on me."

Okay, they were not talking about a board game.

Casey gave him a rueful look and glanced at her wood heater. "I think I'll go out and get another log."

Cage stood and headed outside. "I'll do it."

"Okay, what's going on?"

They were doing a great job at distracting me. Cage had insisted that he needed to watch Casey, too. As I had no family, she was my only weak spot, according to him. As for my mother, he'd sent Spice, a prospect, to park outside her home. When I asked if that would give the game away, he'd laughed. Apparently prospects did what they were told, no questions asked.

"Nothing," she said. "Another water, then?"

"Sure, Nurse Ratched." Cage wasn't the only one who had a pet name. He'd slipped up, too. "It's not nothing."

She paused at the fridge. "If you must know—" A knock at the door cut her off. "I'll just get that."

"Coward," I said as she hurried away.

She returned seconds later with Kitty. I froze in place, my breath catching in my throat like a fist. I often wondered how Sophie felt the day she'd died. Pain-wise, there would have been the prick of a needle, then the heroin would have flooded her body. Perhaps blackness followed. But she would have been terrified, someone taking hold of her, forcing the injection into her body. She'd come to save me, and died as a reward. This man killed her. But my initial fear when Casey had led him in bled away, to be replaced by a hate so deep, my hands shook.

"He's looking for Cage," Casey said.

Finally I could move and I stood, my chair scraping loudly before falling to the floor in a clatter of timber on tiles.

"What are you doing here?" When Ali had told me that he and Cage were certain that Kitty had killed my sister, I'd failed to comprehend. He'd been sweet to me. He'd lost his entire family, and even though it wasn't logic that had ruled him out in my mind, I'd struggled to believe the words.

But when he stood in Casey's home, his eyes drawn tightly on me, I saw him for the killer he was.

"I could ask you the same thing, sweetheart. Why did you come here?" Kitty glanced to the sliding door at the back of the house as Cage came through it. "Hello, brother."

"Kitty." Cage placed the log of wood onto the floor in front of him.

"Keep your hands where I can see them." Kitty stepped forward. "I just want to talk. Do you know who this is? Who Jenna Mitchell is?"

"Why don't you tell me?" Cage's attention flicked to his cut hanging on the back of one of the chairs and my stomach fell. If he had a gun, and of course Cage had a gun, it was likely inside his jacket.

"She's Jack's aunt," Kitty said.

I stilled at that. Kitty obviously didn't know the fatal mistake he'd made all those years ago. "No, I'm not," I said. "I'm Jack's mother. You murdered the wrong girl." His face screwed up in confusion as I continued, "When you took Jack, and you tried to put me out of the picture, you fucked up, Kitty."

"That doesn't matter now," he said. "We can right this wrong. She's going to bring down the club, brother. I admit, her and Ali being together complicated shit—"

"What kind of man kills a fifteen-year-old girl just because his boss tells him to? You're a sick man," I said.

Casey's eyes shot between us all, finally landing on me. I guess she was working out the entire situation now.

Kitty started to laugh, cutting himself off when Cage made a move toward the chair. "Hold it there, Cage. I was never ordered. I knew something was up with Hellion. I followed him to where he had this little whore shacked up. When I confronted him later, he broke down. Seemed Hell was getting sentimental."

"What do you mean?" I said, my mind shutting down. *Hellion did this, I know he did.*

Kitty let out another bark of a laugh. "He knew what he wanted, he wanted his son, and for you to be gone. He'd gotten back blood tests that proved Jack was his, only he was torn up over putting the mother of his child to ground. He never even touched you after that first night. Found it hard to believe, but in the end, I realized it was true. But don't worry, Hellion was very grateful that I fixed things."

"So, you took it upon yourself to sort it out, telling yourself it was for the damn club." Cage shook his head. "The next person to die is you, Kitty. There's no other way, brother. Ali will tear you apart."

"Is that so? Not according to my intel. Heard that shit was over with. She's not club, Cage." He gazed now at Casey. "You all fucked up, gave me another loose end to tie up."

His hand went to the back of his pants and Cage moved.

The gunshot was not silent, but close enough, and echoed in my head when it reached me.

Chapter Forty-Nine

Ali

It appeared to be some kind of barn. There was even a stack of ancient hay bales to one side and some old farm machinery hanging around. They had handcuffed Jack and me to a tall post that stood in the center.

The place hadn't been deserted when we'd driven in. A kid who appeared no older than Jack looked up when we had all entered. He didn't look club. He had messy hair, a mixture of caramel-brown and blond, and a young, innocent face. He wore glasses similar to Jenna's black-framed ones as he sat cross-legged on a table cleaning his fingernails with a knife the size of a baby's arm.

Geezer had been telling him to leave repeatedly from the moment he'd walked through a side door two minutes after we'd been cuffed. So far, the kid had ignored him and Geezer appeared to have given up.

"This needs to go to a vote," the kid said, pointing the knife in the direction of me and Jack.

"Shut the fuck up, Tyler," Needles said with irritation.

This was our meet? I took another look at him and what passed for a Diamond Jack nowadays didn't impress me.

"That's the rat?" Jack said, his voice low.

Tyler looked up—his eyes were almost feline-shaped and seemed to glitter preternaturally. There was something about him that wasn't sitting right. He stood up fast, again appearing unreal. Taller than I had first thought, bigger, too, and possibly a couple of years older. But not old—he was still young, maybe Cage's age, twenty-three or so.

He stalked over to us and knelt in front of Jack. "I'm as surprised as you."

"Why would he think it was you?" Geezer said.

"'Cause I arranged to meet them," Tyler stood again and put his back to them. "You jumped the gun."

"Why wasn't I informed?" Geezer tilted his head. He was white-haired with a long beard. He had to be sixty but his body belonged to someone twenty years younger. There wasn't even the start of paunch in his gut.

"Didn't know they'd show." Tyler shrugged. "Doesn't matter. This still should be discussed. You fuck 'em over and Wraith will come back hard. You looking to start a war then we should get a say in this."

"Here for Uncle Chops?" Needles said. "Last I heard, he had VP on his cut, not president."

"Just got my club's best interest at heart."

Christ, one of those. This could get messy, Jack and me being the resulting mess.

"So" — Tyler clapped his hands together, the knife having disappeared into a sheath he wore strapped to his leg under his combat pants — "what is this? Information or hostage?"

"Neither," Geezer said. "This is example."

"The kid is worth more to you alive," I said.

Tyler turned to us and I schooled myself not to react to the wink he gave me. "He's right there. This other prick can probably give us a few secrets, too."

He crouched again, this time in front of me. "Bet it'll be hard to get them out of him. Still, you never know."

"Tried once before," said Needles.

I smiled at him. "You don't get a second date." I hadn't really enjoyed the first one a couple of years earlier. But it had been short-lived — that time Geezer had called it off. This time, however, the Diamond Jacks' president had some other angle to play.

"Who in the club?" asked Jack. Obviously, he'd been mulling it over.

Wraith had known where we were of course, a few of

the others, but given the secretive nature of our visit, not the entire club. They'd be informed later at the debrief, at least that had been the plan. Still, it made the number of people who knew fairly small and I didn't think any of my brothers had shopped us out. Had to be bullshit. Jack was right, Tyler had opened his mouth.

"We need to stop dicking around and just do this." Palmer crossed the room, his gun out. "Fucking let me, Geezer."

"Settle down, brother," Geezer said. "We'll ask some questions first. Wouldn't hurt to bring something to the table."

He picked up a hammer in his hand and tested the weight of it. Turning to Tyler, he said, "Happy now?"

"Oh, fucking ecstatic. Love that you want to start a war with the Prophets. You're just real special, Geezer."

"And you're looking at losing your patch if you keep that shit up." Geezer rounded on the younger man. "I'll tell you what, you can kiss them better or suck their dicks when I'm finished."

I almost laughed at the infighting, finding it hard to believe that these clowns were who were going to finish me off. But I could see that Tyler used delaying tactics.

"Come on, kids," I said. "Settle down."

Behind me, Jack snickered. "If I piss my pants it's from laughing, okay? Not any shit these morons dish out."

"Same," I said and leaned back. "You need to keep your mouth shut now, little dude. Okay?"

I hadn't called him that for years, but Jack didn't reply.

"Hey," I said, "you fucktards ready now? Or are you going to keep having your pissy little fight? You sound like a bunch of chicks."

Palmer pulled the key to the cuffs from his pants pocket and advanced on us. "Ready to party?"

Chapter Fifty

Jenna

"Cage!" I flew to his side where he'd fallen.

The front door hung wide open, cold air rushing inside. Casey put down the weapon she'd taken from his cut.

"I think he's gone," she said, hurrying over to us.

"We need to call an ambulance," I said as blood pooled on Cage's thigh.

Casey ran from the room, returning with a large metal box. Opening it, she pulled out a packet and tore it open. After pressing the huge wad of gauze against his thigh, she took my hand and held it down over the bleeding.

Next, she took a smaller piece of wadding and put it to Cage's temple. "That's nasty," she said. "I'm going to call this in."

Cage reached for her, his fingers circling her biceps. "No hospital. Cops."

"You idiot," she said. "Last thing you should be worried about is the police."

"It's nothing." He went to move, wincing and squinting, telling me his vision wasn't crash hot. "No cops."

"I'm pretty sure you have a concussion, too." Casey shot me a look before going back to Cage. "You need a doctor."

"It went through," he said. "You can fix this, then we'll get to the clubhouse."

"You are fucking mad," Casey said. "I understand the hospital will ask questions."

"It's not that bad," he said, gritting his teeth. "Please, Casey. The club can handle this."

"You're being ridiculous." She darted her eyes around the room, but a look of resignation crossed her face. "I can't believe I'm doing this."

"Thank you," he said. "I'm not important here, Jenna is."

The room had been warm but with the open door, the music from a neighboring party filtered through, along with the cold.

"She's right," I said. "You need the hospital."

"I promised Ali, princess. I fucked up and Kitty got in here, the least I can do is stay while he's out there." He glanced at his gun and I picked it up. "Ali showed you how to use it?"

"He wanted to, but I kept avoiding it. I'm sorry."

"I can use a gun," Casey said. "Cop for a dad, remember?"

While she set to work on Cage, I locked her front door and came back to help. I didn't know how much assistance I'd be, but Casey seemed to know what she was doing.

"You're right about the bullet," she said. "I'll flush it out and see how it looks. This is going to sting, but I don't have much in the way of painkillers."

"There'd be some at the club," I said. "Right, Cage?"

Casey cut me a worried look and set to work.

Nothing seemed like a hell of a lot of something to me. The hole in his leg was sickening, blood flowing and mixing with the saline solution she used to wash it out with. Her face pinched in concentration, but her hands were steady as she worked on him.

"Do you need to stitch it?" I asked, feeling woozy with the amount of blood.

"Yeah," Casey said. "That's gonna hurt."

Cage said nothing, keeping still, despite the obvious pain he was in.

"What about his head?" She'd placed wadding over the gash and wound a bandage around it, but the blood had started to seep through.

"That's the biggest worry." She looked to Cage with concern. "You have a concussion, but I'm not a doctor. All

I know is it's bad."

When I wasn't watching Cage, I stared at the front door, expecting any minute that Kitty would return. He'd killed my sister, that was only just starting to filter through to me.

"He won't come back," Cage said. "Shooting me is frowned upon." He grinned at me and patted my leg.

"You are nuts, you know that, don't you?" Casey gave him a stern look. "Who was he, anyway? I thought he was one of the club members, that's why I let him in."

It was hardly Casey's fault, I should have warned her, but Kitty coming to her home was the last thing that any of us would have suspected. I'd put her in danger, though, and for that she was owed an explanation.

She would get one too. As soon as we had Cage fixed I'd tell her everything.

"He'll need antibiotics," she said as if to herself. "And this wound has to be kept clean."

"Mick can do that," Cage said. "He's a paramedic."

"That's something. Maybe he'll convince you to go to the hospital. Thank God it went right through." Casey wiped her forehead with her arm.

"Bit like my piercing," Cage said, a smug expression on his face.

Casey's eyes went wide, her look to Cage pleading with him to shut up.

"What piercing?" I knew Cage had several, I'd seen indents through his T-shirts at times to indicate that he had some pretty intimate chest rings. Then I remembered Ali's teasing Casey in my kitchen and shut up.

"It's nothing," Casey said, sitting back on her heels.

"Well, it made you faint." The smugness only increased.

"I passed out drunk, I didn't faint. It wasn't that impressive." She returned his look.

"Admit it, Ratchet. Unless you want me to show you again." He moved his hand slowly toward the front of his pants.

"Stop it," Casey said. "This is not the time."

"This is the best time, it'll take my mind off things." He winced as Casey went back to tending his leg.

"Sorry," she said, meeting my eyes and causing me to gulp. "It's going to hurt, there's nothing I can do about that."

I couldn't, either, and I think when I squeezed Cage's hand, I was more comforting myself.

Chapter Fifty-One

Ali

The minute the cuffs were removed, Tyler threw a gun to me. But I barely had time to use it, he opened fire on his fellow club members and I had no choice but to push Jack to the barn floor and cover him.

Palmer had him lined up as he hid behind the now upturned table. He hadn't managed to get a shot off, I'd pinged him fair in the middle of his head as I'd thrown down.

Tyler got the others, systematically shooting them like ducks at a sideshow. There was no emotion on his face and if Jack and I had been on our feet, I had the feeling we would have been mowed down simply because we were blocking his shots from the others.

It happened fast, bodies on the ground and Tyler walking among them. He kicked at his president. The man groaned and twitched. Tyler got in a head shot, before turning to us.

I pulled myself to my feet, hauling Jack up with me. "For fuck's sake, you nearly took us out."

"Thought you'd be quicker," Tyler said.

He still had his gun out, but so did I. That he'd given me the weapon didn't have me feeling all that much easier in his presence.

Tyler approached me, tucking his gun in the back of his pants and flicking his chin at me. I followed him away from the carnage.

"It was Kitty," he said. "He's been in contact with Geezer for a while now. Wanted a hit on some woman at your club."

I flinched at that. No need to ask who had been the target. "No one took it?"

Tyler indicated Palmer. "He wanted the job, club voted it down. We don't kill women."

"Nah, just your brothers. You could have warned us about the hit. That's my woman he wanted dead."

"There were plans to reach out to your club, it just hadn't happened yet. He didn't have many options — anyone he would have contracted would have run it past Wraith first." As he spoke, I placed the gun on the ground. I was on his territory now and had to play by his rules. But I figured if he wanted me dead, I would be. "What was his beef with the woman?"

Like he really believed I'd tell him that answer. "We free to go?"

Our meet could wait. But when the side door busted open and several Diamond Jacks marched in, I knew I couldn't leave just yet. One pulled up short, the others spreading out around him.

"Your work?" He looked to Tyler. I didn't know him, but the man beside him was Chops, the VP and Tyler's uncle.

"Looks like you're stepping up, Conner," Tyler said to him. "It's simpler this way."

"Bloodier, too." Conner walked over to the dead men. "This everyone?"

"Yeah, got them all in the one room. You're lucky, they were seconds out of getting us in a war with the Prophets."

At that, Chops looked over at us. "Prophets?"

Jack had joined us the moment the others arrived. I folded my arms across my chest, my body slightly in front of Jenna's son. "Yeah, you got a problem with that?"

"You're on our property," Conner said. "So, yeah, we got a problem with that."

"They were here to meet me," Tyler said. "Wraith's got a deal for us."

"You boys got five minutes." Chops righted a chair and

kicked the table back up. Several others grabbed seats of their own and Jack and I joined them.

They'd take what we had, no way they were going to knock back our offer. It meant money for their club, money we were happy to give up now that Wraith had finished signing all the contracts for the new legitimate business.

But first, I needed to call in to Jenna, she was my priority.

"We'll talk," I said. "But I want a phone first."

Tyler tossed me one and I set to dialing.

* * * *

After we got Cage comfortable, Casey and I went into her bathroom to clean up.

"You wanna tell me what the hell is going on here?" She was angry and I didn't blame her one bit.

"Okay, let's wash up first and then I'll tell you everything."

She pulled off her bloody top and hesitated near her laundry hamper before throwing the garment into a rubbish bin.

"I'll lend you some clean clothes," she said, sounding exhausted. "Then we talk."

I nodded and got rid of my own top and pants.

We checked on Cage then I sat her down and I told her everything. I left nothing out, Casey looking blindsided as my story unfolded.

"Jesus Christ," she said when I finished. "Jack is your son?"

"He is. But he doesn't know yet. I'm scared to tell him."

"You shouldn't be. None of this was your fault." She shook her head. "Oh, Jenna, I could never have survived what you did. I'm not that strong." She stood and walked over to the living room entrance where we'd left Cage.

"I'm sorry we brought this to your doorstep. But apart from my mother, you're the only leverage that Kitty would've had over me. Cage thought it a good idea to come here so he could keep an eye on you, too."

"And he's the one that ended up hurt," she said.

"You like him?" I said, wondering if something could be salvaged for Casey out of all of this.

"That night at the club, we almost got together. I was way too wasted, though. And he's been busy, but he's been texting." She let out a long sigh. "But this, this isn't something I can deal with."

"You and Cage?" I had no idea it had gotten that far. I had to smile, despite everything.

"Almost, I came on pretty strong. But he was sweet about it, I guess he didn't tell anyone, but nothing happened. Like I said, I passed out."

"With Cage?" Of course with Cage.

"Um, yeah. Kind of face-planted his crotch." She giggled, this time sounding like she was thinking more of a funny memory.

My message tone chimed and I checked my phone. "It's Ali. He and Jack are on their way."

I shot a text back to tell them that we were going to meet them at the clubhouse, grateful that Ali had messaged and not called. But there was one conversation I had to have, and when I dialed Wraith's number, I filled with dread.

Chapter Fifty-Two

Ali

Jenna's life being in danger had shut down my heart. I've never felt a burn like that in my entire life. I had been fucking petrified. The shit with Pony and Leanne, as bad as it had been, was nothing compared to learning that she'd had a gun on her. That fucking Kitty had taken aim and fired.

Wraith gripped tight around my upper arms, but I pushed him off, determined to go and find her, prove to myself that she was breathing.

"Ali," Wraith said as I walked away from him. "Dusty kept Kitty informed. But he had no idea about what happened to Jenna's sister and Jack. You should've come to me. Jenna told me everything and Cage backed her up."

That was another thing, my brother had been shot. I should never have fucking left. But as I watched Jack head toward a gathering of our members standing outside, I knew that there had been little choice. We couldn't lose him. Jenna wouldn't have survived that.

I hadn't learned of the actual shit that went down until we'd returned. I'd spoken to Jenna on the phone—she'd sounded cool as shit, not letting on one iota of the trouble that she'd been through. I couldn't believe how she'd kept it together like that. Fucking made me love her more, if nothing else.

Still, hearing her voice, but not seeing her, had my blood pressure sky high. I kept walking. Jack was going to learn soon enough what was going on. It was past time for Jenna to talk to him, but I needed to see her first.

She was sitting on the stairs, her shoulder against the railing when I slammed open the front door. For a moment, I just took her in. Dark circles bruised the skin beneath her eyes, her hair was twisted up on top of her head and her clothes were rumpled. She'd never looked more beautiful.

"Ali?" Her eyes flew to mine.

"He's fine. He's outside with his brothers." I crossed the floor, wondering as to the kind of rejection I'd get. Half-hearted, or her flying into a rage like we'd parted on.

"Thank you."

Fuck, she didn't even know yet that we'd run into our own shit storm. That could wait. She and I needed to sort ourselves out once and for all. I didn't want to lose her, but I knew as sure as shit that the chances of her walking were pretty fucking great.

Who could blame her? I was a scumbag biker. Despite the deals we'd completed, I was still a member of an MC. Jenna was good. I was bad. It was that basic.

"Are you going up to see Cage?" Her words were low.

"In a moment. Casey up there with him?"

She nodded, managing a small smile. "He's trying his hardest with her, funniest thing I've ever seen. He's hopped up on painkillers and I don't think he has a clue what he's saying, but I think he's sincere."

"Sounds like him." I sat beside her, shocked, but grateful when her head landed against my arm. "I'm sorry about what happened. I don't blame you for not wanting anything to do with the club."

"He's still out there. Wraith said I had to stay until they find him." She shuddered. "He was good about it all, though. He said if I wanted to go to the police, I could. He'll put more protection on my mother in case there was still anyone who helped Hellion and Kitty. And I can tell Jack in my own time."

I'd been concerned about that. Wraith would consider it club business, Jack knowing who his mother was. But if he was giving her time, I planned for her to be able to take it.

"We'll worry about Kitty later." I would kill him. Done deal. "Right now, I want to know how you are. This kind of stress isn't good for you, or our kid."

"I'm okay. Casey said I should just rest up, but it was hard, with you and Jack not back. But it's okay now."

I let my arm go around her. "Guess you haven't had much time to think."

"I don't need time."

Breathing was impossible. Seconds felt like hours before she spoke again.

"I do feel guilty about Jack and Sophie. I can't help that, Ali. But I can't keep blaming myself for stuff that happened when I was too young to know better. I was a kid. And even though I kept away…"

"He would've killed you. You know that."

She hitched a breath. "I do. And he would never have let me near Jack, I know that, too."

"I love you, Jenna. If the only way we can make this work is for me to walk from the club, I'll do it."

"I need to do this." She stood, her shoulders squaring. "Can we talk later? Right now, I've got to see Jack."

I had to respect that. There was no choice.

Chapter Fifty-Three

Jenna

Jack might have been only eighteen, but he was just over six feet tall and clearly liked spending time in the gym. Already his arms were covered in tattoos and he wore several chunky silver rings. He had also perfected a hard edge to his resting expression, narrowing his eyes and holding his mouth in a straight line. But right at that moment, he looked young and vulnerable sitting behind Wraith's desk, turning side to side in the office swivel chair.

As I entered and closed the door behind me, he looked up. "Oh, hey, Jenna," he said.

"Hey, yourself. What are you doing hiding down here?" The place swarmed with members coming in after being alerted.

I'd had to tell Wraith everything. He'd had no idea about what Kitty and Hellion had done. He, like the rest of the club, had thought that Jack was some junkie's kid. He'd never questioned it and I had seen the regret in his eyes over that.

Now that he knew the truth, he had done everything he could to help, bar letting Cage go to hospital.

There were several brothers out combing the area for Kitty. So far, there had been no sightings.

"Just taking a moment." He smiled, completely disarmed. The slight bruising on his cheek had started to go darker, causing me to frown and lean forward to check it out further. "It's okay. Casey said it's nothing, just a bump."

I snorted. "From talking?"

Something had gone on with the meeting, but no one had said a word to me yet. The conversations seemed to die a quick death when I entered the room. There was no church meeting happening. Of course, that was only a matter of time. Didn't matter to the MC that it was the middle of the night. Or near dawn, I realized, as I looked out of the window.

"Club business, princess," he said with mock-seriousness. "You doing okay?"

I'd had a gun pointed at me and seen Cage jump in front of it and take a nasty hit, so no, I really wasn't. Yet, we were all safe and sound now.

"They're still out after him, aren't they?" I took the seat opposite him. "Kitty?"

Jack shrugged. "There's nowhere for him to go. He knows it, so yeah, they'll bring him in. They got posts. We don't think he's left town yet."

"Unless he did right away."

Jack shook his head. "Don't even go there. We called Ma. She says she hasn't heard from him."

"Oh," I said.

"Yeah. But it's cool, I've known about them for a while." He leaned back in his chair. "My old man was hard, not like he never cheated on her. Kitty made her happy, but that shit is going to be over real quick. I still can't believe he did what he did."

Kitty and Chrissie?

"You were close to your father, though?" I asked.

"Like any other, I guess. He was different. He had the entire club to take care of, not just us. No one has it easy. Families are funny things."

There it was, my opening. If I didn't step through it, I might never have the guts. "We don't talk," I said. "There's only my mother left now."

"You don't have to tell me," he said. "We can just sit and chill."

"No, no, I want to. If you want to listen, that is?"

He sat up straighter, his face growing serious. "So what happened?"

"It was a long time ago. I was younger than Paige." I watched his face, unable to look away as he nodded at me.

"I did something silly. My sister and I did something silly. We went to a biker party." I stopped, but Jack remained still, so I continued, "I was given drugs in my beer. Guess I was too young to be drinking, but it didn't seem that bad. I woke up the next morning with a man and a few months later I found out I was having a baby."

"Fuck, really?"

I nodded. "I was scared, so I ran away from home. I went to the man and he offered to help me."

Jack blinked, but kept staring at me, his body still frozen. "The man who drugged you?"

"You'd think that was the last place, huh?"

"He was the father."

"He was."

"You had the kid." Not a question.

"I did. He was beautiful, perfect. But his father took him from me."

Jack put his hands on the desk, his eyes not leaving mine as he leaned farther forward. "Where's the kid now?"

I finally broke eye contact and Jack sagged in his seat.

"I think I know where the kid is," he said. "He's with his mother, isn't he? Right this very moment, he's with his mother."

"If you want, I can leave. You never have to deal with me again. But I needed to tell you for my own selfish reasons." I looked back. He appeared deep in thought.

"When I was a kid...."

I didn't correct him and tell him that he still was.

"I used to pretend that she—that you—wanted me. That Hellion took me by force and that one day you'd come back. I gave up a long time ago."

I rose to my feet. "I'll give you some time to think about it." How long did that kind of rejection take, anyway?

"Yeah, good idea." Jack spun the chair away from me. "We might catch up later, right?"

"Sure," I said, stumbling blindly from the room.

I shut the door and squeezed my eyes shut. Had I even imagined anything else? What did I expect? Jack to hug me and call me mom?

The sun looked just about to burst over the mountain tops. I wasn't concentrating in that direction, however, as the gate swung open and Chrissie's car drove sedately through. My privacy shattered when she pulled up alongside of me. *Great, this is all I need.*

"You're early," I said, pulling myself together. Of course, she might not have been returning for work. The clubhouse was a hive of activity, and from what I'd gathered, everyone had been called in.

"What are you doing out here? It's freezing," Chrissie said, leaning out of her open window.

"Just getting some fresh air."

"Do you have a moment to talk? Can you hop in? It's way too cold for me to get out and I can tell that the clubhouse is crowded."

Anything to put off Chrissie going inside and running into Jack. I walked around the car and climbed in beside her as she wound up her window. The motor still ran, hot air blowing in through the vents.

"I heard what happened to Cage," she said. "But he's okay, just a leg wound?"

"And a bad concussion," I said. "Casey is worried about it. She says he should be in hospital."

"Well she would, wouldn't she? Just a worrier, typical nurse."

Seeing that she didn't know Casey, I didn't let that go. "No, I think she's right. She's going to keep an eye on him, but even Wraith knows that it could be serious." I turned to her. "I know things could get complicated, but—"

The snick of the gun cut me off. On the back seat, half huddled down in the footwell, hid Kitty. He was mostly covered in a blanket, but the morning sun caught the glint of steel as for the second time the man aimed a weapon at me.

"Now we're gonna go for a drive," he said. "I never meant to shoot Cage. I dropped my aim when he put himself farther in front of you. I need to talk to someone, get a chance to explain."

"Okay," I said. "We go inside and we do that."

"He's not going to shoot you," Chrissie said. "If you behave yourself."

We all looked to the clubhouse as the door slammed open and Jack strode out. He looked to the car, his gaze searching.

"Jenna, wait!"

But we were already backing out. I sat stiffly in the seat watching him.

"He's mine," Chrissie said, her words sharp and halting, but the smile remained plastered on her face. "Don't you get any fucking ideas."

Kitty stayed crouched down and I didn't have to look behind me to know that he'd have kept the gun pointed on me.

Directly in front of us, Jack ran toward the car. "Jenna, I need to talk."

Chrissie gave him a happy wave and turned the wheel. "Did you tell him?"

"No," I said.

"Good, I don't think you should."

"It doesn't matter, Chrissie," Kitty said from behind us. "I'll fix this."

Chrissie's smile widened at me. It wasn't pretty.

Chapter Fifty-Four

Ali

Five minutes with Jenna hadn't been enough. I was beginning to realize that a lifetime might not cut it, either. But I had to start somewhere.

After I checked in on Cage, and yeah, he was making some headway with the nurse, I went off in search of my woman. According to Bel, she had been seen going into the meeting room after Jack. That as good as told me that she'd have laid it all out for him. Jack was a smart kid. His head was in the right place, and I doubted he'd react badly. I really didn't think Jenna had too much to worry about as far as her son was concerned. He liked her. Finding out her true identity was something he'd get used to. I was damn sure of that.

Still, I wanted to be there for her, for that reason, and my own selfish ones.

Once I saw she was good, I'd home in on Kitty. It was time to end that shit. Without the threat of him hanging over her, we could finally relax. He might have been off the grid, but I was a determined enough asshole to track and bury the fucker.

Wraith was going to call church any minute, but I trusted the prez to put a spin on things and keep Jenna's personal details out of it. At least until we knew if there were any other's involved. Dusty fucked up by keeping Kitty in the loop, but that wasn't quite the same thing as killing kids and stealing babies.

The office was empty, but when I left it, Jack was heading

out of the bar. "Wraith called church in ten," the kid said.

"You seen Jenna?" I crossed the floor in long, hurried strides. "She talk to you?"

"Yeah, she did. She told me she was my mother." Jack looked vacant. There was nothing there. "I was a bit shocked."

"Guess you were," I said. "Hearing what your old man did couldn't have been easy. What he did to Jenna, let alone Sophie."

"Sophie?" His face blanked.

Fuck, she hadn't told him that shit. I sucked air through my teeth. I could pull my punches with Jenna, but as young as he was, Jack was club. Out of respect for that, I had to get it out there just how fucking evil his old man was.

"She was Jenna's sister. Kitty fucked up and killed her instead of your mother."

For a moment, he just stood there. "What?"

"You heard me. Taking you wasn't enough, he needed Jenna out of the way. He got that in the end, but he — "

"I had an aunt? Hellion and Kitty killed her?"

I put my arm out to steady him.

"I gotta talk to Jenna. Shit."

"We can do that. We'll go together."

"She got out of here, wanted to give me a minute. But I might have fucked it up. I think she got the wrong idea that I was pissed off." He folded his arms across his chest. "I wasn't. It was just a lot to deal with."

"What did you say?" I'd fucking belt Jack under the ear if he'd upset her. I know it was a lot for him to take in, but he was just going to have to deal. Right now, I was more worried about Jenna.

"Nothing. But when I went out to tell her it was all good, that we'd figure it out, she was leaving."

"She fucking left?" If Jenna had taken off, this time I was tying her the fuck up.

"No, it's cool, she was with Chrissie. Maybe she went home to get changed or something."

"Jenna wouldn't land that shit on you and then walk away." I grabbed him by his upper arms. "Why didn't you try and stop her? She's on lockdown, for Christ's sake."

"It was too late. Jesus, Ali, back off. They were pulling out. She's with Chrissie. She'll be okay." He gave me a lopsided grin. "She can be out of your sight for five minutes, you know."

"Why isn't Chrissie in the clubhouse?" I said, it just hitting me that she shouldn't have been out driving around either.

"She's fine," Jack said.

"Kitty's on the loose, we need to call them back in."

"He's hardly going to go to Chrissie. Shit, Chrissie. This is going to send her right over." Jack shook his head. "We need to get them back here."

"Yeah." But I was worried as fuck that Chrissie had driven away with Jenna. What the fuck could that mean?

His face fell again. "Do you think she knew?"

I sure as hell hoped not.

I ignored him and fished my phone out. It rang four times and she came on the line. *Thank fuck,* I thought as she answered.

"Ali?"

"Yeah, babe. You wanna get Chrissie to turn around and bring you back here. You women aren't supposed to be out driving around. Kitty's still out there."

But it wasn't Jenna that spoke next. "You're right, I'm still out here." Kitty didn't sound too happy and he was going to sound a hell of a lot worse when I finished with him.

Jack blinked at me and I gave him my back. Him I'd deal with later.

"What do you want?"

"Just to talk. I've fucked up, brother, I wanna make things right."

"You can start by bringing my woman back," I said, walking over away from where the brothers were starting to file in for church.

Jack stood there, looking shell-shocked. I guess I could

305

have been easier on him. But I could make that up later. Right now, my mind was on other things.

"She's insurance, you need to come here."

"You're at Chrissie's?"

"Come alone." The phone went dead.

Turning to Jack, I said, "Not a word. You keep this shit shut the fuck down."

He nodded once and I hauled ass.

* * * *

The house was unlocked, so I went straight inside, tossing my phone onto the front yard as I did. Thing was blowing up and I wasn't planning to answer it.

They were in the dining room, Jenna in a chair with her hands taped in front of her. She turned to me, her mouth in a grim line. Chrissie was calmly sitting at the head of the table, Hellion's old spot, sipping a wine and smoking a cigarette, despite the fact that it was early morning. I dismissed her, sizing up Kitty instead. The cunt had a gun on my woman.

"I did this for us, for all of us," he said.

I took in that he was wearing his cut.

"She will bring down the entire club. You included, brother. You need to hear me out."

"No, she can put you inside for murder, you fuck."

"Brother—"

"I'm not your fucking brother," I raged. "Don't you fucking call me that. Put the fucking gun down and man up for once in your miserable life."

"Jack belonged to Hellion," Kitty said. His hand shook as he clutched the gun still pointed at Jenna. "She would've gone to the cops. What good would that have done, hey?"

Chrissie put down her glass. "She lied to you, Ali."

"No, she was protecting herself. She had every right to. She had every right to go to the cops and pull us down. But she didn't. All she wanted was to get to know her son."

Chrissie flinched. "He's mine."

Ignoring her, I turned back to Kitty. It was so fucking hard not to look at Jenna. But right now, I couldn't have the distraction. "You need to turn yourself in."

"Why? So they can slice off my tattoo and shoot me in the head. That's not going to happen. She leaves, or I bury her, and you fucking convince Wraith to let me earn my place back in. I suffered, Ali. Do you think that injecting a hotshot into that girl hasn't kept me up at night? Well, it has. I did what was best for Hellion and the club. Just like you would have and every other brother in that clubhouse."

I knew without a doubt that I'd never have done what Kitty had. I'd followed orders, but never blindly. Killing Sophie, thinking it was Jenna, that wasn't for the club, that was for Hellion's own selfish gain. It was on them, it was all on Hellion and Kitty.

Everything clicked into place. The whole damn thing.

"So it was for the club that you told Geezer that Jack and I were in St. Lorne?"

I stepped closer as Chrissie sucked in a lungful of smoke with a wheeze that rattled her chest. "You put Jack in danger?"

Jenna gasped, and for a moment my eyes fell back to her. "You did what?" she said.

Kitty put up the hand that was not holding a weapon and shook it. "They were fine."

"Yeah, really? So, Geezer thinking it was a good idea to put us both in a grave was fine? If he didn't get taken out by his own man, Jack and I would be dead. You would've known that, you stupid fuck. Were you patching over to them? Was that your back-up plan?"

"Bullshit, he's lying," Kitty snapped, his gaze on Chrissie. "I would never have done that."

"Stop your fucking bullshit, old man. It's only for the fact that Geezer is dead that you aren't planning to join the Diamonds. You can blow a fucking hole in my head, but the club knows what happened."

"Fuck." Kitty staggered. "Wraith knows?"

"What do you fucking reckon?" I stepped forward some more, the gun now on me. That was good, it needed not to be on Jenna.

"So, you were going to them?" Chrissie rose from her spot and started around the table. "You nearly got Jack killed. That's my son, you bastard."

"No, he's not," Jenna said the words low, as if she needed them to be her last. "He's mine. You stole him, you and Hellion."

But Chrissie was paying her no mind. Her fists were clenched and raised as she lunged for Kitty. I saw the opportunity and moved fast, getting to Kitty just as Chrissie started to pummel against him.

I knocked the bitch to the side. She went down with a squeal of protest as I grabbed Kitty's wrist and gripped hard. The gun clattered across the floor going close to Jenna's feet. Chrissie eyed it briefly as Jenna's Converse slammed down on her hand, preventing her from getting to it.

But I had Kitty to deal with if I was going to make Jenna safe. I pushed my entire muscle mass against the big man, sending him down and going with him. Kitty swung, fighting for his life while I wrapped my hands around his throat and squeezed.

There was movement to my left, but I needed all my concentration as I pressed my thumbs deep into Kitty's throat. The man I once called my brother stared up at me with bulging eyes. Pathetic gurgling noises came from his throat as his skin darkened to purple. I pressed harder, torn between wanting his pain and terror to last longer, and needing him to die beneath my hands.

"He's dead, Ali. Let go." Jenna was crouched beside me, her hands out in front, still taped. I had no idea how much time had passed.

The gun. When I turned, Chrissie held the weapon with shaking hands. Only she wasn't pointing it at us. Slowly she brought the barrel up to her face, her mouth opening. It was clear to me that her involvement now in Jack's kidnapping and Jenna's sister's murder had been complicit, at least after the fact. But further to that, she'd helped Kitty take my woman. I wanted her to die, but I wanted fucking answers as well.

Pushing Jenna behind me, I put up my palm. "Chrissie, we can talk about this."

Jenna's hands pressed onto my back. They were rock fucking steady.

Unlike Chrissie's. She vibrated with the sound of the metal clicking against her teeth, as her eyes rounded. She knew her fate, it was written there. Chrissie liked to chug down a few pills on occasion, get herself some attention, but I'd never heard of her trying to shoot herself before. Guns tended to be a hell of a lot more permanent. She stepped back and Jenna pressed her body against mine. "Let her go, Ali. It doesn't matter."

The hell it didn't. But she was right, in a way. I didn't need answers. Chrissie started to lower the gun from her face. I lifted the side of my mouth to a half smile and nodded.

Hellion chose this house because of its isolation. The exploding sound of Chrissie eating a bullet made my ears ring, but it wasn't going to draw much attention from anyone else. As her finger squeezed down on the trigger, I turned, gathering Jenna against me, holding her head to my chest. "I'm sorry, babe," I said as I stroked up and down her spine. Only, I really wasn't.

I winced as I removed the tape from around Jenna's wrists and rubbed her reddened skin. My head had left me for a while there, but I was back, well and truly on my game. For the second time in less than a day, I'd nearly lost her. I didn't do thirds as far as she was concerned. But I was shit scared the odds were against me seeing I'd just strangled Kitty with my bare hands, right the fuck in front of her. I didn't even want to think about what Chrissie had done, and my piss-weak effort to stop that.

Jenna's back was to the bodies, and I expected it to stay that way. When she spun to look at them, my breath sucked in deep.

"I can't believe it's over." Her arms hugged around her middle. "It doesn't seem real."

"Jack was just shocked, babe. We need to get back there, he's not angry at you." I glanced down at the ruin of Chrissie, but had no regret. She was as guilty as Hellion as far as I could see and her death wasn't something I was going to give much thought to.

"Are you sure?" She turned back to me. "He didn't say much. But I guess he wasn't angry."

"No. Right now, we need to get out of here, get someone in to clean up this mess." I reached for her hand, meshing our fingers together. "I thought I'd lost you."

Jenna blinked. "No, unfortunately, you're stuck with me. I don't know how to do this, Ali. But I want to try. Not just for the baby, but because I love you. I thought I could walk away, but when they took me, I really didn't think I'd live through it. All I could think of was you and Jack and this baby. We're a family, I just can't see it any other way."

I pulled her close, surrounding her in my arms. I closed my eyes as I rested my chin on the top of her head. She wasn't the only one new to this. We'd work it out, or we'd just fuck to distract each other, that seemed to work. Grinning, I held her tighter. There's no way I'd let her go.

* * * *

The ride back to the club was brief. We pulled up in the compound to find the brothers gathered and waiting for us in a semicircle. Wraith stood in the center, his fists into his hips. He broke from the group to meet us as we dismounted. Ali's hand sought mine as soon as we were free of the bike.

"I'm going to have a phone surgically implanted inside of you. And you'll be very fucking lucky if it's a doctor that does it, or that it's actual surgery." Wraith stepped closer.

"Had to pick up my woman," Ali said. "We need a clean-up at Chrissie's."

"You do that?" Wraith folded his arms across his chest.

"He shot Cage, took my woman hostage, so yeah, I fucking done that." Ali pulled me even closer. "You aren't going to say I should of run this past you first."

"Jase, Mick, grab the prospect and get over there. Where's Chrissie?"

"She killed herself," I said. "Ali didn't touch her." *No, but he'd given her permission.* I'd felt him move, the small nod of his head just before the gun went off. I couldn't be sure, not really, but something deep down told me that he'd helped her decide. I hugged myself against him tighter.

"Wraith, I didn't want to hurt the club. That was never my intention." I sought Jack's face out among his brothers. He was pale, but seeing he'd just learned the woman he thought of as his mother was dead, and now he knew just how evil his father was, I couldn't blame him. "I just wanted to be with Jack."

The brothers were dispersing. Even Wraith, who gave me a slight lift of his chin, started back for the clubhouse. All that was left was Ali, me and Jack. Beside me, I felt the muscles in Ali's arm ripple. "You want me to go?"

"No, stay. Jack, I'm so sorry. I'm so sorry that I left it so long. And Chrissie—"

Jack put his hand up to halt me. "I know who they were, Jenna, I know who and what Hellion was. If you'd set foot in the clubhouse before he died, you would have been killed. I would never have gotten a chance to get to know you. It's not too late." His bottom lip trembled, his eyes glassed over, but he shook it off. "I'm glad you came, Jenna. I'm glad I know the truth now. As fucked up as it is, it's better to know."

There was no hugging embrace, but he leveled me with his gaze.

For a moment, we were all silent, then the door to the clubhouse burst open. Casey came running outside.

"Where's Wraith? We need an ambulance. It's Cage."

* * * *

Twelve months later

My girls. I cracked an eyelid as Jenna slid into bed beside me, Sophie cradled in her arms.

"I didn't hear you get up," I said, rolling to my side.

"I tried not to wake you. You got up last time." She smiled, adjusting her top to feed our daughter. *My daughter, shit.* I'd known it was going to be a girl.

"That's my job," I said, in a low growl. Sophie loved it when I did that and I watched as her head bobbed, recognizing her daddy even as she fed. "How is my favorite little cockblocker?"

"Ali!" Jenna giggled. "That is so inappropriate. Besides, there hadn't been any blocking of cocks a couple of hours ago."

No there hadn't been. I grinned lazy and wondered if she was too tired for another round. Didn't matter, it was good just to lie here with her, with both of them.

Yawning, I stretched my arms over my head. "I'll put her back when you're finished. Does she need changing?"

"Most likely." Jenna watched our daughter with a soft look. She was so adorable, and if I had my way, we needed to start on another of these perfect little humans. Next time, one who looked like Jenna.

Sophie was all me, or so everyone said. Frankly, I couldn't see it. She looked like a girl, for starters.

"What are you thinking?"

"Nothing," I said. "Did you get on to Cage?"

"He doesn't want to do anything. He brushed us off last year. I really want to do something for his birthday."

"Bake him a cake. Grumpy bastard won't eat it anyway."

My woman just looked fucking sad. Stupid Cage and his hard-ass attitude, only marginally better than the moping around he'd done after Casey had left.

Still, if Jenna got happy about putting on something for him, then the brother would be blowing his fucking candles out for her and be happy to do it, too.

"I'm all over it, babe. Make some calls and this shit is on."

"You sure? He might get annoyed."

"At you?" I blew out a breath. "Doubt that very much."

Her face lit up. *Fucking beautiful.* That glowy thing hadn't ended with her pregnancy. "I'll wiggle this little munchkin in his face. He can't say no to her."

Cage and every other brother. "You do that. Maybe get him a stripper or two."

"If you think that'll help."

I burst out laughing. "That was a joke."

"I know that." She kept her face straight. "Jack's coming for dinner tomorrow night."

"So, what else is new?"

"He's bringing Paige. She's home from school."

"You good with that?"

"Yeah, I'm good."

Jack had pulled his socks up, as Jenna liked to say. Ever since his mother had been in his life, he'd ditched club girls and gotten serious with the prez's daughter. Wraith had doubled his antacids, but dealt okay. Jack treated her well. Made a man proud, especially when Jenna said Jack had taken a leaf from my book.

"Babe, you know I love you?"

"You poor bastard, you know I love you, too."

I was the richest man in the whole fucking world.

More books from
Totally Bound Publishing

Book one in the Deadly Intent series

Danger, desire, death.

Book one in the Corporate Heat series

Taylor's suddenly thrown into the dangers of the corporate world and her only protector is her hot, anonymous one-night stand.

Some things are best left forgotten.

Book one in the Brass Ring Sorority series

Think archeology is just dead bones? Think again

About the Author

Pauline Hornsby

Pauline lives in a quaint country town where she writes, reads, and is lucky enough to, live romance. Having found the love of her life early, she has no issue with her friends reading her stories, and being unable to make eye contact with her for weeks after. It's all about love, and the trials of finding a happy ever after in her world.

Pauline Hornsby loves to hear from readers. You can find contact information, website details and an author profile page at https://www.totallybound.com/

Home of Erotic Romance